Scorched

Broken Bow

Book Five

Ashley A Quinn

TCA Publishing LLC

Copyright © 2021 by Ashley A Quinn

This book is a work of fiction. The names, characters, events, and places are either products of the writer's imagination or have been used fictitiously and are not to be construed as real. Any resemblance to persons, living or dead, actual events, locales, or organizations is entirely coincidental.

No parts of this book may be copied, reproduced, and/or distributed in any way without express written consent from the author.

ISBN is 9781733160087
Library of Congress Control Number: 2021913894

ONE

Sweat dripped down Fire Lieutenant Declan Briggs's forehead to sting his eyes as he broke through the cloud of smoke and stepped outside. Walking to the firetruck, he set the hose down before lifting his helmet and taking off his mask. He tucked both under his arm as he inhaled a breath of smoke-scented air and swiped at the sweat on his face. A quick glance at his partner, Sam Reeves, showed him doffing his own gear.

"Hell of a fire, Lou." Declan's newest firefighter, Jameson Gehring, walked up, carrying water bottles.

Declan took the bottle held out to him and downed half of it before answering. "Yeah. It's a hot one, that's for sure. But we're winning now."

"About time. Need me to tag in?"

"No." Declan shook his head. "Keep doing what you're doing. This one is a bit wild for you yet." Jameson was a good kid, but he was very young and very green. Declan wasn't about to send him into a fire like this without more training. "Can you get me a new oxygen tank? Something is wrong with this one." The one he'd been using should have lasted twice as long, but a few minutes ago, he'd glanced down to see the oxygen level in the red. He figured it had a bad seal or valve.

With a nod, Jameson hurried to the other side of the truck to grab another tank. Declan unhooked his old one while he waited, then checked in with the other two units on scene, helping to tackle the house fire and keep it from spreading to the neighboring homes. They were making progress on the blaze, but it was slow-going. The house was fully engulfed when they arrived. It had taken one look for Declan to call in additional units.

Jameson returned with a fresh tank. Declan hooked it up, testing it before nodding to Sam. "I'm good. Let's get back in there."

Sam drew his mask down. "Let's get it."

"Make sure that tank doesn't get put with the others," Declan instructed Jameson. "It needs to be fixed."

"You got it."

Declan settled his gear into place and followed Sam back to the house. They picked up their hose and mounted the porch steps. As Sam crossed the threshold, the air around them changed. The fire sucked away from them, and Declan's eyes went wide as he realized what was happening. Before he could utter a word of warning, an explosion of heat and flames sent him flying backward through the air as the fire flashed, growing exponentially in the blink of an eye.

Pain jolted through his hip and back as he hit the ground. The air left his lungs, and he rolled to his side, gasping as he tried to draw a breath. When his lungs finally worked again, pain lanced his ribs. Groaning, he rested his head on the wet grass. His ears rang, the noises around him fading as the ringing took over.

"Lou! Lieutenant! Are you okay?"

Declan cradled his ribs, rolling to look up at Gehring, whose worried face loomed over him.

"Sir, are you okay?"

"I think so." He tried to sit up, but fire raced across his ribcage. Moaning, he clutched his side and maneuvered himself to a sitting position. "Where's Sam?"

Gehring pointed ahead of them to the left. Declan squinted, trying to bring his vision into focus, and saw Sam sprawled over the grass, not moving.

"Shit." Still clumsy from the blast, Declan got to his knees. Jameson helped him stand, and he stumbled over to Sam. Two paramedics arrived and kneeled over him to assess his injuries.

"Sam!"

One of the paramedics looked up. "Lieutenant, you shouldn't be moving around." She glanced around, presumably for another medic to take care of him.

Declan ignored her and dropped to his knees. "Sam, can you hear me?"

"He's out cold," the second paramedic said. "His pupils are equal and reactive, but a little sluggish." He wrapped a blood pressure cuff around Sam's arm. A third medic came up and squatted next to Declan.

"Lieutenant, can I take a look at you?"

Declan turned to the young man at his shoulder, Denton Truesdale. Denton's voice—and everyone else's around him—sounded as though he were shouting through a tunnel.

"You can't do anything for Sam right now. Kara and Mike have things under control. Let me assess you. The blast threw you both quite a distance."

Declan nodded reluctantly, wincing as he pushed to his feet, wobbling a bit. Denton and Jameson grabbed his arms to steady him.

"I'm fine." He shook off their grip and headed for the ambulances. Denton hurried ahead and opened the back of the one on the right. On legs shakier than Declan wanted to admit, he climbed inside and sat on the stretcher. He looked at Gehring, who stood outside, watching. "Go find Walters. Tell him he's in charge and find out where he wants you. If he has to send you into the house, you do *everything* your partner says, understand?"

Jameson nodded. "Yes, sir." He ran off to find Sergeant Walters, who headed up Ladder Three.

Feeling the blast now, Declan let his head fall back against the stretcher and closed his eyes. Everything hurt.

"I'm going to take your vitals."

"Go for it," Declan muttered.

A blood pressure cuff went around his arm and a pulse oximeter clamped over his finger. He heard some beeps as the machines got their results.

"Vitals look good, considering."

Declan opened his eyes. Denton held up a penlight.

"Follow the light."

He did as asked.

"Good. Where do you hurt? And don't say you're fine. You flew twenty feet."

A corner of Declan's mouth quirked. His people knew him well. "My ribs hurt." He pointed to the left side of his chest. "And my left hip. It took the brunt of my landing."

"Can you take off your coat so I can examine your chest?"

With a groan, he sat up. His chest was on fire. Broken ribs were just what he needed. He pulled his right arm out of his turncoat, then let the jacket slide off his left. Denton leaned forward and probed his ribcage. Declan bit back a grunt of pain as he hit a sore spot.

"You should probably get some x-rays. Just to make sure there aren't any shards or dislocated breaks lurking that could puncture your lung. I'm pretty sure you broke at least two.

There's some crepitus around the sixth lateral rib, and you're tender above and below that."

He nodded. "I'll get checked. Can I go, now?"

"So long as you promise not to go back into the fire. You need to man the radios now, sir."

Seeing as he could barely lift his arm, wrangling a firehose under pressure was most definitely out. "I'll behave." He slid off the gurney. "I'm going to check on Sam."

"I hope he's okay. After what happened to his brother, it doesn't seem right he'd get hurt badly, too."

Declan agreed. Austin was just beginning to recover after being shot in the line of duty a few weeks ago. It was touch and go for several days. He'd lost a lot of blood and infection set in. The kid spent two weeks in the hospital before he was well enough to go home. He still had a ways to go, though, before he regained full function of his arm and shoulder.

Cradling his ribs, Declan stepped out of the ambulance and went looking for Sam, finding him in the next bus. He'd come to, but looked dazed.

"How's he doing, Ericson?"

Kara Ericson, the female paramedic from earlier, glanced at him before turning her attention back to the IV line she was busy hooking up. "He'll be okay. A little concussed and some contusions, but otherwise good. You both were lucky."

"We all were." He and Sam were the only firefighters close to the house when the fire flashed. If any of them had been inside when it happened, it would be a much different situation.

"Did you get checked?" she asked.

He nodded. "Broke a couple ribs. I'm all right."

"Good. You want to ride with us to the hospital for x-rays?"

He shook his head. "No. I need to stay here and help coordinate."

She gave him a sharp look.

He held up a hand, staving off the ass-chewing. "I'll go after my shift, I swear."

"Or if you start to feel short of breath. One of those ribs could shift and puncture a lung."

"I'm aware." He reached in and patted Sam's boot. "Take care, buddy. I'll check up on you later."

Sam offered him a weak smile and nodded. Declan stepped back and closed the doors. A moment later, the ambulance pulled away. As he wandered over to Ladder Three to find Walters, he wished he'd asked Truesdale for some ibuprofen, at least. He'd have to check the firetruck. There was a bottle lurking somewhere. If not, he knew there was one in his office at the fire station.

"Walters." He walked up to the older man standing beside the ladder truck, staring up at the fire. It was still burning, the progress they made earlier erased by the blast.

"Jesus, Briggs. Are you and Reeves okay? That was some explosion. I can't believe the house is still standing."

"We're fine. Cracked ribs for me and a concussion for Reeves. He's on his way to the hospital. Do we know what caused the blast? I thought we had it contained."

"So did I. There's no word yet, though. It's too hot to get inside, but we're getting there."

Declan nodded. "Okay. Sam and I didn't make it to the back of the house before it blew, so we never checked the rooms back there."

"I'll make that the priority, then. I hope the place was unoccupied. The neighbors said it's vacant because it was a flip, but that doesn't mean there wasn't a squatter they didn't know about."

"Or a contractor working late. Okay. I'll take over here. You go coordinate an entry team."

"On it." He jogged off, and Declan sagged against the

truck. He lifted the radio mic to his mouth, pressing the talk button. "Gehring."

The radio squawked. "Sir?"

"Bring me some water, would you?"

"Yes, sir."

Declan pressed the button again, this time checking on his teams. He continued to coordinate their efforts to knock down the blaze for the next couple hours. Because of the intensity, they weren't able to get inside again until they reduced it to a smolder. The fire burned through the floor to the cellar, and they needed the visibility to walk through the house without falling through. Well aware of the danger, Declan sent Walters inside with another experienced firefighter once it was safe.

His radio crackled to life. "Briggs."

"Yeah, Walt."

"Call the coroner. We've got a body."

Declan swore, loud and long, before replying. "Copy." Switching channels, he radioed dispatch and asked them to call Dr. Randall as well as Sheriff Archer.

Dammit! Could this scene get any worse? He pushed away from the truck and went looking for the med kit. He needed that pain medicine now. His ribs weren't the only thing throbbing anymore.

"Forensics just pulled in," Gehring said, running up to Declan an hour later.

Declan lifted his head from where he rested it against the doorframe of the firetruck.

"You all right, Lou?"

"I'm fine." He hurt everywhere. The pain pills only dulled

his aches to a loud roar, but he still had a job to do. He would just have to deal. "You said forensics is here?"

The young man nodded and pointed to his left. "They're over there."

"Thanks." Declan swung his legs out the open door and lowered himself to the ground, biting back a moan as the movement shifted his broken ribs. He tucked his left arm close and walked over to the forensics van. As he got close, he could hear Dr. Randall and the chief forensic scientist Katie Mitchum arguing.

"All I'm asking for is paint, Alex."

"Of the entire room. I had to hire a crew to do it the first time because of the high ceilings."

"So, we do that again."

"What's wrong with the color it is?"

"It's—boring."

He laughed. "Not everything needs to be shades of the rainbow, love."

"I'm not asking for purple or red. A nice shade of sage would be great. I mean, if I'm going to live there, I should love it, right?"

"I thought you did love my house."

"I do. Just not the white in the living room. It's too harsh with all that natural wood."

Declan stopped in front of them at the back of the van. Alex stood on the ground, taking the things Katie handed him as they bickered. "Why are you two arguing about paint colors?"

"The walls are finally getting repaired from the shooting," Alex said.

"And I'm moving in," Katie interjected.

"She wants to paint the entire room a different color instead of just repainting the new dry wall the same color."

"Have you seen his house?" Katie asked.

Declan shook his head.

"It's all beautiful hardwoods. With white walls."

"They're eggshell," Alex countered.

She rolled her eyes at him. "Same thing. My point is, the color sucks. It's not asking much to repaint, is it?"

Declan held up his hands. "I am not getting involved in your domestic dispute. You two can work that out all on your own." There was no way she was going to get him to pick a side. He was friends and colleagues with both of them.

She huffed. "Where's a woman when you need her?"

Alex laughed and helped her out of the van. "You know I'm going to let you do whatever you want. Leave the poor man alone." He pressed a kiss to her cheek.

A pretty smile spread over her face. "Fine." She scooped her multi-colored hair into a ponytail. "So, what do we have? Dispatch said you guys found a body in the house."

"Yeah. You two have what you need?"

Alex nodded. "Lead the way."

Declan spun around and led them toward the burned-out structure. "Walters will lead you to the victim." He pointed to the man in turnout gear standing near the house, his helmet tucked under his arm as he drank a bottle of water.

"You're not going in?" Alex asked. He frowned, running an assessing gaze over Declan. "What happened? You're standing funny."

"The house flashed on us. Sam Reeves and I were too close and were thrown. I broke some ribs. Sam's at the hospital with a concussion."

"Oh my goodness!" Katie glanced up at Alex. "Who's going to take care of Austin with Sam out of commission?"

"I don't know, but I'm sure the police and fire departments will come together to make sure the brothers are properly looked after while they recover."

"Damn straight. And if they're not, I'll do it myself."

Alex patted Katie's shoulder. "Down, girl."

She huffed. "Sorry."

Declan waved her off. He knew she had a soft spot for Austin after what they went through. "Alex is right. We'll make sure they're taken care of."

"Good."

They reached Walters. "Keith will lead you to the body and help you remove it. Watch your step in there. The floor is a minefield."

Walters waved them forward. "It'll be easier if we go in through the back. The victim is in the kitchen."

Declan headed back to the truck, needing to sit. Would this call ever end?

While Alex, Katie, and Walters worked to bring the victim outside, Declan kept busy doing his best to distract himself from the ache in his chest. He raided the med kit again, this time for acetaminophen.

Another vehicle pulled up on the scene as he downed the pills. Declan watched the sheriff, Sebastian Archer, emerge from his truck. Seb spotted him and jogged over.

"Sorry it took me so long to get here. I had to go to Colorado Springs earlier. Any news yet?"

Declan shook his head. "No. They'll probably be out soon. It's been close to thirty minutes since Walters took forensics in there."

"Have you talked to the neighbors at all?"

"They said the house is vacant, so we don't know who the victim is."

"Damn. Okay. I'll go talk to them again and see if any of them remember seeing anyone hanging around lately." He took in Declan's pinched expression. "You okay? I heard about the flash over on the scanner."

"I'm fine."

Seb arched a brow. "Sure. How do you really feel?"

"Like I got blown up," he replied honestly. "I'll be okay."

"You sure? Walters can handle things. Or we can call Crichton." He mentioned the other lieutenant, Matt Crichton.

"I'm fine," he growled, his voice hard. There was no way he was going to leave and give the higher-ups another reason to doubt him. He was still recovering from being labeled a murder suspect a few months ago.

Seb held up his hands. "Okay. Do you know what caused the blaze yet?" he asked, changing the subject.

Declan shook his head. "No. We haven't been able to go in and assess the structure yet for an ignition point. It was probably electrical, though. The house was under renovation."

"Is that why it burned so hot?"

"Yeah. If there were construction materials inside, it would help fuel it."

Commotion from the side of the house drew their attention. Walters emerged, helping Dr. Randall carry a body bag. Seb and Declan walked forward, and Seb opened the back of the forensics van, climbing inside to help them stow the body.

"What can you tell me?" Seb asked as he stepped down.

Alex frowned and propped his hands on his hips. "Not much yet. It's a male. I need to get him back to the lab before I can give you anything else."

"Okay. I'll locate the owners and find out who might have had access to the house."

"And I'm going to walk through it to see if I can determine the ignition source," Declan added.

"Sounds good," Seb said. "Everyone keep me informed."

The group split up, and Declan wandered back to the firetruck to get his gear.

"Lou, what are you doing?"

Declan glanced back at Gehring after shrugging into his jacket, wincing with the movement. "My job."

"You really should stay out here and let Sergeant Walters handle things."

"Probably, but this is still my scene, and I have the most training on ignition points." Declan might be young for a lieutenant at thirty-six, but he had almost two decades of experience. He joined the Marines right out of high school, and they'd put him in a firefighting unit. The work fascinated him, and he'd taken every course the military would let him until he had high-level certifications in both hazardous materials and arson. No one was better qualified to determine the source of the fire than he.

"How about you come with me? You can be my hands." Declan picked up his helmet and gloves.

The young firefighter's face lit up. "Sure."

The two of them picked their way over the soggy grass to the back of the house.

"Watch your step. Test your footing before you put your full weight on any one point and try to step where I step."

Gehring nodded and followed Declan inside. As he did, Katie poked her head around from the garage side of the wall, a camera in her hands.

"Find anything?" Declan asked.

"Maybe. Come look at this."

He walked closer, stepping into the garage through the opening exposed by the fire.

Katie pointed at the doorjamb of the steel door. "Right there."

Declan leaned in as much as his ribs would allow and inspected the spot she indicated near the doorknob. A small piece of wood sat between the door and the frame. "Is that a wedge?" He looked up at her.

She nodded. "I think so. Someone didn't want this door to open from the inside."

He closed his eyes for a brief moment. *Shit.* "This fire wasn't an accident."

"Nope. I'd say it was also probably a deliberate homicide."

"Dammit. Okay. I'll let Seb know. Have you seen any signs of an accelerant?"

She shook her head. "Not yet, but I haven't really been looking."

"Okay." He glanced back at Gehring, who stood just inside the kitchen, wide-eyed from their conversation. "Let's go find the source of this blaze." Declan stepped back into the house, his eyes roaming the walls and floor for the telltale signs of arson. "Go get the PID from the firetruck. It's in with the field-testing equipment." The photoionization detector would give him a good idea if the arsonist used an accelerant like gasoline or something similar.

Gehring nodded and left through the back door. Declan continued his perusal of the house, noting a spot near the door where the floor was charred more than it should have been. He exited the kitchen, entering what was likely the dining room. More spots like in the kitchen darkened the floor beneath each window. He took careful steps and rounded the staircase into the living room, seeing a similar pattern. Whoever set this fire made sure every exit was obstructed. The person in the kitchen never stood a chance.

Two

A slight shiver ran through Maggie Archer's body as she stood outside Declan's front door. She should have grabbed a heavier coat this morning. Winter was well on its way. But she hadn't been counting on doing more than walking from her car to her office and back. A whole twenty steps, at most, both ways. She certainly hadn't imagined she would be standing outside Declan's house, waiting for him to answer the door. How she let Macy talk her into stopping over here, she didn't know.

She knocked again, louder this time. Maybe he just didn't hear her before. He'd had quite the day, after all. She bounced on her toes and hugged herself. Damn, it was cold.

"Declan! Open the door. It's Maggie." She pounded again.

A few seconds later, she heard the lock twist. The door opened, revealing the thunderous expression on Declan's handsome face. It also revealed his naked torso and a pair of black athletic pants that hung low on his hips.

Her mouth watered and heat licked her belly at the sight of all his hard muscles on display. At least, it did until she caught sight of the deep purple bruises coloring the left side of his chest.

"Oh my God. Declan, that looks terrible."

"No shit. It doesn't feel good, either. What do you want, Maggie?"

"Macy asked me to check on you. She was going to stop by, but got hung up at the coffee shop."

"I'm not a child. I don't need her or you to check up on me."

She arched a brow, still bouncing. How was he not freezing? "Did you go get an x-ray like you were supposed to?"

His frown darkened. "No."

"Ha! Then you do need a keeper. Go put on a shirt and some shoes. I'll take you."

"I'm fine. I'll go tomorrow. I just want to get some rest."

She stopped bouncing. "You really think you can do that without stronger pain killers? I'm betting you were lying in bed—or more likely sitting in your recliner—trying to sleep, but not having much success because you hurt too much. Am I right?"

His blue eyes glittered as he glared at her. She just grinned.

"This is ridiculous. Go home. I'll be fine."

"I'm not going home. I promised Macy I'd make sure you were okay. You're not, so I'm staying. Can we go inside? It's freezing out here."

He rolled his eyes. "That's your own fault for wearing that trench coat. I know it looks good with your outfit, but it's not very practical on a day like today."

She moved closer, forcing him to take a step back, giving her enough room to slip inside. Maggie crossed the threshold, then turned to look at him. "I wasn't planning on standing outside. You could have answered the door sooner." She wiggled her toes inside her heels. They were frozen, too.

His eyes roamed over her, lingering on her legs and her

breasts. A tingle ran up her spine at his obvious appreciation. As nice as it was, though, she wanted to move this party along; she still had to prep for court tomorrow and would like to get to bed before midnight. That was probably already a fantasy, since she had to sit in the ER with him now.

"I was hoping whoever it was would go away. When I heard your voice, I knew you wouldn't."

"Persistence is my middle name." She walked further into his house.

"Where are you going?"

"To find you a shirt." She glanced over her shoulder at him. "Unless you want to go to the ER like that? I mean, the nurses would probably love it, but..." She trailed off and shrugged, offering him a sassy grin.

He growled, following her. "I told you I would go tomorrow."

"Uh-huh. Just like you told Seb and your colleagues you would go after your shift?"

The muscles worked in his jaw, but he stayed quiet.

"That's what I thought." She poked her head around a doorway, looking for his bedroom. She'd never been any further than his living room and kitchen. This room held a desk and stacks of papers and books. She kept going. "Just agree with me and let me take you. It'll save us both a lot of time and stress." She stuck her head in the next door and saw a rumpled bed. Bingo.

Maggie walked inside and went to the dresser, pulling open the top drawer. Stacks of underwear and socks met her. An image of Declan wearing nothing but those tight gray boxer-briefs flitted through her mind. Her cheeks flamed, and she shoved the drawer shut, then opened the next one. Neat rows of folded t-shirts laid inside. She took out the top one and held it out to him.

He crossed his arms, muscles bulging, and stared at her, defiant.

Lady parts fully awake now, she looked up at the ceiling, both to get away from the sexier than sin visage in front of her and to express her exasperation. "Just put on the damn shirt, Deck." She looked back down and threw the aforementioned garment at him. It hit him in the face, then dropped into his hands.

"You're not going to go away if I don't, are you?"

"Nope."

He sighed and slipped the shirt over his head. When he tried to put his left arm through the sleeve, he grunted in pain. Maggie hurried forward.

"Let me help."

"I can put on a damn t-shirt." He tried again, sweat popping out on his brow.

"Maybe we should try a button-up," she suggested as she watched him struggle.

"Yeah," he groaned. "Let's do that."

She helped him take off the shirt, then walked into his closet and found a zip up hoodie. It would be warmer than a button-up, and he wouldn't have to put on a coat too.

Maggie walked up beside him, holding the sweatshirt open. He slid his left arm inside, and she drew it over his shoulder so he could put his other arm in. He took the two ends and zipped them together.

"Happy?"

"Yes." She pointed at the bed. "Sit."

"Why?"

"So you can put some socks and shoes on. It's a bit nippy for flip-flops."

His lips twitched, but he held his glare as he sat on the bed. She retrieved a pair of socks for him, eyes deliberately avoiding the stacks of underwear in the drawer, then went in search of his shoes, finding them lined up on the floor of his closet.

Once he was dressed, she ushered him back into the hallway and out the front door, only allowing him to stop to grab his wallet and phone.

"You realize we're going to be stuck at the hospital for hours, right?" he said as he buckled himself into the seat.

"Yep." She backed out of the driveway.

"I'm sure you have other things you'd rather be doing than babysitting me. Just drop me off."

She snorted. "Like you'll stay if I leave? And all I was going to do tonight was prep for court tomorrow. But I can do that anywhere. Everything I need is in my briefcase." She inclined her head toward the leather satchel on the backseat.

He made a low hum and slumped in his seat. Maggie suppressed a smile. She had won. For now, at least.

They made the short trip to the hospital in silence. She parked the car, and they walked inside. The woman at the registration desk made quick work of taking his information. The ER wasn't busy, so a patient care assistant waved them through to the back as soon as Declan was registered.

"You can stay out here," Declan told Maggie.

The look Maggie leveled on him could have withered even the hardiest plant. "Yeah, no. I know you. You'll get in there and tell the doctor you're 'fine' when you're not." She air-quoted. There was no way she was going to sit in the lobby while he did that. She knew how much trouble broken ribs could cause. Her brother, Brady, fell off a horse years ago and broke several. He'd needed surgery to fix them. Declan's chest didn't look misshapen, so she was hopeful the doctor could just give him some stronger pain killers and send him home. But there was always the chance he needed more serious treatment.

He rolled his eyes. "Whatever. Let's just get this over with."

Smiling sweetly, she walked past him to follow the PCA through to the back. In a triage room, the young woman took Declan's vitals, then put them in an exam room to wait on the nurse.

Maggie sat in the lone chair, leaving the bed for Declan. He eyed it with disdain, but sat on the edge, wincing.

"Would you rather sit here?" she asked, eyeing his hunched posture.

He shook his head. "It hurts no matter how I sit."

Her face pulled in a frown. "I'm sorry."

"It's not your fault. You didn't set the fire."

She shrugged. "I know, but—" She broke off. "Wait. Set the fire? It was deliberate? Macy didn't mention that."

"Yeah, it was. We found a body in the kitchen and someone set fires at all the entry points on the first floor."

"Oh my goodness. That's terrible! What is going on around here lately?"

"I don't know, but it needs to stop. I'm tired of all the drama." He winced again as he shifted.

"I'm sure Seb is, too. He's hardly had a day off since Abigail found Amy Beckett."

The cubicle door swished open, admitting the nurse, whom Maggie recognized as a classmate from school, Jodie Dunlap.

"Lieutenant, hello. What lands you in my ER as a patient? Oh!" Jodie paused as she caught sight of Maggie. "Maggie Archer, is that you?" She smiled.

Maggie returned her smile. "Hi, Jodie. It's good to see you. It's been a long time."

"It has." She glanced at Declan, a curious frown on her face. "I didn't know you two were together."

"We're not," Declan said, his tone dry.

"Geez, Deck. Can you make that idea sound any more distasteful?" Maggie shook her head. "He's right, though. We're just friends. I'm here to make sure he actually sees the doctor and doesn't duck out the moment no one's looking."

Jodie laughed. "He wouldn't be the first man to do that." She sat down on the rolling stool and scooted up to the computer. "What brings you in, Lieutenant?"

"I was injured in the same fire as Sam Reeves. He came through here earlier with a concussion."

"Oh my. Okay. What hurts?"

"Everything, but mostly my ribs and hip. The medics on scene thought I broke a couple ribs, which I agree with."

She typed that into the computer. "Did you ever lose consciousness?"

"No."

"Good. Which side is it?"

"Left."

Her head bobbed as she entered that into his chart, then switched screens to go over his medical history. Once finished, she pushed away from the computer and stood. "I'll let the doctor know you're ready. It shouldn't be too long."

Declan thanked her, and she left.

Maggie opened her briefcase and took out her case files and a pen. She really did need to prep for court tomorrow.

"What are you working on?"

She glanced up. "I have court in the morning. I just want to make sure I'm up to speed on all my cases."

"Shouldn't you know that by now?"

She rolled her eyes. "It never hurts to double check. And some of these landed in my lap this morning. They're arraignments from arrests made in the last couple days."

"Why did you choose to be a defense attorney, anyway? I mean, I'm grateful. You were great when I needed you. But why?"

"Why not? I know we have a reputation as money-grubbing, but we're not all that way. And I didn't go to law school intending to be a criminal lawyer. I was going to do corporate law. But we had to do some job shadowing as part of the curriculum. Criminal law was much more interesting. The more I looked into it, the more I realized it was what I wanted to do. And I chose defense because I met too many prosecutors who wanted to railroad defendants just to get the conviction. I wanted to make sure the truth was known, and that everyone got a fair shake with the system."

"Even if it meant you had to defend some truly guilty people?"

She nodded. "Yep. Even the guilty deserve a fair trial."

"So, are you defending Judge Brandt or the Paulsons?"

"Hell, no. Even if they asked me, I'd say no. After what they did, not just to those kids, but to Rayna, I hope they rot in jail." She gave him a sheepish smile. "I might think they deserve a fair trial, but that doesn't mean I want to be the one who finds a loophole that gives them a lighter sentence."

"You could just ignore it."

"Not really. It would show up in appeals, eventually. Then I could lose my law license on an ethics violation."

"Seriously? How is it unethical to look the other way to make sure people who rented children like cars and ruined them get what they deserve?"

"Morally, it's not, but legally? That's why I won't touch that case. I'll leave it and those like it to someone who has no scruples and can sleep at night if one of those monsters walks."

"What kinds of cases do you take, then?"

"Mostly just domestic stuff and civil disputes. You were the first murder case I ever took on."

"How is it you can pick and choose? Aren't they assigned to you?"

"No. I have my own practice. Mom and Dad put down the capital to help me set it up."

"Huh. I thought you worked for the public defender's office and just took me on as a pro bono side case."

"I did. Take you pro bono, that is. But no, I'm not a public defender."

"So, how did you get assigned those cases, then?"

"They weren't assigned. I was hired. People are given a choice when they're arrested, if they want a public defender, or if they want to hire someone. These people chose to hire an outside attorney. I may be new to the job, but I've already built a reputation as competent, tough, and fair." Maggie worked hard while in law school to learn what she could about being a skilled attorney. She knew she wanted to come home and practice law in Boone County, but not in the public defender's office. She still worked hard to be the best she could be.

The cubicle door opened again, and a woman with light brown hair, wearing a lab coat and blue scrubs walked in. "Hello. I'm Dr. Demarco." She sat down on the rolling stool. "You were injured in the fire earlier today?"

"Yes, ma'am."

"Do you remember what happened?"

He nodded. "I never lost consciousness."

"Okay. What *did* happen? I wasn't here when your partner was brought in, but I heard a firefighter came through."

"The fire flashed over on us, causing a small explosion. It threw me and Reeves about twenty feet. I landed on my hip and the side of my chest."

"And that's what hurts, correct?"

He nodded.

"Do you have any bruising?"

"A little."

Maggie snorted. "The entire left side of his chest is one giant purple bruise. I imagine his hip looks the same way."

Declan glared at her.

She stared back, but spoke to the doctor. "Have him take off that hoodie. You'll see."

Dr. Demarco raised a brow. "Is she correct?"

Declan stared at her, stoic.

"Oh, for heaven's sake, Declan. Just show her your chest. It might help her decide what to do first so you can get out of here sooner," she said, playing to his desire to go home.

"Fine," he ground out. He yanked down the zipper and slid the sweatshirt down his arms.

The doctor rolled closer, her eyes on the bruising. "Boy, she wasn't wrong. That's quite colorful. Does it hurt to breathe?"

"Yes."

"In general? Or just when you take a deep breath?"

"Mostly just deeper breaths."

"That's good. I don't see any deformations, and I won't go probing around to find any bumps or dips that shouldn't be there, because that looks painful. An x-ray will tell us everything we need to know. Now, about your hip. Do you notice any clicking when you walk?"

"No. It just aches."

"Any swelling?"

"Maybe some."

"Bruising?"

"Yes."

"Okay. I think we'll x-ray that too, just to be safe. After your films come back, we'll go from there. Sound good?"

Declan nodded.

She rolled to the computer and entered information into his chart, her fingers flying over the keyboard.

"Someone from radiology should be down soon. We'll talk in a bit."

"Okay. Thanks, Doc."

She exited the room, the curtain fluttering behind her as she pulled the door shut.

Maggie kept her eyes on her files and not Declan's sculpted chest. He'd opted to leave the shirt off rather than shrug into it again. She couldn't really blame him. He'd just have to take it off for the x-ray.

True to the doctor's word, an x-ray tech showed up minutes later. Maggie stayed in her seat and continued to work while Declan left. He returned a short while later, still shirtless.

She did her best not to stare. The man was too sexy for his own good. She knew he wasn't trying to be—especially right now—but he still was. With his wavy reddish-brown hair, deep blue eyes, and chiseled body, he embodied the type of man that went on a firefighter calendar.

"How are you not cold? I would freeze, walking around without a shirt."

He flashed her a grin. "I'd like to see that."

Maggie's cheeks flamed as she realized what she said. "I didn't mean it that way. And I thought I wasn't your type."

He sat down on the bed, letting out a little moan as he settled. "I never said you weren't my type."

"Not in as many words, but you made it clear what you thought of the idea."

"It's not because I don't find you beautiful."

His words produced a warmth in her chest, but it was tempered by the fact that something about her he found irritating.

"What is it, then, that you find so abhorrent?"

Declan sighed. "I don't find you abhorrent. You're just pushy. And a lawyer."

What the hell did her job have to do with anything? "Why does that matter? I mean, I get the pushy part. I grew up with four older siblings. I had to be pushy to survive. But my job?"

He attempted to shrug, his right shoulder lifting only a fraction. "I don't like lawyers. My experience with them hasn't been the greatest."

"When have you had experience with lawyers other than me?"

"As a kid." His voice was quiet.

Maggie's eyes widened. She wanted to smack herself. Declan and Macy grew up in and out of foster care. She could imagine why he would have an unfavorable view of the legal system. "I'm sorry, Deck. I didn't mean to drudge up bad memories."

"You didn't. I don't think about my childhood. It's not worth it."

She frowned, her heart aching now. That was sad. She had fond memories of being a kid.

"Well, for what it's worth, I try my hardest not to be that kind of lawyer. People like that disgust me. Kids deserve better."

He offered her a kind smile. "I don't think you could be like those people if you tried. You and your family are some of the best people I've ever met. Being friends with your brothers probably saved my life. And what your parents are doing for those kids from the trafficking ring is amazing. They have a shot at a normal life now, thanks to them."

Maggie smiled at the mention of her parents. They were pretty awesome. She hadn't really been surprised when they announced they were fostering the kids who didn't have any other family. Her mom and dad had the biggest hearts of anyone she knew.

"I wish they'd taken you and Macy in when you were young. Maybe things would have been different for you."

"They tried."

"What?" That was news to her.

"Dad got arrested again and Mom was God only knows where. I was twelve and Macy was ten. The court put us into yet another foster home. Your parents petitioned to be our foster parents, but got denied."

"Why?"

"It had to do with that land dispute; when the developer was trying to lay claim to part of the Broken Bow. The court ruled that until the matter was settled, the home wasn't stable enough. Too much of a risk that the Archers could lose everything."

She stared at him, nonplussed for several moments. "I didn't realize they came so close to losing the ranch."

He gave her that half-shrug again. "I don't know the details or what went down. I just know Brady told me they were trying to foster us, then later that they couldn't because there was a question about where we were all going to live if the developer won."

She would have to ask her parents about that. Her knowledge of the whole thing came from what she'd been told. She was only four when it happened.

"How come you didn't end up with them later, then? Once things were settled."

"Mom showed up again and managed to get a job and stay sober long enough to get us back. We went into the system only for brief periods after that. Mostly when Dad got out of jail long enough to come home and cause problems. He left for good when I was sixteen."

Maggie's heart hurt for the boy he'd been and all he and Macy endured at the hands of the people who were supposed to love them and from others who were supposed to help them. The system needed fixed.

"But it doesn't matter. It's in the past," he said. "And I don't have anything to do with my parents anymore."

"It's probably best they're out of your life, but I don't know that it all doesn't matter. It shaped who you are, so it matters to some degree."

"All it did was make me tougher. And for that, I'm thankful. The world is not a pretty place."

She wouldn't argue with him there. Even though she'd been raised in a wonderful home, she knew how ugly the world could be. She saw it every day. But she didn't think it was as bleak as his tone implied. There was still a lot of good in the world, too.

He scooted up on the bed, leaning against the back with a grunt as he tried to get comfortable. "I'm going to try to get some rest. Wake me when the doctor comes in if I'm asleep."

She nodded, and he closed his eyes. With a sigh, she flipped her case file open again.

The minutes ticked by quickly as she worked. Declan's soft snores soon accompanied the rustle of her papers. Before she knew it, an hour passed.

Needing a brain break, she took out her phone and opened a jigsaw puzzle app. She scrolled through the pictures, finding one of the beach she liked. She was partway through reassembling it when the door opened and Dr. Demarco stepped inside.

Declan sucked in a breath, and his eyes fluttered open at the sound. He scrubbed a hand over his face as he yawned.

The doctor sat down on the stool and logged onto the computer, talking as she worked. "Okay. Your hip looks fine, but you did break some ribs. The sixth and seventh. The seventh rib is a clean break, but your sixth rib has me a bit concerned." She pulled up his x-ray and turned the monitor so they could see it. "It's in three pieces." She pointed to the screen. Two obvious fractures stood out. "This piece here is slightly out of place." She traced one of the breaks. "Normally, with this minor degree of displacement, I would recommend we do a nerve block and you take it easy for four to six weeks, but I have a feeling you wouldn't follow orders very well."

"So, what do you suggest, then?" Declan asked, not contradicting her, Maggie noticed. "I grin and bear it until they heal?"

"No. I think you should let me admit you for surgical repair. They'd probably do both ribs to be safe."

"What? How is that any better?"

"I know it sounds worse, but in your case, I think it would be beneficial. You'll get more mobility faster, and you won't have to worry about that fragment slipping further if you don't follow instructions. My concern is that with the angle of displacement, it's going to slide deeper into your chest and puncture your lung. Then you'll be in the hospital with a different set of problems. And still end up with the surgery to fix the rib."

Declan groaned, closing his eyes. Maggie leaned forward and took his hand, sensing he needed to know he wasn't alone. He looked over at her, then at the doctor.

"How long would I have to stay?"

"Just a day or so to make sure you don't have any complications. I don't see any evidence of free air in your chest, so it should be pretty straightforward. Within a few weeks, you should be mostly back to normal."

"And if I opt for no surgery? How long, then, until it's healed?"

"If you behave and don't do any lifting, pulling, or pushing, you're looking at four weeks minimum. And this is assuming it heals on its own. With the displacement, there's a chance it won't."

He muttered a curse. "Fine. Do the surgery."

She smiled at him. "Excellent decision. I'll call the cardiothoracic team and we'll get you sorted. Hang tight." She stood and breezed out of the room.

Maggie squeezed Declan's hand, a little in shock herself about how things turned out.

"You okay?"

He grunted. "Peachy."

"Look at it this way—you'll actually heal faster with the surgery."

"Yeah, but I still have to stay in the hospital."

"It won't be all bad. Macy will baby you."

He moaned. "God, don't remind me. The last major injury I had, she parked herself on my couch for two weeks. I love her, but I also love my space."

Maggie giggled, and Declan smiled. "I'll head her off."

"How? Have you met my sister?"

"Yes." She rolled her eyes. "I'll tell her I'm taking care of you."

He scoffed. "That won't stop her."

"Sure it will. She might come check on you, but it'll keep her off your couch."

"Not when she realizes you're not there to watch over me."

"Who says I won't be?"

His eyes widened. "I'm not trading one pushy woman for another."

Maggie's lips flattened. "Well, you can either take pushy, hovery Macy, or just pushy me. Which is it?"

"Jesus, what did I do to deserve such obstinate women in my life?" He ran a hand through his hair and rested his head against the bed, looking up at the ceiling.

Maggie grinned. "You love us, don't lie." She poked his shoulder.

A corner of his mouth quirked, but he glared at her. "Sure."

She giggled again, then patted his hand and stood. "I'm going to go call your sister and tell her what's going on. She's probably already freaking out because I haven't yet. If you're not right here when I get back, I will not only ask her to help track you down, I will also call Brady, Thomas, and Seb. You won't be able to hide."

He waved her off. "Yeah, yeah. I'm not going anywhere. I might not like it, but the doctor's plan is a good one. I'll be here."

"Good." She picked up her phone. "I'll be back soon." Spinning on her heel, she walked out of the room to go break the news to Macy.

Declan clicked through the hospital's TV channels for the fourth time, hoping for something different. He rarely watched television, and now he remembered why. He turned it off and picked up his phone, opening his internet app to read the news. The gloom and doom he saw didn't improve his mood.

His door opened, and he looked up, eager for a distraction, even if it was a lab tech coming to take more blood. It wasn't, though. It was Maggie.

After she talked to Macy, and he was admitted, she left to fetch his toiletries and some clean clothes. She'd stopped at her house to change, too, from the looks of it. He scanned her outfit, which differed from earlier. Black leggings hugged her long legs and a ruby red sweater hung down to the tops of her thighs. Her long, dark hair fell over her shoulder in waves, released from the twist it was in. She took his breath away with her beauty.

"Hi. Settled in?"

He nodded. "I guess."

"When's surgery?"

"Seven a.m."

"That long?"

"They needed time to run bloodwork, and I ate when I got home. But I'm first on the docket in the morning."

She sat on the edge of his bed. "Well, shoot. I was hoping I could be here, but I have to be in court at nine."

"That's okay. Macy will be here. She called while you were gone. Thanks for keeping her in the loop."

"Of course. She's the one who roped me into this. And you should also be thanking me for convincing her to stay home this evening and not come hover over you. She was ready to drive up here in her pajamas when I told her what was going on."

He grinned. "Yeah. She still was when I talked to her. But I could tell how tired she was. She kept yawning while we talked. Speaking of, you should get home so you can finish prepping for tomorrow. I appreciate you bringing me in and then going to get my stuff. Macy could have brought it up with her in the morning."

"She could have, but then you wouldn't have this." She opened the tote she carried and pulled out the book from his nightstand.

Declan took it with eager hands. "Thank you. I'm so bored. TV sucks." He hadn't asked her to bring the book, but was so glad she did.

She chuckled. "I remembered you talking about how you would rather read than watch TV. You and Brady are a lot alike in that regard, so I figured you'd want that."

"I do. You just saved my sanity, thank you."

"You're welcome." She laid her hand over his.

Warmth spread up Declan's arm from her touch. He turned his hand over and laced his fingers through hers. Her eyes widened a fraction before she cleared her throat and looked away, standing.

"I should probably get going. It's getting really late."

Disappointment shot through him. He'd just said the same thing, so he wasn't sure why he felt that way. "Yeah. Thanks again for all you did for me tonight."

"You're welcome." She offered him a soft smile. "I'll stop in tomorrow as soon as I can. I hope everything goes well."

"I think it'll be fine, but thanks."

She hummed a non-answer and backed toward the door, leaving the tote bag on a chair. "Good night, Deck."

"Night, Maggie."

He held her gaze until she finally turned and left, then blew out a breath as hard as his ribs would allow. He needed to do something about that woman. About this hum of desire that punched him in the gut whenever she walked into a room. Even broken bones couldn't stop it.

Declan hadn't been entirely truthful when he told her why he was against the idea of a relationship with her. It didn't have anything to do with her chosen profession. The truth was, she scared the ever-loving daylights out of him. She held such a power over him. The more he was around her, the more he wanted to do whatever she asked of him, just to make her happy. Only Macy had that power. His mother had once, but she betrayed him, and he vowed she was the last person he would ever allow to devastate him like that. But if he wasn't careful, Maggie could do that in a heartbeat.

THREE

Heels clacking on the tile floor, Maggie hurried down the corridor to Declan's room, finally free. Work dragged today. She didn't want to be in court or her office. Just here with him. Which was crazy. They were friends. And not even particularly close ones. They didn't hang out. She saw him when he was with her brothers or Macy and she happened to be around. But it didn't matter. Her mind was on him all day. She just wanted to see him and make sure he was all right.

She reached his room and pushed the door open, entering as quietly as her shoes would allow in case he was asleep.

Macy looked up from her seat beside the bed. "Hi," she whispered.

"Hey. How's he doing?" Maggie tiptoed across the floor to stand next to them. Declan was asleep, his mouth parted slightly. His rusty hair fell over his forehead in soft waves, and stubble dusted his jaw. An IV snaked out of his forearm and a white bandage covered the left side of his naked chest.

"Good. He's just been resting. Nothing's really changed since I talked to you earlier."

Maggie was glad. Macy called her after he was out of

surgery to tell her it was a success and that he was resting comfortably. She shrugged out of her coat and laid it over the back of a chair before sinking into the seat. "Have you eaten?"

Macy shook her head. "Not yet. The doctor was going to come in again for evening rounds. I didn't want to miss him."

"Do you know when he'll get to go home?"

"Not yet, no. I'm hoping they'll be able to tell me that. I need to make arrangements for the shop."

"I can help. Not at the coffee shop. You don't want me anywhere near your espresso machine. But with Declan. I can work from his house. I don't have to be in court again until next week."

"That would be great. He mentioned something this morning about you staying, but I wasn't sure if you could actually do it. London and Rayna manned the coffee shop today, but they have their own responsibilities to tend to, so it would be nice to have the help."

"Let's plan on that, then. I'll stay with him."

Macy's shoulders drooped, some tension leaving her. "That would be great. I've been stressing all day about what I'm going to do."

"It's not a problem, really." She preferred it, actually. She would be useless at her office. All she would do was wonder how he was, even though she knew Macy would take good care of him.

The door opened. Maggie and Macy turned to see a man in his fifties walk in, dressed much like Dr. Demarco in the ER yesterday. A younger doctor and a nurse followed him inside.

"Hello. I'm Dr. Calvin." He held out a hand to Maggie.

"Maggie Archer. It's nice to meet you." She shook his hand.

He smiled, then turned to Declan, who was now awake with the commotion. "How's our patient?"

"Sore." Declan's voice was gruff from sleep.

"That's to be expected. Any nausea or vomiting after you woke up?"

"No."

"Good. How about shortness of breath?"

"No."

"Perfect. You did very well, Mr. Briggs. I suspect you'll be right as rain in no time. I suppose you're ready to get out of here?"

"Hell, yes."

"Tomorrow morning. After rounds. Let's make sure we have your pain under control and give your sister a chance to prep for your arrival home. You're going to need help for a few days."

"How soon until I can go back to work?"

"You should be able to resume light duties—and by that, I mean desk work—in about a week. After that, you can gradually increase your workload. But no running into burning buildings or training for at least four weeks. We'll reassess at that point."

Declan nodded, his expression grim.

"Okay. We'll get you switched over to oral pain control and see how you do. Get some rest."

"Yeah. Thanks, Doc."

Dr. Calvin gave him a nod. "Have a good night." He and his entourage left the room.

Maggie leaned forward and took Declan's hand. "How do you really feel?"

"Like I got hit by a truck. My chest feels like there's an elephant sitting on it."

Macy frowned. "Why the hell didn't you say something?"

He cast a glance at her from the corner of his eye. "I'm fine, Mace. It's just uncomfortable."

"You're not fine, you stubborn mule." She swatted his arm.

"Macy. I'm okay. Really."

She sniffed. "Never do that again. You really scared me this time."

"I know. I'm sorry. It's not like I planned to get blown up."

She rolled her eyes, huffing a short laugh. "I know. It's just —you're the only family I have, Deck."

He let go of Maggie's hand to grab Macy's. "I love you, Macy. I'm sorry I scared you."

She bent over and pressed a kiss to his temple. "I love you too, you big oaf. I'm glad you're okay."

"Me too."

"All right." She sniffed and wiped her eyes. "I'm going to leave you with Maggie. I haven't had any dinner and I need to go check on the coffee shop. She can explain the plan for when you come home." She dropped another kiss on top of his head. "I'll see you later." Picking up her purse and coat, she left.

Declan struggled to sit up, having slouched while he slept. Maggie stood, helping shift his left side while he pushed with his right arm.

"God, this sucks," he said through clenched teeth. He tipped his head back against the bed once they got him situated. Sweat dotted his forehead, and he puffed short breaths.

"You okay? Should I get the nurse?"

"No," he growled, staring at the opposite wall. "I'll be fine. I just need a second."

Maggie took his hand, and he gripped her fingers. She ran the fingers of her other hand over his forearm, trying to soothe him. After a few moments, his breathing calmed and his grip loosened.

"You sure you don't want more pain medicine? It's not macho to suffer."

One side of his mouth lifted. "I know. And it's not being macho. I just don't like the way the stuff makes me feel."

"So extra-strength ibuprofen it is, huh?"

"Yeah. So, what's the plan Macy mentioned?" he asked, changing the subject.

She settled back into her seat, still holding his hand. "Oh, that. It's what we talked about last night. I'm going to stay with you for a few days until you're more mobile. Macy has to take care of the coffee shop. I can pretty much work from anywhere. It just made sense."

"I still don't need a keeper."

"You can't move without almost passing out."

He blinked at her.

"It'll be fun. Like a sleepover."

"If you paint my nails while I'm sleeping, I will give all your high heels to charity."

"No, you won't. You like my heels."

His eyes lit, a bit of fire displacing the pain. A shiver went up her spine. That backfired on her.

"Fine. Your purses, then."

She waved a hand at him. "You're an invalid for the foreseeable future. It will give me time to hide them elsewhere."

He laughed, then groaned, clutching his ribs. "Oh, don't make me laugh. That hurt."

She giggled. "Sorry. But you're still stuck with me for the rest of the week."

"I don't get a choice, do I?"

"Nope. It's what's best for you and for Macy. And I don't mind helping my friends."

"So, since when did you and Macy become so buddy-buddy?" He lifted one brow.

She could tell he didn't like the thought of her conspiring with his sister behind his back, even though they'd already discussed her staying with him instead of Macy. Maggie shrugged. "We've gotten closer since I came back to town after law school. Coffee is the lifeblood of any lawyer, so I spend a lot of time at Peppy Brewster."

Declan hummed. "I guess that makes sense. I'm not sure I like it, though. There doesn't need to be a fifth in that group of friends. The four of them get into enough trouble."

She grinned. "They do, and I think that ship has sailed. They invited me to their monthly book club."

He started to laugh again, but quickly reined it in. "You mean the book club where they never discuss the book?"

She laughed. "That's the one. I don't even know what book we're supposed to read for this month. I just know I'm supposed to show up. We'll probably end up talking about Tara's wedding, since it's that weekend."

"I hope this pain is a lot better by then. I don't relish spending hours in a tux with my chest on fire."

She patted his arm. "I think you'll be almost good as new by then. But only if you rest like you're supposed to."

He rolled his eyes. "Why do I get the feeling you're going to be more of a pain in my ass than Macy?"

Maggie tipped her head, glancing up. "Probably because I will. And I'm going to start now. Get some sleep." She stood and picked up her coat. "I'm going to go home and pack some things to take to your house. I'll be back in the morning." She shook a finger at him. "Do what the nurses tell you."

"Yes, dear." A cocky smile split his tired face.

She grinned. "Just be good."

"Yeah, yeah. Scram, so I can rest." His head fell back against the pillow and he closed his eyes.

"I'll see you in the morning. If you think of anything you need before discharge, let me know and I'll bring it when I come." She put on her coat as she talked, walking toward the door.

"Okay. Maggie?"

She paused with her hand on the knob and looked back in question.

He cleared his throat, those indigo eyes latched onto hers. "Thanks. For everything."

A soft smile spread over her lips. "You're welcome. I'll see you tomorrow."

"Good night."

"Night." With a wave, she opened the door and left his room. Warmth filled her chest at their exchange. She didn't quite know what to make of this shift in the dynamic of their relationship. She wasn't even sure what to call it. A deeper friendship, maybe. But that didn't explain the way he looked at her when she mentioned her shoes.

Tired and confused, she pushed those thoughts to the back of her mind. She had a million other things she needed to concentrate on to be ready to bring Declan home tomorrow. Pushing through the lobby doors, her heels making a steady clack on the pavement, she walked to her car so she could do just that.

The door to Declan's hospital room opened. He looked up to see Seb stride through.

"Seb. Hey. What are you doing here?"

The tall lawman crossed the room in two strides and sat in the chair by the bed. "I wanted to talk to you."

Declan struggled to sit a little higher, frowning at the serious note in Seb's voice. "About what?"

"Alex performed the autopsy on the man from the fire. He was stabbed before he was doused in gasoline and set alight."

"Are you serious?"

"Yeah. The knife nicked the spine and Katie found gasoline residue on him."

"Do you know who he is yet?"

Seb shifted, taking a deep breath. "That's where it gets weirder. I'm not a hundred percent certain yet, but I think it's one of the ranch hands from the Broken Bow."

Declan's eyebrows shot up. "What? Why would he be in that house, and what makes you think it's one of your hands?"

"Brady told me a few days ago that one of the hands, Jed Stafford, didn't show up for work. He thought it was unusual, because the kid was a hard worker. I asked the others if they'd heard from him and no one had, but a couple of them mentioned he'd taken on some side jobs in construction. I guess he was trying to save up enough money to buy a new truck."

"And you think he was working on that house?"

"Yeah. I don't have anything concrete. It's just a feeling. Too much of a coincidence for me."

"Why would someone stab him, though, and then burn the house down?"

"To cover up the crime."

"Maybe." Declan stared out the window as he considered Seb's theory. Something didn't add up.

"What?"

"What?" Declan looked at his friend.

"I can see the gears working. What are you thinking?"

"Whoever set that fire knew what they were doing. I don't think it's the first time they've done it."

"We haven't had any other arson cases in the county lately."

"Right, but that doesn't mean he hasn't practiced on other structures we don't know about. If he lives somewhere remote, he could have built and burned small sheds on his own property. My point is, what if this isn't about your ranch hand, but about the arsonist? Maybe Stafford was just in the wrong place at the wrong time."

"Collateral damage?"

"Exactly."

Seb sat back in his chair, running a hand over his jaw as he thought about that. "Well, damn. If that's the case, I'm back to square one without the slightest clue where to look for a suspect."

"I could take another look at the crime scene and—"

Seb waved his hands, cutting him off. "No. Macy and Maggie would have my hide. Then so would my wife, because I upset them. No. You are to stay away from work until the doctor says you can go back."

"Then why the hell are you here and telling me all this?"

Seb gave a self-deprecating laugh. "Hell if I know. I guess I figured you deserved an update since you were hurt fighting the blaze. I wasn't counting on you throwing out alternate theories."

"Well, I still think you should share all the evidence and crime scene photos with me sooner rather than later. If I'm right about Stafford being collateral, this guy's going to strike again. I can work on Maggie and soften her up to the idea."

Seb frowned. "Work on her how? And why is she the one staying with you and not your sister?"

Oh, here we go. Big brother was taking a stand. Declan decided to have a little fun. "Didn't you know? We've been secretly dating since you arrested me for murder in June. She practically lives at my house."

Seb's frown turned thunderous. "What? I swear to God, Declan, if you break her heart—"

Declan fought to hold in the laughter, wincing as some broke free. "Relax. Nothing's going on. Macy asked her to check on me the other night because she was busy, and it's just snowballed from there. I haven't touched her." Though, that idea was becoming more appealing with every moment he spent in her company.

"If you weren't all busted up, I'd punch you. Jackass."

Declan held back another laugh. "You're such an easy mark."

"Yeah? Well, wait until you find out some clown is dating Macy, then come talk to me."

"Hell, I'd be happy. Maybe she'd stop trying to run my life."

Seb grinned. "You'd be lost without her, and you know it."

Yeah, he would. He loved his sister to distraction. She was the one person who truly understood him, because she'd been right there beside him, experiencing the same life. They'd needed to depend on each other, because there hadn't been anyone else. She did have one serious character flaw, though. "I could do without her obsessive neat-freak tendencies when she's stressed. She reorganized my cupboards when she was worried about Rayna. All my canned goods are alphabetized now, and my dishes are stored by size, then color."

Seb shook his head and grinned. "At least she's trying to be productive."

"That's true. But it still took me forever to get used to where she put everything, especially the dishware."

The door opened again, and Maggie waltzed inside, looking fresh and young in a pair of jeans, red flats, and a yellow cardigan over a deep purple t-shirt. Declan felt a pang of disappointment she wasn't wearing heels.

She paused when she saw her brother. "Hey, Seb. What are you doing here? He's going home, you know." Her eyes narrowed. "Wait. You're not here discussing work, are you?"

Seb stood. "Well, that's my cue to leave."

"Sebastian." She glared up at him.

He bent and pressed a quick kiss to her cheek. "It was just an update. He needs to stay in the loop." He glanced back at Declan. "I'll let you know if we uncover anything else."

Declan nodded. "Keep my theory in mind."

"Like I could forget it. Put a damn monkey wrench in my investigation. Take care of yourself." He looked down at Maggie. "And you, don't hover."

She rolled her eyes. "Yes, Dad. Now, shoo." She gave him a soft shove toward the door.

"I'll see you guys later." He waved and closed the door behind him.

Maggie turned those dark eyes on him as soon as the door shut.

Declan held up his hands as high as his ribs would let him, hoping his expression was innocent because he was anything but. "It really was just an update."

"Hmm... sure it was." She put down her coffee and the brown tote she carried, then sat in the chair Seb vacated. "How are you feeling?"

He put his hands down, thankful she dropped the matter. "Still like I got hit by a truck, but that it was a slightly smaller truck."

"That's good. How soon until you can blow this pop stand?"

"The nurse said the doctor would be in soon to give me a final once over. After that, we just have to wait for him to input the orders."

"I guess it's good I brought breakfast, then." She opened her bag and pulled out a sack from Peppy Brewster. "London got ambitious while she was helping at the coffee shop yesterday and made all kinds of stuff for Macy to sell. I snagged some of her cinnamon rolls." She handed him a clear plastic box and a fork.

Declan's mouth watered as he took them from her. He didn't care that he already ate some powdered scrambled eggs and chewy bacon. London's rolls were legendary.

"Wait!" She laid a hand over his. "You're allowed to have that, right?"

"I have no idea, and I don't care. They're sending me home, so it's not like I wouldn't just eat it in a couple hours, anyway." He flipped open the lid and speared a forkful of the roll, making sure to get lots of icing. "We'll just hide it fast if the nurse comes in." He stuffed the bite in his mouth, his eyes rolling up as the flavors exploded over his tongue.

Maggie giggled. "It's a cinnamon roll, Declan. Not caviar."

He made a face at her and swallowed. "Have you ever had caviar? It's disgusting. Like salty, gelatinous ground beef."

Her nose wrinkled. "That sounds... lovely. When did you have caviar?"

"In the Marines. I was in France on leave and trying to impress some French girl."

"Did it work?"

"No. I couldn't stand the texture and spit it out in my napkin. She muttered something in French that I think probably meant I was a disgusting pig, then got up and left."

Maggie laughed. "What did you do then?"

"Found a pizza place, bought some beer, and went back to my hotel."

"That sounds much better than caviar."

"Oh, it was. But not as good as this." He continued to eat while they talked, demolishing the roll in just a few bites, and now scraped the container for the last bits of icing. "I don't suppose you have another coffee hiding in that purse, do you?"

She shook her head. "No. I figured the food would be safe —even if it's against the rules—but I wasn't sure about the caffeine." She picked up her cup and held it out to him. "I doubt a few sips will hurt, though."

He accepted the cup and took a drink, quickly scrunching his nose at the sweet flavor. "I should have asked what was in it first. Why do you girls like the sweet stuff so much?" He handed the cup back to her.

"You just ate an entire cinnamon roll, but you're complaining about some flavored syrup in coffee?"

"Well, yeah. It's supposed to be black."

"Only when there are no other options."

He grinned.

The door opened, drawing their attention. The doctor walked in with his entourage again. "Good morning, Mr. Briggs. And Ms. Archer."

"Good morning," Maggie said.

The doctor walked around to stand next to the bed. "So, how's your pain level?"

"Better."

"Good. Do you feel like it's under control?"

Declan nodded.

Dr. Calvin leaned over to check his incision and asked a few questions before declaring him well enough to go home. "I'll get your paperwork in as soon as I finish rounds. We'll have you out of here by lunch. Take it easy for the next few days. I am hereby ordering you to be lazy. Let this pretty lady take care of you."

Declan glanced at Maggie, who waggled her eyebrows at him and grinned. He smiled back, shaking his head.

"I'll make sure he's good," Maggie said.

"I have faith you will, Ms. Archer." Calvin said, before turning his attention back to Declan. "Rest really is the best thing for you. You do that and your breathing exercises and you'll be on the fast track to being one hundred percent."

He knew the doctor was right, but it didn't mean he liked the idea of resting on his laurels for days on end. He would do his best, though. Being injured was for the birds. "I will."

"All right. I'll see you in my office in a week. We'll talk about you returning to work then."

"Okay. Thank you, doctor."

"Not a problem." Calvin and his team left with a wave, leaving Declan and Maggie alone again.

He glanced down at the cinnamon roll container he still held. "I guess it wasn't against the rules."

She laughed. "I guess not."

Four

Maggie's jaw cracked as she let out a huge yawn. She padded down the stairs to the kitchen to start her morning coffee, shivering slightly. Declan kept his house on the cooler side, and even in her flannel pjs, she was still chilly after having been tucked under warm blankets all night. Coffee would fix that, though.

She tiptoed through the living room, trying not to wake him. He hadn't been able to sleep in his bed yet, preferring the semi-upright position the recliner offered. She'd slept on the couch the first couple nights, just in case he needed her. The poor man tossed and turned most of the night, so she did her best not to wake him when she got up in the mornings.

As she entered the kitchen, she reached for the light switch, flipping it on, only to let out a yelp when it lit up Declan's half-naked form sitting at the table.

"Holy crap, Deck! You scared the shit out of me! I thought you were still sleeping. Why are you sitting in the dark?"

He squinted up at her in the bright light. "Thinking."

"What? Why does that require you to sit in the kitchen in the dark?"

"I was thirsty. My ribs hurt, so I sat. Then I started thinking."

That explained everything. She rolled her eyes and walked to the counter, turning on the coffee machine. She needed caffeine to process this conversation. "What were you thinking about?"

"Stuff. The fire. How many emails are probably in my inbox at work. You."

She paused, coffee filters in her hand, and glanced back. "Me?"

He nodded.

"What about me?" She put the filter in the machine, then reached for the bag of coffee.

"How I'm attracted to you, even though I shouldn't be."

Coffee grounds fell over the counter as she missed her target. The plastic scoop clattered against the counter as she laid it down, turning to look at him. "Why shouldn't you be attracted to me?" Because she was certainly attracted to him. "Is this about the lawyer thing again?"

He smiled. "No. It's more because you're almost ten years younger than me. *And* the kind of woman I swore I wouldn't get involved with again. And numerous other reasons, to include the lawyer thing."

She frowned, her mind latching onto the woman thing. "Okay. What type of woman is that?"

He gave her a one shoulder shrug. "High-maintenance. Prissy."

Maggie blustered. She hated that word. Just because she liked high heels and dresses did not make her prissy. She was just as happy in jeans and flannel, covered head to toe in dirt and manure. "I am hardly either of those things. I can do without all the trappings just fine."

"Prove it."

"Excuse me?"

"You heard me. Prove it. Except for work—outside this house—you have to give up your creature comforts. No frilly dresses, no heels, no makeup, *no fancy lattes*," he eyed the coffee on the counter, "for a week."

"What would that prove? And why do you want me to?"

"Call it a test."

"A test?"

"Yes."

"A test of what?"

"Suitability."

A clearer picture started to emerge in her mind. "Suitability? Between you and me, you mean?"

He nodded.

She puffed a breath through her nose and shook her head. "You sure it was your ribs they worked on and not your brain? If you need me to prove I'm suitable for you to date, I'm not." She swiped up the coffee grounds and tossed them in the sink, then closed the coffee bag and shoved it back to its spot on the counter. "I'm going to go put on a pretty dress and heels, then take my *prissy self* to Peppy Brewster for a latte." Glaring at him, she stormed out.

Declan watched her go, running a hand through his hair as she stomped out of the room in her thick wool socks. He knew he'd been an insensitive jerk, but the thoughts he'd been entertaining before she walked in left him feeling a little raw. The last few days with her around were nice. They reminded him of what it was like to be in a committed relationship. The desire to have her around even after she went home was strong.

She was worming beneath his defenses at an alarming rate, so he latched onto any reason he could to put her at arm's length, which in this case was his last serious relationship. He met Lilah in Colorado Springs. Beautiful, smart, sexy, she'd captivated him, but she was also high-maintenance. In the end, they hadn't been able to make it work, neither of them willing to give up their lifestyle and move for the other. The whole thing left a sour taste in his mouth.

But Maggie wasn't anything like Lilah, other than her love of sky-high heels and pretty dresses. She was a rancher's daughter, one who worked alongside her father growing up, and wasn't afraid to get dirty. She was the total package, which was a good part of what he found so attractive about her. He didn't want to be attracted to her. He didn't want to be attracted to anyone. He liked his solitary life. Fewer possibilities of having his heart smashed to bits.

He groaned and covered his face, scrubbing his hands over the stubble dusting his jaw. He shouldn't have taken his frustrations and fears out on her, but it just popped out. Now, he had some groveling to do to get back in her good graces. God, what a mess.

The sound of water running as the shower started upstairs drew his attention. Unbidden, thoughts of her naked and slick with suds floated into his head and stuck there. He growled and pushed out of his chair. Sexual frustration was just what he needed to add to his misery.

He flipped off the kitchen light as he left the room. It was slow-going as he ascended the stairs to his bedroom. He knew he needed to apologize and try to make amends, but there was no way he was going to do that with her fresh out of the shower. It could wait until she returned from court later. He was going to hide out like the coward he was until she left.

Ribs on fire, he reached his room and sank onto the bed, groaning as he shifted. He couldn't wait until he no longer felt as weak as a kitten.

The shower cut, and Declan stayed put, hoping she would

think he went back to sleep. Her anger at him was more likely to keep her away, though. Fifteen minutes later, he heard her heels click on the hallway floor, then down the stairs. When he heard the garage door rise, then close again, he got up and went back downstairs.

Maggie's light floral scent lingered in the air. He couldn't even get away from her when she wasn't here. Frustrated, he wandered into his office. He still had a couple days before he was allowed back to work, but he didn't care. He needed the distraction.

Declan sat down at the desk and logged into his computer, navigating to the fire department's employee portal. He logged in and clicked on the tab for his email. Hundreds of messages greeted him. Sighing, he clicked on the oldest one and got started. Most of them were nothing important, but as he weeded through, he found several related to the fire. Katie had analyzed the trace evidence and discovered the accelerant used was gasoline. There was a higher concentration of it near the kitchen, and she found melted plastic from a gas can there. He also had a message from Seb. They'd made a positive ID on the victim. It was the ranch hand from the Broken Bow.

He picked up the phone on the desk and punched in the number for his sergeant, Keith Walters. The line rang twice before he picked up.

"Walters."

"Hey, it's Briggs."

"Lou! How are you doing?"

"Getting better."

"That's good. Are you bored? Hell, you must be if you're calling me." He chuckled.

Declan felt a smile tug at one corner of his mouth. "Just a bit, yeah. Can you tell me anymore about the fire investigation? I just read the reports from the lab."

Walters blew out a breath. "There isn't much more to

report. No one saw anything. The only trace was the accelerant and the gas can, which could have been bought anywhere. The sheriff's department is working the victim angle, trying to find out if he had any enemies. That's about all I know."

His mouth pulled in a frown. "Damn. I was hoping there was a stronger lead on the arsonist. I don't like this. That scene was organized."

"I agree. I don't think we've seen the last of this guy."

Fire tones sounded before Declan could reply.

"I gotta go, Lou. I'll talk to you later."

"Stay safe."

"Always."

Declan hung up, perturbed. The lack of evidence bothered him. It meant this wasn't the first fire the arsonist had set. But he couldn't think of any other unsolved suspicious fires in the area. He made a mental note to have Seb check for similar fires in surrounding counties. Maybe they would get lucky.

He turned back to the computer to comb through his emails again, but the fire tones still clanged through his head. He wanted to be there! It was driving him nuts to sit around doing nothing. His eyes flicked to the door and back to the screen.

Screw it.

He pushed away from the desk and went in search of his truck keys. He couldn't drive yet. Not because he wasn't allowed, which he wasn't, but because he couldn't lift his arms high enough to turn the wheel. But he could sit in the truck and listen to the radio traffic.

Back in the living room, he grabbed his phone from beside the recliner, then headed to the kitchen. He snagged his keys off the hook by the door and stepped into the garage. The truck's door locks clicked as he unlocked them with the remote. Opening the door, he hoisted himself into the driver's seat and turned the key to the accessory position, then flipped on his fire radio. It only took him a moment to find the correct channel.

Declan sat back in the seat and listened to the traffic, learning they were on-scene of another residential fire. He just hoped the occupants got out. It was early yet; most people were still at home.

He stayed in the truck until the fire was out. It was another hot one. As he waited to hear Walters give the all-clear, his cell phone rang. He looked down, frowning as he saw Walters's name come up on the screen. Dread filled his belly as he swiped to answer the call.

"It's the same guy, isn't it?" Declan asked in lieu of a greeting.

"Yeah. I think so. There are burn marks in front of the doors and under all the windows."

"Did everyone make it out?"

"With some burns and smoke inhalation, yes. Home-owners are Mark and Lorraine Meyers."

"Wait. Did you say Lorraine Meyers?" Declan's mind worked as he mulled over that tidbit of information.

"Yeah. You know her?"

"I do. She's Thomas Archer's veterinary assistant."

"Weird. What are the odds both arson cases would be connected to the Archer family?"

That was an excellent question. What *were* the odds?

When Maggie walked in the door that afternoon, Declan pounced.

"I need you to take me to the Meyers's house."

She paused just inside the front door, one hand still on the knob, and blinked at him. "Who? And why?"

"There was a fire at Lorraine Meyers's house this morning. Walters found the same burn patterns there as at the vacant house where I was injured."

Her eyes widened. "Oh my goodness. Are Lorraine and Mark all right?"

"They were taken to the hospital with some burns and smoke inhalation. I don't know how bad their injuries are, though. Can you take me to their house? I need to walk through and confirm it was the same arsonist. I also need to talk to Seb."

She stepped inside and closed the door, then held out a hand and waved it in a small circle. "Hold on a second. You're not supposed to be working. How do you even know all this?"

"I checked my email after you left. The forensics reports from the fire that injured me were there. I called Walters to see if he knew any more. He got a fire call while we were on the line, so I went and listened to the radio traffic in my truck. They were wrapping things up when he called me direct to tell me they found the same burn pattern at all the egress points as the previous fire," he summed up. "So, can we go?"

She sighed and closed her eyes for a moment, then looked at him. "You're not supposed to be working."

He rolled his eyes. "Come on, Maggie. It's a walkthrough and a conversation."

"Wearing turnout gear, which weighs like forty pounds."

"I shouldn't need it. The fire's out. All I need is my jacket and badge to identify me as part of the department and my helmet."

She grumbled under her breath. "I'm going to regret this, but okay."

He resisted the urge to pump his fist.

"With two suspicious fires, your expertise is warranted." She held up her hand again. "Just promise me you'll be careful?"

"Scout's honor." He held up three fingers.

She narrowed her eyes at him. "Were you even a boy scout?"

He grinned and shook his head, dropping his hand. "No. How about Marines' honor instead? I'll be careful, I swear."

"Fine. Let's go." She put her briefcase down next to the entryway table and turned around to go back to her car.

Declan opened the closet and took out his department jacket, doing his best to put it on as he followed her out the door. He was glad he grabbed his badge and put on his shoes before she got home. She wasn't waiting. He got both arms in the jacket as he reached her car, climbing inside as she started the engine.

"Where am I going?"

"The fire station, so I can get my helmet."

She put the car in reverse.

"Thank you."

Maggie glanced at him as she pulled onto the street, a question in her dark eyes.

"I know I promised to stay away from work, but—"

"No, I understand. I'm not mad. Just worried you'll hurt yourself."

"I was a Marine. I can handle some broken ribs. It's not the worst injury I've ever had."

"No, but you're stubborn."

He couldn't argue there. But he had no intention of overdoing it. He wanted to get back to fighting fires as soon as possible. "I'll behave." He gave her outfit a once over. "I'd offer to let you come in and supervise, but you're not exactly dressed for it."

"What? Am I too prissy for a fire scene?"

He groaned. "I'm never living that down, am I? I'm sorry. I know you're at ease in anything you wear and aren't afraid to get dirty. But you still remind me of Lilah in some ways. She was always very polished, and God forbid if I messed up the polish."

She wrinkled her nose and made a turn out of his neighborhood. "I'm not sure I like being equated with her. I remember her from some party we all went to. She seemed a bit stuck up. What did you see in her, anyway?"

He shrugged. "She wasn't all bad. So long as we did things on her terms, she was great. But she wasn't ever willing to do anything that would mess up her nails or her makeup." Looking back on his relationship with Lilah, he knew now they should have ended it sooner. They weren't well-suited. It was a bit of a blessing neither of them wanted to move so they could take their relationship to the next level.

"I'll never understand that. Both those things can be fixed. You miss out on life when you aren't willing to get dirty. Some of my favorite memories are when I was covered in dust and engine grease. Or horse manure." She laughed.

He grinned. "Same here. Not the manure part, but the other stuff. Messy can be fun."

"So, does that mean you'll stop thinking of me as high-maintenance?"

"No."

She turned a sharp glare on him.

"What? You are. But you're also not when you want to be. How about I promise to see you as both?"

Maggie gave a short laugh. "I'm not sure how that works, but okay."

"It just does, trust me." Declan smiled. He took his phone from his pocket. "I'm going to call Seb and have him meet us at the house."

While he talked, she drove the rest of the way to the fire station, soon pulling into the parking lot.

"I'll be just a minute if you want to wait here."

She arched a brow. "You've been out almost a week. Do you really think you'll be in and out of there quickly?"

"Normally, I'd say no, but it looks like most of the squads are out on runs." He pointed to the open doors in front of the bays where firetrucks and ambulances normally sat. There was one firetruck and one ambulance remaining.

She nodded. "Point taken. I'll wait here."

He opened his door and climbed out, walking inside as fast as his ribs allowed. The garage was quiet, and he made his way to the equipment room, finding his helmet hanging above the rest of his gear. He took it off the hook and grabbed a pair of gloves as well, then went back out to Maggie's SUV.

"Let's go," he said, climbing inside and buckling up.

"Where am I going?" She backed out of her parking space.

He told her the address. They crossed town, pulling up outside the burned-out shell that used to be the Meyers's house a few minutes later. Seb was already there, standing outside the house, staring at the ruined structure.

"Oh my God," Maggie breathed. Tears welled in her eyes. "This is awful. Why would someone do this?"

Declan's jaw worked. "I don't know, but I'm going to stop them. Come on." He got out of the car, and she followed. "You can stand at the front door just in case something happens."

"What? I thought you said this was safe."

"It'll likely be fine." He walked toward the front door, waving at Sebastian.

"Declan!"

"Relax, Mags. The biggest risk is the weakened floor joists, but I know what I'm doing."

She growled, following behind him, her heels clacking on the sidewalk.

Seb's brows quirked as they reached him. "What's got your dander up?"

"She's just worried about me," Declan replied before she could answer.

"Why?"

"Because he's injured and should be at home resting, not traipsing through this death trap."

Seb looked at the house, eyes a little more wary. "Is there something I should know before we go in there?"

"You're not going anywhere," Declan said. "I don't have any safety gear for you. A helmet is a necessity in a place like this."

"Then what do you need me here for?"

"To replace the crime scene tape, for one. And I have questions about both fires." He settled his helmet on his head, then took a knife from his pocket, flicking it open and slicing through the seal on the door.

He stepped over the threshold. "I'll be back in a few."

"Watch yourself," Seb said.

"Yep." He walked further into the house, noting the char pattern near the door as he entered. It was a match to the other house. So were the markings under each window and at the back door. At the master bedroom, there was a burn pattern outside the door. Declan stepped over the mark and went over to the window. There was no charring there.

He bent closer to inspect the frame, poking his head through to look at the outside. A small piece of wood was wedged between the frame and the casing.

"Sebastian! You should come take a look at this."

Seb and Maggie stepped around the side of the house, coming toward him when they saw him leaning out of the window.

"Look at what?" Seb asked once they were close.

Declan pointed at the window casing. "It was wedged closed just like the garage door at the other house."

Seb cursed. "I don't know if Katie saw that. I'll call her

and ask." He stepped away, already bringing his phone up to his ear.

Maggie looked up at him, her eyes shining with concern. "Mark and Lorraine should have died this morning."

He nodded, his mouth a grim line.

"Why didn't they?"

"I'm not sure. I don't even know where they were in the house or how they got out."

"Maybe Seb knows." She glanced at her brother, who hung up the phone and walked back to them.

"She said she didn't. She's on her way over to catalog and remove it."

"Good. What can you tell me about how the Meyers escaped?"

Seb blew out a breath and ran a hand through his hair. "Lorraine said they woke up to smoke. The door was hot to the touch, so they tried the window, but it wouldn't open."

"Why didn't they just break it and climb through?" Maggie asked.

"She said they couldn't find anything heavy enough to break the window with all the smoke obscuring their vision. Mark wrapped a piece of clothing around his hand and opened the door. The hallway was on fire, but they didn't have a choice. She said they wet themselves down in the attached bathroom, then walked through the flames."

"That was good thinking," Declan said. "It probably saved their lives."

"Yeah. They both have some pretty serious burns, though. Especially to their feet."

"Did you get any more on Stafford? On why someone would want to kill him?"

Seb shook his head. "And what I don't get is if the two fires are related, why didn't the arsonist murder the Meyers before he set the fire like he did with Jed."

"Maybe Jed caught him in the act of torching the place," Maggie mused. "Mark and Lorraine were asleep."

"That could be, but it doesn't help explain the connection between the victims," Declan said.

"What do you mean?" she asked.

"Stafford and the Meyers are both connected to your family. If Jed wasn't meant to be at the house, that means that fire isn't connected to you guys."

"It's possible there's another connection," Seb said.

"Like what?"

"I don't know yet. I'm just saying it's possible."

"It is." Declan's head bobbed. "I think we'll know soon enough, though. I don't think this guy is done."

"Jesus, don't say that," Seb said.

"Sorry. It's true, though. The scenes are just too sophisticated. He's practiced all this somewhere, and now he's showing off. He's just getting warmed up."

FIVE

Maggie entered the fire station, ready to get Declan and go home. The doctor gave him the okay to go back to desk duty last week, but he still wasn't allowed to drive, so she offered to take him and pick him up every day. She just hoped he was ready to go. She had to peel him away from the station the last few days. She was starving. All she wanted was a giant slice of pizza and a glass of wine. It was officially the weekend.

She waved at several of the firefighters as she walked through the station to his office.

"I'm not ready yet, Maggie," he said through the open door before she even showed her face.

"How did you know it was me?"

"I could hear you coming."

She glanced down at her shoes, then shrugged. "How much longer do you think you'll be? I'm ready to eat."

"So go eat," he said, not looking up from the pile of papers on his desk. "I have plenty to keep me occupied."

She heaved a sigh. "You're terrible. I don't think working twelve-hour days, even behind a desk, is what the doctor had in mind when he said you could go back to work."

"Well, it's the reality. I have annual reviews to process."

"It's October."

"It's almost November. And raises from these start in January, so they all have to be completed in time for the paperwork to get sent over to the budget office so people get their increase on time."

"I guess that makes sense." She sank into the chair opposite his desk. "How about I order us a pizza? We can pick it up on the way back to your house. That'll give you an extra twenty minutes." She stared at him, waiting for him to look up.

"I might be done by then," he said, meeting her gaze.

"I hope so, because I might have to get your guys out there to back me up if you aren't. You need to rest, Declan." She could see the fatigue pulling at his face. The lines around his eyes were deeper than normal.

"Why don't you go get the pizza, and we'll eat it here while I work?"

"Not gonna happen. I need wine too. And you need to rest." She knew she sounded like a broken record, but it was true.

He arched a brow. "You're not going to let this go, are you?"

She shook her head.

He huffed. "Fine. Twenty minutes."

Maggie beamed and hopped up out of her chair. "I'm going to order the food and mingle. Twenty minutes, Deck. Not a second more."

"Yeah, yeah." He waved a hand at her. "Go away."

She stuck her tongue out at him, but flounced out the door, smiling, knowing she won. As she walked down the hall, she took her phone out of her purse and called the local pizza place she had on speed dial. She placed her order, then entered the common room, where several of the firefighters were hanging out.

They looked up when she came in. A couple of the younger ones stumbled out of their chairs, eager to greet her. Sam Reeves stood more slowly, sauntering over to wave off the rookies.

"Leave her alone, boys. Unless you want to suffer Lou's wrath."

Maggie smiled up at him as the younger men dispersed. "Thanks, Sam. It's good to see you. Declan said you were coming back. I'm glad your injuries healed quickly. I know with Austin still recuperating, things were tough."

"Yeah. But the boys here pitched in. I still have a freezer full of meals and a stack of gift cards to use if we don't want to reheat something."

"I'm glad. So, how *are* you doing?"

"Pretty good. I've got a hard head."

"Apparently so. How's your brother?"

"He's doing well. His P.T. is progressing, and he's steadily regaining function in his arm. The therapist is hopeful he'll get most, if not all, of it back."

"Really? That's amazing."

"Yeah. He's tough, too. Gets it from me."

They chuckled.

"So, you here to pick up Briggs?"

Maggie nodded.

"You're a brave woman. He's been a surly bear all day."

"He has? He seemed like himself to me." Maybe a little preoccupied with work, but himself.

Sam smiled. "That's because you're you. You make him happy."

She did?

"Don't look so shocked."

"Sorry. I just didn't think I had that kind of effect on

him." She knew their relationship had changed in the last couple of weeks, but she still didn't think she had that sort of influence over him.

"Well, you do. I just wish you'd shown up earlier. He was barking orders at us all day and growling anytime one of us walked into his office and interrupted him."

"He was? Hmm. I'll have a talk with him and see what that was all about."

Sam waved a hand. "You don't need to. He's probably just pissed he can't take part the way he usually does. He went on runs with us today, but only in a supervisory capacity. A couple times, he started walking toward the scene to help, then realize he couldn't, and would plant his feet and scowl."

Maggie giggled. "It's been hard on him."

"That's for sure. And I know how he feels. Sitting at home, waiting on the concussion symptoms to go away was torture."

She opened her mouth to reply when her phone rang. "Sorry. Hang on a second." She looked at the screen, frowning when she saw Tara's face. "It's my sister. I need to take this."

He nodded. "Tell her I said hello."

Maggie nodded, swiping her thumb across the screen as she walked away. "Hello?" She headed down the hallway to go outside for privacy.

"Where are you?"

"At the fire station, picking up Declan. Sam Reeves says hello. Why, what's up?"

"Oh, hello to him too. And good! Can you run to the grocery and pick up some things for me? I'm at London's, and we're working on cake flavors. She ran out of a few items."

London ran out of stuff to bake with? That didn't seem possible. She always had plenty of those items on hand. "How much cake did you make?"

Tara cleared her throat. "Probably more than we should

have. But I couldn't decide!" she rushed to clarify. "I'm still on the fence, and I keep thinking of other flavors... Why does this have to be so hard?"

Maggie laughed. "Because you want it all to be perfect. And it will be. Not because you have the perfect flavor of cake, but because you're marrying a great guy. That's all that matters."

Tara sighed. "I know. But I still want a kick-ass cake. So, can you bring me what we need or not?"

"Yes. Just text me what you need. We'll be over in a little while. I ordered pizza, and we have to stop and get it too."

"Sounds good. Thank you!"

"Yep. There better be samples for my trouble."

Tara laughed. "Girl, there are more than samples. I'll see you soon."

They said goodbye, and Maggie hung up as she went back inside to find Declan. His twenty minutes were getting cut short.

She rounded the corner to his office hallway, stopping in his doorway.

"It hasn't been twenty minutes," he said, not looking up, writing.

"No, but Tara called. She needs us to go to the store and bring her some things to make cake."

He looked up with a frown. "Shouldn't she have had all that before she started?"

Maggie smiled. "She did, but she and London used it all and need more. Apparently, pregnancy has made my sister indecisive. They're at the inn, baking a bunch of different flavors because she can't decide which one she wants for the wedding."

"Wait. Are you saying there are several kinds of cake at the inn? That London baked?"

Maggie nodded, sensing victory. She had him now. His sweet tooth was as bad as Seb's, she'd discovered.

He clicked his pen closed and tossed it on his desk, rising from his chair. "Let's go."

"I'm not sure if I should be offended that you're more willing to leave for cake than my growling stomach." She stepped back into the hallway as he came toward her.

He grinned. "Cake will always win. And I like messing with you. Take that as you will." He sauntered past her.

She rolled her eyes, laughing, and followed. Outside, they climbed into her car, and she headed for the grocery store to get the things on Tara's list.

Once the groceries were bought, they swung by the pizza place, then drove out of town toward the inn. Maggie pulled into the drive and parked around the side of the house, noting that most of the family was here.

"I hope they don't expect us to share our dinner," Declan said, glancing around at all the cars. He held the pizza box in his hands.

She looked up from looping grocery bags over her arms. "*Our* dinner?"

"Don't even pretend like you weren't going to share with me."

"Well, only if you asked nicely." She snagged the last two bags with her fingers, then backed up. "Hit the button to close the hatch, would you?"

He pushed the button just inside the vehicle and stepped back. They made their way to the front door. Declan twisted the knob and let them inside. The noise of her family assaulted her right away. They followed the sound into the kitchen.

"Oh! Yay!" Tara spotted them. She hurried around the island, hands outstretched, to take the grocery bags from Maggie. "Did you get everything I asked for?"

"Yes." Maggie took in the array of cakes scattered over the

counters. "Geez, Tara. How many different flavors did you bake?"

Tara looked up from emptying the bags. Her eyes roamed over the pans littering every available surface. "A lot."

"Eight." London piped up. "We made eight."

"Holy cow. What happened to good ol' chocolate and vanilla?"

Tara sighed.

"It's boring," Jace said. "She doesn't want boring."

"Well, I think you've avoided that. How many more were you planning on making?"

"Too many," London moaned.

Tara shot her a look. "You don't have to help. I can do this on my own."

"No, I'll help. I'm just tired. The sooner we get finished, the sooner I can go put my feet up."

"Which you should do, too," Rayna told Tara, ever the voice of reason. She pointed at Tara's distended abdomen.

Tara waved a hand. "I'm fine. I've got my kitchen shoes on, so I'm good to go. Let's do this."

Jace sighed and ran a hand through his golden hair. Seb, Thomas, Brady, and Declan laughed at him. He narrowed his eyes and glared at them. "Just you wait. They'll all be the same, especially Maggie."

"Me?" Maggie pointed at her chest. "Why me?"

"Because you're sisters, and honestly, the two of you are a lot alike."

Her mouth flattened. She couldn't exactly deny that, but she would never admit it, either. She snatched the pizza box from Declan and walked over to the table tucked against the wall. "The first part is true, but I'm much more laid back."

Declan snorted and joined her. "Whatever. You've been bossing me around for two weeks." He lowered himself into the chair across from her and took a slice of pizza from the box.

"Well, you need to rest, and you don't listen." She took a bite of her food.

"I'm fine."

"Now you sound like Tara," Jace said.

The others laughed, including Tara, and they fell into easy conversation as London and Tara baked. While Declan and Maggie ate, Macy made frosting for the cakes already done. Rayna sliced them once they were frosted and passed out pieces. Maggie tried not to stare at Declan as a look of pure ecstasy crossed his face when he took a bite of the double fudge cake.

He glanced up, and she wasn't quick enough to look away. Those deep indigo eyes met hers, seizing them as heat flared between them.

Two glasses of wine landed on the table, making them jump.

"Damn." They looked over to see Macy standing beside them. "Drink that and cool off before you set the kitchen on fire."

Maggie snatched up her glass, using it to hide her flaming face. She resisted the urge to fan herself. She really needed to move out of his house. Now that he felt better, she struggled to keep a lid on her attraction.

But would it really be so bad if she didn't? He was a good man. Nice, funny, intelligent. Gorgeous. Why shouldn't she let herself be attracted to him? So what if he was her brothers' friend and her friend's brother? London married her brother's best friend. Rayna was marrying her friends' brother—though Thomas and Rayna were different. Those two were destined for each other since birth. Maggie had a sneaking suspicion, too, that Macy and Brady were headed the same direction. So why shouldn't Maggie date Declan?

She didn't care that he was almost ten years older. She liked older men. The guys her age—at least around here—were more interested in partying it up at the local bar and having casual sex. She didn't do casual. Never had. Maggie was a bookworm, preferring her books to boys. Between school, ranch chores, and sports, she had little time for dating during high school. Not that she hadn't, but none of her relationships ever got serious.

In college, it was more of the same. Her studies sucked up all of her time. She went on a few dates, but no one ever got too close.

But she was an established career woman now. Why couldn't she have a serious boyfriend?

She cast another glance at Declan. A shiver went down her spine at the thought of *him* being her boyfriend. Their relationship would be much more than the heavy petting sessions she had with the others.

His blue eyes sparkled with laughter at something Thomas said. Desire punched her in the gut.

So much more...

She looked away from him, her gaze landing on her sister, who grinned at her. Flushing to the roots of her hair, she schooled her expression and took another sip of her wine.

The trill of Seb's cellphone, closely followed by Thomas's, then Declan's broke through the din in the room. Maggie held her breath as they answered. She saw shock and disbelief cross Thomas's face. Rayna clutched his hand, anchoring him. Urgency had Seb striding toward the door. Declan stood to follow more slowly.

"Thomas's clinic is on fire," Seb announced.

"Oh my God!" London spun and turned off the oven, yanking out the pans. "Let's go."

"What? No," Seb said. "We don't all need to go."

"You're wasting time, Sebastian," Maggie said, getting out of her chair. "We're all going."

"Fine," he growled. "Thomas, Declan, Jace, you can ride with me. The rest of you can follow. At the speed limit." He gave a pointed glance at Tara and Maggie.

"If anyone is going to speed, it'll be Macy," Maggie said, on her way to the door.

"No argument there," Macy said.

"Behave!" Seb yelled, entering the garage, while the rest of them went out through the pocket door to the main living area, then out the front door.

Outside, Brady commandeered Macy's keys. She didn't protest and climbed into the passenger seat. The rest of them piled into the back two rows of the car. He took off down the drive after Seb.

Despite telling Seb they wouldn't speed, Brady kept pace with Seb as they barreled down the country roads toward Thomas's clinic. Rayna clutched Tara's hand in the middle seat, worry etching deeper on her face with every mile. As they neared, Maggie could see an orange glow in the sky, and her heart sank. She'd hoped it was a small fire the fire department could quickly knock down.

They rounded the bend, and the clinic came into sight. A collective gasp went through the car. Flames shot toward the sky, overpowering the flashing lights of the firetrucks just arriving on the scene. Smoke billowed, the roar of the fire audible even inside the closed interior of the SUV.

Tears sprang into Maggie's eyes. It was a total loss.

Brady brought the car to a halt at the perimeter of emergency vehicles, and they all rushed out. Rayna dashed toward Thomas, who stood with Declan near one of the trucks. Horror shone all over his face as he stared at the flames.

From the barn at the rear of the property, Maggie heard the terrified screams of several horses. It drew Thomas's attention as well. Without asking for permission, he ran around the flaming building. Maggie kicked off her heels and followed.

Declan snagged her hand as she ran past.

"Let me go, Deck!"

He slapped a radio in her hand. "Be careful."

More tears welled in her eyes at the look he gave her. He understood she had to do this and wasn't going to stop her. Every fiber in his being wanted to, though. It was written in the lines of his tense muscles and the tick in his jaw. On impulse, she closed the distance between them and pressed a quick kiss to his lips. "I will." With one last look, she turned around and ran after her siblings and friends.

The animals' screams grew louder as she got closer. The barn was just starting to catch from the embers that landed on the roof; the flames contained to the rafters. Thomas had his keys out and was unlocking the doors when she reached them. He pushed inside as the lock opened, the rest of them following.

"Just let them out. We'll worry about rounding them up later," Thomas yelled.

Maggie stopped at the closest occupied stall and opened the door, making sure she was to the side so she didn't get trampled. The horse ran out, the whites of his eyes showing. Her eyes watering from the growing smoke, she ran to the next stall and repeated the process. A loud crack sounded overhead, and embers rained down. Pockets of fire roiled in the rafters now.

She hurried through the barn, checking stalls, leap-frogging with the others. Through the haze of smoke, she caught a glimpse of glowing eyes peeking around some hay bales in the corner. A cough wracked her as the smoke grew thicker, but she stepped toward the stack, getting on all fours to crawl across the floor. As she got closer, she saw a kitten huddled in the hay.

"Come—" she coughed "here, kitty."

The roof creaked again, and she heard something besides embers fall behind her. Praying hard that she would make it out of the barn, she edged toward the cat. It shrunk back against the hay, hissing. "It's okay, baby." She coughed some more. "Let's get out of here."

"Maggie!" She heard Thomas shout her name. "Maggie, where are you?"

His voice distracted the kitten, and she snatched the cat by the scruff. It yowled, but calmed as she got a better grip.

"I'm coming!" she yelled back as best she could. The smoke was really getting thick. She turned toward his voice and bent low to stay out of the thickest smoke. She was glad for the barn's high ceilings. It helped keep the air at her level a little clearer.

Another wracking cough shook her. It was still pretty smoky down here, though. Tears streamed down her face now. "Thomas?" Her voice cracked and broke on the end of his name.

"Out here, Mags!"

She was still on the right path, his voice directly in front of her. A flashlight bobbed through the haze, and she made a beeline for it, cradling the kitten to her chest. The roof cracked again, and more debris fell. Maggie screamed as a beam crashed down in front of her. Fire blocked her path.

Panic made her breath come in quick pants. She tamped down the fear, knowing it wouldn't help her escape. *Think, Maggie!* The hard plastic in her hand registered. *The radio!* She pressed the mic button and brought it to her mouth. "Declan? Are you there?"

"I'm here, Maggie."

"I'm trapped. A beam fell, and it's on fire, blocking the exit. I don't think I can go back the way we came in, either. I heard a crash somewhere back there."

"Okay. Hang tight. Stay low. I'll get you out."

She dropped to her belly on the floor, keeping the kitten tucked close. It let out a pitiful meow, and she knew it was feeling the effects of the smoke, too.

"It's okay, baby. Declan will find us. We'll be okay." Another crack ripped through the barn, and she heard another crash behind her. Fear sent a fine tremor through her body. She prayed no more beams dropped near her.

"Maggie!" Declan's voice carried over the roar of the fire.

Relief drew more tears to her eyes. She turned toward the sound, trying to see the door, but failing. "Declan!" She tried to yell, but the smoke made her voice hoarse.

"Hang on, baby, I'm coming! Just stay put, I'll find you."

She could do that. The cat meowed again, and she whispered to it, trying to keep it calm. A bobbing flashlight grew closer.

"Over here!" She got on her hands and knees and waved, trying to yell again and failing. It didn't matter, though. Since she was in the pathway, he walked right up to her.

He grabbed her bicep and pulled her up, then pressed a mask to her face. Maggie took a deep breath of the clean air, then promptly fell into a coughing fit.

"We need to go!" he yelled through his face mask.

She nodded.

"Keep that over your face. And stay close."

Maggie tucked herself into his good side, then shut her eyes and let him lead. It wouldn't have mattered if she kept them open, anyway. Between the tears and the smoke, she couldn't see. They broke free of the barn, and he kept going until she was out of the smoke plume. She sank into the grass, still clutching the little kitten as she coughed.

Declan kneeled beside her, doffing his helmet and raising his mask. "Take deep breaths, honey."

She nodded, holding the oxygen mask to her face.

The others hurried over. She thrust the cat at Thomas. It was lethargic and wheezing and covered in soot.

"There's extra oxygen in the firetruck," Declan said.

Thomas took off at a run with the kitten, Rayna with him.

Maggie hoped the little cat would be all right. It was so tiny, and they were in there for what felt like an eternity. Another coughing fit doubled her up as her lungs expelled the smoke and soot.

"I told you to be careful," Declan growled.

She looked at him through red, scratchy eyes. "I was." She coughed. "Then I saw that kitten's eyes."

He ran a hand over her back, his jaw working as he looked down at her. Without a word, he leaned down and pressed a kiss to the top of her head, holding her close. She clutched his shirt in her free hand.

"I'm glad you're safe," he whispered into her hair.

She was too. More tears spilled from her eyes, this time from relief.

SIX

Exhaustion pulled at Declan as he and Maggie walked into his house. He needed the max dose of pain pills, a shower, and eight hours or more of sleep. In that order.

"I'm going to go take a shower," Maggie said, her voice not much louder than a whisper thanks to all the smoke she inhaled. After Declan rescued her, Brady drove them to the hospital so a doctor could look at her at Declan's insistence. Maggie hadn't wanted to go, but he didn't give her a choice. She hadn't been able to stop coughing. She was now the proud owner of a bronchodilator inhaler and under orders to rest.

"Same. You can use the shower in the guest bath down here and sleep on the couch if you don't want to climb the stairs."

She shook her head. "I'll be all right. Thanks, though. Good night."

He offered her a tired smile, and she retreated upstairs. Declan found his pain medicine and swallowed as many as he was allowed. His ribs hadn't hurt this much since he broke them. He hoped he didn't damage the repair job or

Maggie would have his head. It wouldn't make any difference that he did it saving her. But he would do it again. There was no way he was going to trust her life with anyone else.

Declan downed the rest of his water, then turned off the kitchen light and made his way upstairs to shower and go to bed. He could hear the water running from the other bathroom and tried not to think about Maggie naked only feet away.

A chuckle slid past his lips as he entered his bedroom. He was in no state to do anything about his need for her. It was all he could do to stand up straight right now. And she wasn't in any better shape. Her breathing was okay, but he could tell the ordeal had been hard on her.

He undressed as he crossed to the bathroom, leaving his shirt until last. Gingerly, he eased his left arm through the hole, then pulled it over his head and dropped it on the floor. Multiple colors covered his chest, an angry red line cutting through them. He examined the incision and bruising in the mirror. It didn't look any worse than this morning, which made him think he just overdid it tonight.

Happy with how things looked, he turned and started the shower, letting the spray grow warm before he stepped in. The hot water sluiced over his gritty skin. Declan squirted some soap in his hands and ran it through his hair and over his body. The suds slithered down his frame, turning a light gray on the shower floor from the grime.

Once he was sufficiently clean, he stepped out, running a towel over his hair, then wrapping it around his waist. He stepped into his room to find clothes, but stopped short at the sight of Maggie sitting against a mound of pillows on his bed. Her long legs peeked out from beneath cotton pajama shorts, and a large t-shirt swallowed her upper half.

"What are you doing in here?"

She bit her lip, her gaze glued to his exposed body. Shaking her head, the glaze over her eyes disappeared.

"I know it probably isn't wise, but can I sleep in here?"

Dear God, was she trying to kill him? "What's wrong with the bed you've been sleeping in?"

"Nothing. I just—" she broke off and sighed. "I don't want to be alone. My mind won't shut off, and all I can think about is what would have happened if you hadn't given me that radio or come in after me." She finished on a soft whisper, tears welling in her eyes. One spilled over, and Declan was lost.

"Let me put some clothes on quick." He crossed to his dresser and took out a pair of underwear and some athletic shorts, skipping the t-shirt. He'd never get it on. He walked back to the bathroom to dress, quickly donning the clothes. With his hand on the doorknob, he took a breath, tamping down his desire and locking it firmly away. He tugged open the door and stepped out.

She was under the covers now and curled on her side with the blankets tucked up under her chin. At least those long legs of hers were no longer in sight. Now, she just looked cute as hell.

He stifled a sigh and flipped off the light, then joined her. Easing into the bed, he stuffed the pillows behind his back. Lying flat still hurt too much. Once he was settled, the sleep he thought would come didn't. His body hummed, sensing the woman beside him.

Her fingers curled over his arm, and he jumped.

"Sorry," she murmured, withdrawing her hand.

"No, it's okay. You just startled me." He'd thought having her touch him would only ramp him up more. But it didn't. It was comforting. Neither of them were in any condition for more than cuddling, so her touch was soothing instead of arousing. Like sitting by the fire with a good book and a beer after a long day.

He reached for her hand under the blankets. Instead of just holding it, he tugged her closer. She was on his good side, so he tucked her into his body. Her arm crossed his abdomen to curl around his waist. She drew slow circles on his hip at the top of his shorts.

He closed his eyes, enjoying her touch.

"Declan?"

"Hmm?" He kept his eyes closed.

"Thank you."

He turned his head to look at her. Gratitude shone from her pretty brown eyes. "I will always come for you, Maggie. Always."

Her hand slid up to his shoulder, and she scooted higher to press a kiss to his jaw. A shot of lust zinged through him, but he put a lid on it. He turned his head and pressed a kiss to her hair. "Go to sleep."

She nodded against his shoulder, and he felt her settle. Declan inhaled a breath, catching her sweet scent and letting it relax him. He cradled Maggie against him and let sleep take over.

The doorbell brought Maggie out of a deep sleep. That and Declan shifting under her in response to the bell.

"What time is it?" she asked. *Good God, I sound like a frog!* She sat up, trying to work up some saliva to moisten her sore, parched throat. Smoke inhalation was no joke. She felt like she had a bad case of strep.

"Seven." He pushed off the covers and got out of bed, wincing at the movement after being in one position for so long.

"Who's ringing the damn doorbell at seven in the morning, especially after the night we had?" She lowered her voice to a whisper. Ack, she needed a drink!

"Someone with a death wish." He headed for the bedroom door.

She scrambled out of bed and followed him downstairs. Declan unlocked the front door and threw it open. Seb stood on the other side.

"I know it's early," he started before either of them could say anything, "but I need you." He pointed at Declan.

"What? Why? What happened now?" Declan stepped back to let him in.

"We've been digging into Jed Stafford's life. Katie found the remnants of an Apple watch on him, and he had his password written down at his apartment. Jace spent the night going through his cloud account and discovered he had the fitness app enabled, which gave us a record of his movements up to his death. One place he visited was out in the middle of nowhere. On a hunch, Jace drove out there and found another torched building. A hunting shack. I need you to come look at it and tell me if you think it's from our guy. I also need you to confirm the fire at Thomas's clinic was lit by the same person. Walters is pretty sure it was, but I want you to look at it."

"Wait, so Stafford's the firebug?" Maggie asked. "How can that be if he's dead? Is he dead?"

"He is dead. DNA confirmed it, but that could be why he died. He knew who the arsonist was."

She wanted to smack herself. "That makes sense. Sorry, my brain isn't working yet. Who owns the property where Jace found the hunting shack?"

"He's working on that now." He frowned down at her. "How are you doing? You sound awful."

"Gee, thanks. I hadn't noticed."

"Well, you do. Other than sounding like a frog climbed in

your throat and died, are you doing all right? You gave us all quite a scare last night."

"I'm fine. My throat is sore, and I'm still exhausted, but otherwise, I'm okay. How's the kitten?"

"Doing well. Thomas and Rayna took it home with them. I imagine Mason and Emma are spoiling it rotten already."

"Good." That made Maggie happy and made the smoke inhalation worth it.

Seb looked at Declan, raising a brow. "So, is she really fine?"

Maggie huffed and spun away, her happiness fading, and headed for the kitchen. She hated that Seb treated her like a kid still. She was twenty-eight!

"She's fine," Declan said. He and Seb followed her.

"So, how come you're still here?" Seb asked her. "Declan was cleared to go back to work. Surely he doesn't need a nursemaid anymore."

"No, but he needs a housekeeper and a chauffeur. He's still not allowed to lift anything or drive." She shrugged, reaching for a box of tea and a mug. She wanted coffee, but the tea would be better on her throat. "It just makes more sense for me to stay here than to have to drive past my office and come get him in the mornings. And I only have to clean one house this way."

Declan filled a glass with water and handed it to her. She took it and smiled her thanks. The cool liquid slid over her raw throat, offering some relief.

Seb's gaze flicked between them. "That's all it is?"

Maggie's cheeks heated as she thought about falling asleep in his arms last night. It was completely innocent, but it felt more intimate than any make-out session she'd ever had.

"What it is, is none of your business," Declan said.

She could kiss him. Seb needed to butt out. She loved her

brother, but she was an adult, and Declan would never intentionally hurt her.

Seb sighed and shook his head. "My sister? Really?"

"Don't start. You married your best friend's sister."

He held up his hands. "I know. I just hope you two know what you're doing. Relationships between friends can be messy. If it doesn't work, well, it's not pretty. It's a large part of what kept London and me apart so long."

"Duly noted," Maggie said. She filled her mug with water and put it in the microwave to heat. "Can we talk about something else, please?" Her love life, or lack thereof, was not something she wanted to discuss before she had her morning caffeine jolt.

"Yep." Seb looked at Declan. "How soon can you be ready?"

"Five minutes."

"Good. Go change."

"I'll make you some coffee," Maggie told him.

"Thanks. I'll be back down in a few." He left, leaving Maggie alone with Seb.

He stared at her while she put water and coffee grounds in the coffeemaker. She pressed the start button, then turned to look up at him.

"What?"

"What do you mean, what?" he asked.

"Why are you staring at me?"

"Just trying to figure you out. You've never shown much interest in boys—men," he quickly amended. "I'm just trying to understand why you've set your sights on Declan."

"Who says I have?"

"Well, your cheeks are red again and neither of you denied it." He narrowed his eyes. "Do I need to get my shotgun?"

Maggie rolled her eyes, crossing her arms. "You mean like

you did with Tara?" Seb had been overjoyed at their sister's pregnancy.

"That's different."

"Not really. And I've known Declan a lot longer than she's known Jace."

"Which is what makes it different."

She glared up at him. "You're annoying, you know that?"

He grinned at her. "Yep."

Maggie smiled back. "At least you're honest. And while it drives me crazy that you want to butt into my life, I *am* thankful you care. You're an awesome big brother, and I love you."

He mussed her hair. "I love you too. Just be careful, is all I'm saying. I don't want to see either of you with a broken heart."

"We will be. If we can ever figure this out. I'm not even sure where we stand. I just know he makes me want what I've never wanted before."

"Damn. You really are all grown up. I feel old."

She laughed. "Wait till you and London have kids. I'm told that's when you really start to feel old."

"That might not be all that far off for you, you know."

She held out a hand. "Hold the phone. Let's not get ahead of ourselves. We need to go on an actual date first. Plus," she pointed a finger at him. "I'm still eleven years younger than you. And don't think I've forgotten you turn forty in January. We've already started planning that birthday bash."

The coffeepot gurgled out the last of its coffee, and she reached for a travel mug.

"Who's we?"

Maggie gave him an evil grin.

"Oh, geez. It's the girl squad, isn't it? How has London kept this hidden from me?"

She giggled. "Your wife doesn't tell you everything."

"I don't doubt it. She's entitled to her privacy, even from me. So, is this going to be a topic of conversation at book club next week?"

Maggie blinked. She'd forgotten all about it. "If we even still have it. I'm not sure what's going to happen. I'll have to call the others and find out."

Seb frowned. "Yeah."

"How's Thomas? He looked pretty devastated before we all ran into the barn."

"He is. But he's also pissed. And he's not letting it shut him down. He and Rayna were going to call all his clients today—thank God he backs everything up to a cloud server— and let them know there would be a temporary clinic on the ranch opening in a couple days until a new facility is built. They're going to use his house for domestic pets. Dad and Brady are going to set aside some space in one of the barns for stock animals."

"Did anyone get any sleep last night?"

Seb shook his head. "Not really, no. Everyone was too keyed up."

"What about the animals at the clinic? Did he lose many?"

"He didn't lose any, actually. With Lorraine still off, he referred all his patients who needed round-the-clock care to another vet. The horses in the barn were boarders."

"That's fantastic. And I'm glad there's a plan. If I can do anything to help, let me know."

"Right now, just take it easy. At least it's the weekend, so you can relax."

She snorted, or at least tried to. It came out more of an airy huff. "Weekends are for people who aren't taking most of next week off and didn't get a complicated domestic case dropped on them yesterday."

"You didn't have to take the case, you know."

"Yes. I did. You didn't see that woman."

His mouth pulled. "Angie Tulley?"

"Okay, maybe you did."

"Her husband is a piece of trash I've been trying to take out for a long time. I'm glad she's finally doing something about her situation. What prompted it? I know my deputies were out at their place yesterday, but I haven't read the report. The clinic fire has usurped everything else. Did she finally just have enough?"

"He hit one of their kids. And she's pregnant again. When she tried to stop him from beating their oldest, he punched her in the stomach. She picked up a kitchen knife and stabbed him four times. He's in the hospital, but going to live. Kerr charged them both with domestic violence. She called me to represent her."

"Jesus. Is she out on bail? What about the kids?"

Maggie nodded. "She posted her own bail, and I got the judge to allow me to place her and the children in a women's shelter. It's one recognized by the courts, so he didn't have a problem with it. And she doesn't want to run. She just wants away from her husband."

"You shouldn't have any trouble proving self-defense."

"Maybe. Four stab wounds could be considered more than self-defense. But she didn't kill him or aim for the places that would."

"If their history gets brought into the trial, I think she'll be fine. Let me know if there's anything I can do to help."

"I will."

"When's the first hearing?"

"Tuesday. It's my only case next week. I hope my voice clears up some by then."

"You need a partner. Someone you can hand things over to when you're sick."

"I have an arrangement with another law firm in Pueblo, but I try not to give them things on such short notice. They handle my cases for me when I'm on vacation, or if I'm too sick to move. I'll just get some throat lozenges, take a giant water bottle, and apologize to the court for my funky voice."

He frowned down at her.

"I'll be fine."

Seb hummed. "Okay, just don't overdo it today, all right?"

"I won't. I'm going to camp out in Declan's recliner with my laptop and a mug of tea and prep for Tuesday."

"That sounds fun," Declan said, entering the room fully dressed.

Maggie lamented the loss of the sight of his bare chest. Those pants did something fabulous for his hips, though. Deck was one of those men who knew how to wear a pair of jeans. They were snug in all the right places.

She shook off her lustful thoughts and tore her eyes away from his delectable body. "Not exactly fun, but not stressful, at least."

"That's good. You need to rest up. Drink lots of water, use your inhaler if you feel like you need it. No cleaning. Stay in the chair and *rest*."

She saluted him. "Yes, sir."

He swatted her hand down, a smile tugging at his lips. "Just behave. I don't know when I'll be back. I might have Seb drop me at the fire station, then catch a ride home later."

"Okay. I'll be here. Bring dinner if you're going to be that late."

"Boone's okay?"

"Yes. I want a grilled chicken sandwich and fries. Oh! And chocolate pie."

Declan's smile grew, and he glanced at Seb, amused. "Looks like I'm bringing dinner."

Seb just shook his head. "You two act more like an old married couple than an old married couple. Come on. Let's get going. We'll see you later, Mags."

Maggie handed Declan the travel mug filled with coffee. "You take it easy too. I know you stressed your ribs last night rescuing me."

"I'll be okay," he said, taking the mug. He leaned in and pressed a kiss to her cheek. "I'll see you this evening."

She nodded, watching them walk out of the kitchen. Seb's words echoed through her head. He was right. They did act like an old married couple. Being with Declan was easy. It had only been two weeks since she moved in to help him out, but her old life seemed foreign now. The thought of going back to her house once he was well enough to clean and drive felt unsettling. She didn't want to go back to that empty home.

Maggie groaned, swiping her hands over her face and through her hair. How did she get to this point so fast?

Was it really that fast? Her subconscious niggled at her. She thought about their relationship, trying to pinpoint when it started to change, and realized it was when he was accused of murder in June. They spent a lot of time together in those few days before Seb cleared him, and she'd come to know him better than she ever had. To learn what made him the man he was and how deeply he felt things. It gave her an insight into his character she hadn't forgotten.

She sighed and pushed away from the counter. It didn't matter when she started to see him as more than a friend. All that mattered was she did. And what she was going to do about it. That part she still had no clue about.

SEVEN

The truck rolled to a stop in the clearing, and Seb shut off the engine. Declan glanced around, his eyes going to the burned-out shell at the edge of the trees. "It's amazing he didn't start a forest fire." He climbed out of the truck, looking over at Seb as they rounded the hood.

"Yeah. Could be he doused the surrounding vegetation before he set the building on fire."

"Maybe. Where did he get the water, though?" They started walking toward the shack.

"Trucked in? We use those portable water tanks on the ranch all the time."

"It would take a couple of them to soak the ground enough. And he'd have to find a way to spray it up into the trees above the building."

"Well, he did something, because the fire didn't spread."

They paused in front of the structure that was little more than a large shed. Declan walked around the outside, noting areas where an accelerant was used. "You should have Katie come take some samples here."

"Jace was working on a warrant. As soon as it comes through, she'll be out here. What can you tell me?"

Declan pointed to the areas with significant burn scars. "Something was poured here. You can see where it pooled." They walked around to the front again. "Can we go inside?"

"Yeah. Just don't move anything. Visible evidence only right now."

"Got it." Declan stepped over the threshold, his eyes sweeping over the debris. There were more burn patterns under the lone window and by the door. In the back corner, he made a gruesome discovery. A charred body lay partially buried beneath a piece of the roof. "You don't need that warrant."

"What?" Seb stepped closer to look over Declan's shoulder. "Fuck."

"Yep." He sighed. "Damn. How did Jace miss this?"

"He didn't go inside. He saw the burned building, called me, then came back to town to get a warrant." Seb ran a hand through his hair.

"What do you want to bet this is why Jed Stafford ended up in that house?"

"I'm not taking that bet. The question is, why was he out here?"

Declan stepped closer, leaning in to examine the body. "I think finding out who this place belongs to, and who this is, might answer that question."

"Yeah. I'm going to call in the calvary and see where Jace is on figuring out who owns this land."

"I'm going to poke around some more."

Seb nodded, already heading to his SUV to radio for backup.

Taking care not to disturb anything, Declan crouched near the body, looking for telltale burn patterns. A large burn scar was just visible under the debris. It surrounded the body and went up the wall. Someone had doused the victim in accelerant—likely gasoline if the other fires were anything to go by—and lit him or her on fire. He hoped the person was already dead when that happened.

Footsteps alerted him to Seb's return.

"Find anything?"

"Just more areas where our guy used an accelerant."

Seb nodded. "Okay. Katie and Alex are on their way. And I got a text from Jace. The land is part of the national forest."

"So, whoever built this shed did so illegally."

"Likely, yes. This is nowhere near the cabin rental place."

Declan's mouth flattened. "This isn't good. Whoever this is, is very smart."

"Agreed. I hate that we have another body, but he or she may be our only hope of catching this guy before he kills someone else."

Unease crept up Declan's spine, making him edgy. He had a feeling the person responsible was only getting started.

The sound of the front door opening and closing drew Maggie's attention. She looked up from her laptop. Declan stood in the doorway to the living room.

"Hi." She smiled.

He smiled back and held up the white paper bags in his hands. "Hungry?"

"Yes!" She closed the lid on her computer and set it on the floor, standing. "Did you remember my pie?"

"Of course I did."

"Good. Who brought you home?" She followed him into the kitchen.

"Gehring. Your voice sounds better." He set the bag down while Maggie took two plates from the dishwasher.

"Yeah. Once the sleep wore off and I drank some hot tea, it really loosened up. It's still sore, but it's not that bad."

"Good. It should get steadily better. Did you have to use your inhaler at all?" He handed her a sandwich and a box of fries.

"Thanks." She put them on her plate, then opened the fridge to get the ketchup. "I had to this morning after you left. I started coughing and couldn't stop." She squirted some on her plate, then handed him the bottle. "It cleared up after that."

He nodded and added ketchup to his plate. They walked over to the table to sit down.

"So, how was your day? Did the hunting shack offer any information?" She took a bite of her sandwich.

He sighed, putting down the sandwich he just picked up. "Just more questions. There was another body inside."

"What?" Who were they dealing with and how many more people were they going to find murdered because of this guy?

"A woman this time. Seb called before I left and said Alex determined she died in the fire. Katie was hoping she could get DNA from a bone. There wasn't much usable soft tissue. The killer doused her in gasoline."

Maggie set down her sandwich. "That is a horrible way to die."

"Agreed."

"What else did you find out there? Anything that might give you a clue about who's doing all this?"

"Not really, no."

She wrinkled her nose. "Well, I hope that woman offers some clues. Seb needs to find this person before more people die."

Declan nodded, taking a bite of his food. Maggie swirled a fry through her ketchup and ate it, lost in thought. "That woman has to be the key. Especially if Jed was killed to cover up her death."

"She could just be some random person, too. There haven't been any missing people reported around here. Seb checked."

She frowned and ate another fry. He had a point.

"Whatever it is, we're not going to solve it over grilled chicken sandwiches and fries. Tell me about your day."

"My day? I prepped for court Tuesday. I'm so thankful for the internet. And that our county digitized its case files."

"And that's *all* you did?"

"Yes." She held up three fingers. "Scout's honor."

"You weren't a scout, either, Maggie."

She grinned.

He chuckled. "I guess I deserve that. So, what did you do you weren't supposed to?"

"Laundry."

He narrowed his eyes at her. "And?"

She huffed. "How can you tell I did something else? I'm literally just sitting here eating." She held up another fry and stuffed it in her mouth.

"It's in your eyes. Now, what did you do?"

"Fine. I cleaned the bathrooms." She wasn't sure she liked that he could read her so well.

"Was this before or after the coughing fit?"

"After. And I didn't deep clean them. Just a quick wipe down. After I picked up the laundry, I noticed your bathroom could use some sprucing up. I figured mine could too, because I did them both at the same time the last time I cleaned."

He took a bite of his sandwich and stared at her, saying nothing.

She huffed again. "I went right back to the recliner after I finished. I swear."

His eyes crinkled as he smiled. "I believe you."

"Oh, thank you, my Lord." She rolled her eyes and ate some of her sandwich.

Declan laughed, breaking off as it jostled his ribcage.

"Serves you right." She pointed a fry at him.

"Vindictive woman." He scowled, but spoiled it when one corner of his mouth lifted. "So, do we know if Tara picked a cake flavor?" he asked, changing the subject.

"I have no idea. I haven't talked to her."

"Me either. I hope she's not stressing too much with everything that's happened. It's not good for her or the babies."

"Tara's the queen at handling stress, so I think she'll be okay." Maggie hoped what she said was true. Her sister was a strong woman, but between the fire drama, her wedding, and the fact she was at the same point in her pregnancy when she miscarried Lucy, her stress level had to be at an all-time high.

Declan and Maggie fell into an easy conversation about the wedding while they finished their food. There was a lot to do over the next week. Maggie, as maid-of-honor, had a full plate. She vowed to take as much responsibility from Tara as she could. There was no way she could keep her sister from stressing out, but she could at least minimize it.

She stuffed the last fry in her mouth and got up, taking her plate to the sink. The chocolate pie called her name, and she retrieved a fork from the drawer and flipped open the clear plastic container to take a bite.

Declan got up, done as well, and put his plate in the sink. "You gonna share that?"

Maggie frowned. "You didn't get your own?"

"I got peach, but that looks good."

"It is. Eat your peach." She tucked the container close to her chest as she took another bite.

His mouth quirked. "Come on, Mags. Just one bite."

"You have your own. Don't get between a girl and her pie." She stabbed another bite with her fork and lifted it, but it didn't make it to her mouth. He swooped in and stole it off her fork.

"Hey!"

"Hmm, I was right. That is good." He made to swipe his finger through the whipped cream.

"Declan!" She laughed as she twisted away. "Go eat your own pie."

"But I want the chocolate now." He followed her, reaching around to grab her hand with the fork.

"Then you should have bought chocolate for yourself instead of peach." She turned around, laughing, but being careful of his ribs, hoping to twist out of his reach. But all it did was allow him to trap her between the counter and his body. The pie took a backseat as the feel of him pressed the length of her registered.

He noticed too. His eyes darkened, the pupils growing large. The hand holding hers loosened to slide up her arm so he could thread his fingers into her hair.

"Maggie." His voice came out as a low whisper.

In response, she tipped her face toward his, then watched as he descended toward her. Anticipation sent goosebumps rippling over her skin. Her eyes fluttered closed a second before his lips touched hers. Excitement raced over every nerve in her body. She wanted to wrap her arms around him, but her hands were full.

He didn't have that problem, though. The hand in her hair tightened, holding her head in place. His other hand curved over her hip to bring her closer as he deepened the kiss. Her knees turned watery as his tongue swept into her mouth to taste the inner recesses. She'd imagined what this would be like—dreamed about it, even—but it didn't hold a candle to the real thing.

By the time he pulled back, her brain was mush and her legs were noodles.

He rested his hand on the back of her neck, staring at her.

"Wow," she whispered.

He nodded. "Yeah." He let go and took a half-step back. His eyes dropped to the container squished between them. The whipped cream was smeared all over the sides, but had thankfully stayed in the box. He snatched the fork from her numb fingers, scooping up a bite of the sweet confection.

She wasn't even mad. The opposite, in fact, as she watched the plastic fork slide through those delectable lips that just kissed her senseless.

"That's still good pie. But it tastes better on you."

Lord have mercy! Heat rushed south at the low gravel of his voice uttering those words. She leaned into the counter for support.

His mouth quirked.

The rat! He knew exactly the effect he had on her. But she still couldn't bring herself to be angry. She was too damn aroused.

He stuck the fork in the pie. "I'm going to go take a shower. Maybe find a book and relax. You should too. You're very tense."

She found her voice again at his light-hearted teasing. A smile spread over her face. "I wonder why?" She put the pie down. He wasn't going anywhere until she got to fully participate. She took his face in her hands and pressed her lips to his.

That was the last bit of control she had over the kiss. He closed the gap between them with a groan. She swept her hands into his dark copper hair and held on as he drove her higher with his tongue and masterful hands. They ghosted under her shirt and over her back, raising more goosebumps and leaving behind a trail of fire.

Maggie broke the kiss long enough to hop up on the

counter. He stepped between her legs, and she locked her ankles behind his back, returning her mouth to his. His fingers dove back beneath her shirt to find her breasts. He pulled down the stretchy fabric of her sports bra and cupped their heavy weight in his hands.

She wanted to touch, too, and tugged his polo from his jeans. Her first touch to his abdomen elicited a quick intake of breath. Too quick. He hissed sharply and pulled back.

"Did I hurt you?" she asked. "I'm sorry."

"No. It wasn't you. My body just isn't healed enough for this. Not with the way you make me feel. I forget I'm not a hundred percent when you touch me."

"Ditto." She unlocked her ankles, and he stepped back. She hopped down.

"I'm going to take that shower now."

She nodded. His eyes stayed on hers for another moment before he turned and left. Maggie sagged against the counter, the starch gone from her legs. She picked up her fork, taking a bite of the rich treat as she stared after him. It was good, but it wasn't what she wanted now; that had just walked upstairs.

EIGHT

The trill of the doorbell early Monday morning drew Declan out of sleep. He cursed as he scrambled out of bed. What the hell was up with these early morning wake-up calls? He didn't get enough sleep as it was between his ribs and thoughts of Maggie running rampant through his brain until all hours. He pretty much avoided her yesterday. Not because he didn't want a repeat of Saturday, but because he did. His body couldn't handle what it thought it wanted. It was better just to not torture himself.

He stumbled into the hallway and almost ran her over as they both responded to the doorbell, which rang again.

"Why does this keep happening?" she asked.

"I don't know. But it's undoubtedly Seb. Does he ever sleep?" They descended the stairs.

"Apparently not."

Declan twisted the locks and threw the door open. Seb stood on the porch, a fierce frown on his face.

"Dude. It's even earlier than the last time."

"I know, but this couldn't wait."

Declan stepped back so Seb could come inside.

"Can we sit?"

"Seb, what's wrong?" Maggie asked.

He gestured toward the sitting area to their right. "Let's have a seat."

Declan shared a glance with Maggie, neither of them certain what was going on.

Seb stepped toward the furniture and sat in the recliner. Declan pulled Maggie down on the couch with him.

"Okay, we're sitting. Tell us why you're waking us up again, looking so grim," Declan said.

Seb took a deep breath, his gaze fixed on Declan. "Katie got some usable DNA off the woman from the hunting shack using her CRISPR technique."

"That's great. Why don't you look excited?" Declan said.

"She got a match. Well, a partial match."

Declan rolled a hand. "And? Just spit it out, Seb."

Seb clasped and unclasped his hands. "The match was to you."

"What?" He sat a little straighter. Confusion pulled his mouth down and his brows together.

"It was a fifty percent familial match to you. Katie thinks it's your mother."

Maggie sucked in a breath beside him and reached for his hand. He clutched her fingers as he digested what Seb said.

"My mom?" Declan cleared his throat and looked away, trying to put a leash on his emotions. The intense grief was unexpected. He hadn't seen her since he left home after graduation. When he came back after his time in the Marines, she was long gone, and not even Macy knew where she went. Cutting ties with both his parents was the best thing he ever did. Sherri Briggs was an absent mother at best. He had only a few truly good memories of his mom. When she wasn't drunk or high, she was working and ignoring him and Macy. Her shining achievement was she never hit them.

He glanced at Maggie, whose own eyes telegraphed her disbelief, before returning his attention to Seb. "Why would my mother be in that shack? Who would want to burn her alive?" He might not have liked his mom, but she didn't deserve to die that way.

"I don't know. Can you think of anyone she used to associate with who might be capable of doing that?"

"God, I don't know, Seb. I haven't seen or heard from her since I left for basic training. She ran around with some lowlifes, including my dad, but they were all stoners and drunks, not murderers."

"Do you know where she was living recently?"

"No. I didn't keep tabs on her."

"Did Macy?"

He frowned. "I'm not sure. I can go talk to her and ask, though."

"What about your dad? Do you know where he is?"

"Last I heard, he was in prison again. But that was years ago. Someone read it in a Denver paper and told me about it. I don't know if he's still there."

"I'll check. He might know where she's been and who she's come into contact with." Seb sighed again. "I'm sorry to bring such bad news so early."

Declan scrubbed a hand over his jaw, the rasp sounding loud to his own ears. "This is all very surreal. What the fuck is going on? How is my mother connected to three arson fires and a murder?" He paused as he thought about what two of the fires had in common. "You don't think this has something to do with that child trafficking case, do you?"

"It wouldn't surprise me. Not now that Thomas's clinic was targeted."

"No." Declan stood, needing to move, as agitation churned in his gut. "I can't see her being part of that, though. She was a crappy parent, but she would never exploit a child.

She had plenty of chances with me and Macy, but she never did."

"Maybe she knew something and was killed to keep her quiet."

He scoffed. "They could have just kept her high if they wanted her silence." He sighed and stopped at the window to stare out at the dreary day. Low, gray clouds scuttled across the sky and dry leaves swirled down the street with the wind. It was supposed to rain later before changing to snow.

Maggie's soft touch on his bare back brought him out of his thoughts. He turned, looking down at her. She stared up at him with her chocolatey eyes, wrapping her arms around his waist. He held her close, resting his cheek on top of her head and welcoming the comfort she offered.

Seb stood. "I'm going to try to track down your dad. Talk to Macy and let me know what she says."

Declan nodded. "I will."

He tipped his head in acknowledgment, then let himself out. Declan didn't move from where he stood, soaking in Maggie's presence. It was a balm to his mixed-up emotions.

"I'm sorry, Declan."

He pulled away far enough to look at her. "Thank you. I'm not sure why this has me so out of sorts."

She shrugged. "She was your mother."

"In name only. I think it's more the shock of how she died that's thrown me for a loop. Who burns someone to death?" He couldn't let himself think about how horrific that must have been for her. He hoped she was unconscious long before the flames reached her.

"Someone very disturbed." She hugged him tighter.

He hugged her back before dropping a kiss on her head and pulling back. "Let's go get dressed and talk to Macy. Maybe she has some answers." He hoped to God she did, because he needed to know what the hell was going on. Not just to stop an arsonist and murderer, but for his own sanity.

"She's going to hate us, you know that, right?" Maggie stepped out of her car and rounded the hood. "Dropping a bombshell like this on her at work."

"Yeah, well, I'm not willing to wait until she closes to hopefully get some answers." Declan frowned as they walked toward the door. Macy would just have to deal. If anyone could fake a happy façade for the rest of the day, it was her.

He opened the door and let Maggie precede him out of the blustery drizzle that had started to come down.

Macy looked over as they walked in, a smile on her face. It faded as she took in the severe expression on Declan's face.

"I'd say good morning, but it doesn't look like you've had one. What happened now?"

Maggie and Declan walked closer.

"Can we talk in the back?" Declan asked. The shop was busy, and he didn't want their conversation to end up all over town.

"Damn. I'm not going to like this. Yeah, okay." She turned to the young woman working alongside her, telling her she would be in the kitchen if she was needed.

The three of them pushed through the swinging door to the back. Macy stopped at a stainless-steel table and faced them.

"What's up?" She crossed her arms and leaned a hip on the table.

"Did you hear about the body Seb and I found at that illegal hunting shack in the national forest?"

She nodded. "London mentioned it." She straightened, dropping her arms. "Wait, did they identify the body?"

"Yeah." Declan cleared his throat. Maggie slipped her hand into his. He gave it a squeeze, silently thanking her for the support, and continued. "Katie got a DNA match. It's mom."

The color drained from Macy's face. "What?" she breathed, her eyes wide. "She's sure?"

"Yes. My DNA is in the system from when I was arrested for murder. It's a half-match, indicating it's a parent."

"Oh my God." She pushed away from the table, pacing several feet away before turning around. Her hand curled around her ponytail, and her eyes darted around the kitchen as she processed what he told her. "Why would someone want to kill her? Like that, anyway. I can imagine she's made some enemies, but to burn her in a fire?"

"I don't know as if it had anything to do with her."

"Seb and Declan have a theory it has something to do with the child trafficking ring Thomas and Rayna busted up."

Macy's eyes grew larger. "No way. She wouldn't be involved with something like that."

"That's what I said. But maybe she knew something? Have you talked to her lately? Or know where she was living?"

"Not in a couple years. She was in Denver then. She called me one night, drunk, rambling about how she was sorry. I managed to figure out what city she was in, but not much else before she apologized for disturbing my evening and hung up."

Declan frowned. "Why didn't you say something to me?"

"Because I knew it would just upset you. There was no point when I knew any effort to help her would just turn out like the last time."

"Last time? What do you mean?" They tried talking to her when they were teenagers to get her to quit and stay sober, but she always promised she would, then never did. They'd never done more than that.

"While you were in the military, before she left town for

good, she went through a long dry spell. Even went to AA meetings regularly and had a job. I thought she was finally clean. I went over to pick her up for a lunch date, and she was stoned out of her mind. She offered me her drugs, telling me I should try it because it felt so good. I asked her if she was sorry for relapsing. She smiled and said no. That she was tired of fighting it and just wanted the high. That it was better than the misery of real life." She shook her head. "After what I went through to get her clean, I left and vowed not to go back. That's when I went to California. She moved away not long after I did."

Declan stared at his sister in shock. "Why didn't you ever tell me any of this?"

"You were deployed, and I didn't want to distract you with the troubles here at home."

"Yeah, but she was sober for a while. Why did you keep that secret?"

"It wasn't exactly a secret. She just asked me not to. Said she wanted to tell you herself when you came back. Except she didn't make it to that point."

"Geez." He pinched the bridge of his nose. "So, you didn't hear from her after that until a couple years ago?"

She nodded.

"What about Dad?"

"That asshole could be rotting in a ditch for all I care."

Declan agreed. "Did she ever mention him? When she was sober or when she called you?"

"No. Not that I remember. I think she hated him as much as we did."

He rubbed his temples, feeling a headache starting. "Why was she back here?"

"Maybe she was sober and looking to make amends," Maggie suggested.

"But why?" Macy asked. "It's been years, and we didn't part on good terms."

"Maybe she was sick and wanted to mend fences."

"If that's the case, we might never know. I doubt Alex could tell much about her overall health from his exam. She was in bad shape." He tried not to think about what she looked like when he found her. Now that he knew who it was under all that rubble, the image was even more horrific. He inhaled through his nose, trying to bring his mind back to the present.

"We'll let Seb know about your conversation with her. It'll at least give him a place to start," Maggie said, saving him from having to speak as he brought himself under control.

"Okay. This is crazy. I hope he can figure out what she was doing here."

"He has to. I think she's the key to whatever's going on." Declan sighed. "Thanks, Macy. We'll let you get back to work."

"Oh, yeah. Work. Like I'll be able to focus now."

"You had a boatload of customers out there. I'm sure you'll get back into the groove quickly," Maggie said as they all turned to go out front.

"Yeah, probably. You guys want coffee before you go?"

"Is the sky blue?" Maggie replied.

"Not today." Macy pointed out the front window. Rain came down in earnest now.

"Forget the analogy. The answer is yes. Seb woke us up at six-thirty. We came straight here after he left."

Macy walked over to her industrial coffeemaker and picked up a cup, pouring Declan a cup of coffee. "Maggie, do you want a black coffee or a latte?"

"Latte." She cast Declan a glance. "Today calls for some prissiness to dress up the angst."

He groaned. "We're going to be old and gray and you're still going to hold that over me."

She patted his cheek. "You betcha."

Macy frowned, curious. "What? What'd I miss? There's an inside joke going on here, isn't there?" She glanced at them as she steamed milk for Maggie's latte.

"He thinks I'm prissy."

"I already walked it back." He rolled his neck, turning to look at her.

Macy giggled. "You are a bit. But you're also not."

"See?" Declan said.

"But shame on you for calling her that." Macy poured the steamed milk into the espresso and put a lid on the cup before handing it to Maggie.

"Ha!" Maggie took the cup, smiling her thanks. "Vindication."

"Whatever. Can we go? I'd storm out and leave without you, but you're my ride." He grinned.

"I should leave you here."

"No!" Macy said, holding out her hands to ward him off. "He'll drive me bonkers. Take him, please."

Declan hooked an arm around her neck, pulling her close. "You love me."

"Do not. Let me go, dork!"

He placed a smacking kiss on her head and released her. Macy straightened her apron, glaring at him. He just grinned at her. It was still fun to tease his little sister.

"Shoo!" She pushed him toward the end of the counter. "Go talk to Seb."

Declan sobered at the reminder of why they were here. "Yeah. Keep your eyes and ears open. We don't know who could be a target."

She nodded. "I'll be careful."

He lifted his coffee cup in a wave, then walked with

Maggie out of the café. They hurried through the rain to her car, shutting themselves inside. She started the engine and drove them the few blocks to the police station.

"You know, I almost wish it was snow," Maggie said, pulling into a spot as close to the door as she could find.

"Why?"

"Because I hate rain without thunder. It's usually cold and just blah. At least storms are exciting."

"True. But it's fall, and this is what it does." He took off his seatbelt. "Ready?"

She unfastened her belt and took the keys out of the ignition, grabbing her purse. "Yep."

They flung their doors open and dashed to the overhang, shaking the water off as they reached shelter.

"Man, it's really coming down." Declan pulled open the door and held it for her.

She walked inside and smiled at the desk sergeant, Alaina Wilder.

"Hi, Maggie. Lieutenant. Are you here to see the sheriff?"

"We are," Maggie answered.

Alaina pushed a logbook toward them and two visitor's badges. "Sign in for me."

They scrawled their names on the book and pinned the badges to their shirts. Alaina pushed a button to unlock the door and it buzzed.

"He's in his office."

"Thanks." Maggie smiled at her and led the way through the door. They walked down the hallway, following the perimeter of the bullpen to get to Seb's office. His door was cracked. She knocked softly and gave it a push.

"Hey." He sighed and sat back in his chair. "Did you talk to Macy?"

"Yeah." Declan followed Maggie inside, and they sat in the chairs in front of the desk. "She said she heard from her a few years ago. I guess she was blitzed and a little incoherent, but Macy said she learned she was in Denver at the time. She didn't know anything more precise than that."

"Well, that gives me a place to start. I'll call up there and see if they have an address for her. If she was using, she might have been arrested recently."

Declan leaned forward, propping his elbows on his knees and pressing the heels of his hands into his eyes for a brief moment. "I just don't understand why she'd be back here. There was nothing here for her. Nothing. She knew Macy and I didn't want anything to do with her. Why would she come back?"

"I don't know, but I'm going to do my damnedest to find out."

He nodded. "Yeah, I know. I'm just frustrated. And worried. Did you find my dad?"

"Not yet. He was in prison at the state penitentiary until about a year ago. I called the warden, and he pulled his file. I got the name of his P.O. and was getting ready to call him when you arrived."

"Do it." Declan motioned to the phone on the desk.

Seb picked up the receiver and punched in the number on a sticky note.

"Hi, this is Sheriff Sebastian Archer, down in Boone County. I'm looking for some information on one of your parolees, Cole Briggs."

Declan steepled his fingers, resting them against his chin. He tapped the toes of one foot as he listened. Maggie sat quietly next to him, staring at her brother.

Seb picked up his pen and scrawled an address across the sticky note. "Okay, thanks." He hung up. "Last known address is in Denver. Feel like going for a drive?"

"Hell, yes." He stood.

"How about you, Mags?"

She rose. "No. You two go. I need to make sure I'm ready for court tomorrow. There were a few things I needed to run down yet, and I need to meet with my client."

Declan touched her shoulder. "Watch yourself. I hate that my messed-up family might have put you in danger."

"It's not your fault. And I'll be fine. I know how to take care of myself."

"I know you do. Doesn't mean I can't worry." And he would. She'd picked up jiu jitsu with Rayna, but there were still situations she would never see coming.

She stepped closer and pressed a kiss to his cheek. "I'll bug you with texts, how about that?"

"Sounds good."

"I'll see you two later." She left the two of them alone.

Declan looked away from the doorway after she disappeared to see Seb watching him, shaking his head.

"What?"

"Nothing. Still trying to wrap my head around the two of you." He stood up and took his sidearm from his desk, clipping it to his belt beside his badge before picking up his coat and putting it on. "Let's go."

"There still isn't an us." Declan followed him out the door.

"You sure about that?"

He wasn't sure about anything when it came to Maggie Archer, except that he wanted her. His desire for going solo through life had taken a backseat to his desire for her. He didn't care, though. That kiss unleashed something. He craved more. But he was beginning to question if being around her was a good idea, considering today's revelation. Rehashing his past left him feeling dirty. He didn't want to tarnish her image by dragging her through his family's filth.

"No," he snorted.

Seb looked back and arched an eyebrow, but said nothing.

They walked out the back door of the station and climbed into Seb's police-issued SUV. While Seb drove, Declan pulled up his email on his phone, going through departmental memos. He still had annual reviews to complete, but they would have to wait.

The drive to Denver was longer than normal, the weather slowing them down. Declan yawned as he watched the scenery pass and wished he hadn't left his coffee in Maggie's car. Before they left the city, he'd make Seb stop for some. It was nearly lunchtime, anyway.

They exited the interstate and wove through neighborhoods until they stopped at a house in a rundown part of town. A rusty, ancient sedan sat in the driveway. A few children's toys were scattered around the yard. Their presence made Declan's stomach sink. Something told him he wouldn't find his father here.

Declan stepped out of the SUV and walked up the crumbling sidewalk to the front porch. Seb knocked on the door. A small dog barked. He could hear its nails scrabbling on a wooden floor as it ran toward the door. A woman yelled at the dog to shut up.

The lock clicked, and the inner door opened to reveal a woman around forty with dull blonde hair scraped up into a messy bun, wearing a baggy sweater and jeans. She held the dog, trying to shush it as it growled at them. "Yeah?"

"Ma'am, I'm Sebastian Archer, Boone County Sheriff. We're looking for Cole Briggs. Is he here?"

"I ain't seen that bastard in months. He came home after he got out of prison late last year. Long enough to satisfy his parole officer, then he split. Just like he always does."

Declan blinked. Maybe they did have the right place. He glanced at the toys in the yard. "Who is he to you?"

"My good-for-nothing baby daddy." She frowned at him. "You look familiar. Who are you?"

The world spun. Declan put a hand on the house to steady himself. "I'm his son, Declan."

The woman's eyes widened. "He mentioned he had a couple kids when we first met, but hardly ever talked about you. Just said you weren't part of his life."

He swallowed hard, then pointed at the toys. "You have children?"

She nodded, more subdued. "Three. My oldest is nineteen and left to find work in the oil fields up north after he graduated last year. I have two daughters too. Twelve and seven."

"What are their names?"

"My son's name is Michael. My daughters are Hannah and Jessie."

Declan's mind reeled. What the actual fuck? How did he have three siblings and not know about them? He mentally scoffed at himself. Because his old man was a selfish prick, that's why. He reached into his pocket, pulling a business card from his wallet, then looked at Seb. "Do you have a pen?"

Seb reached into the inside breast pocket of his coat and handed him one. Declan wrote his cellphone number on the back of the card with shaky hands.

"I know you don't know me from Adam, but I would really like it if you would call me sometime so my sister and I can meet our siblings." He handed her the card.

She took it and looked at it, tracing the emblem with her finger and reading his title out loud. "Lieutenant Declan Briggs, Boone County Emergency Services." She looked up at him. "You're a firefighter?"

"Yes, ma'am. What's your name?"

"Denise James. What's your sister's name?"

"Macy. She owns a coffee shop in the town we live in."

"What about your mother? Does she live near you? Cole only said they weren't together anymore. I tried a few times to get him to talk about his life before we met, but he just told me it was in the past and to shut up."

That sounded like his father. "Mom's dead."

"That's actually why we're here, Ms. James," Seb said. "Sherri Briggs was found murdered a few days ago. We're trying to track down her last known whereabouts so we can find her killer."

"Oh my goodness! You think Cole had something to do with it?"

"We're not sure. We're just exhausting every angle. Why? Do you think he's capable of murder?"

She snorted and readjusted the dog. It now sniffed the air around them, assessing the newcomers. "I think he's capable of just about anything." Her eyes shifted to Declan. "I don't know how much you remember about him, but your father is slick. He could talk a bird into buying an airplane."

"I was a teen when he left. I remember his silver tongue. He had a temper too."

"Yeah. I know."

Declan frowned, feeling for this woman. "Why did you keep taking him back if you knew what he was like?"

"Because he's my kids' father. I should have left him not long after I met him, but I got pregnant with Michael. I was young—only eighteen—and had nowhere to go. Cole supported me. At least until he ended up in jail. I swore when he got out I wasn't going to let him back into our lives, but he would sweet talk his way in the door and then I was lost. Hannah came after his first release from prison. Jessie after the next one. I learned my lesson after she was born and made sure I was current on my birth control this time. I don't need any more mouths to feed."

Anger swelled in Declan's chest, building to a fury that his dad continued to take advantage of this woman. She wasn't blameless, but he played to her weakness.

"Do you know where he could be?" Seb asked.

"A bar. Some dark alley, shooting up heroin. Hell, he could be dead for all I know. He took off out of here in March. Haven't seen or heard from him since."

"Assume he's alive. What bars did he frequent? Did he have any friends he might contact?"

She rattled off a few names and gave them a couple bars to check out. Seb typed them into a notepad app on his phone.

"I'm sorry he's such an asshole," Declan said as they prepared to leave. "And I would still really like you to call me sometime. Macy and I would love to meet the kids."

She smiled. "I think they'd like to meet you, too. Michael could probably use a stable man in his life." A troubled frown creased her forehead. "He's a little too much like his dad. He had a few run-ins with the law in high school. Thankfully, he's kept his nose clean since he left for North Dakota. As far as I know, anyway. He doesn't call home as often as I'd like." She shook off the melancholy on her face and smiled again. "I wish the girls were home. They're at school, though."

He wished they were home, too. He had more sisters! Macy's face floated through his mind, and he couldn't help but wonder how much they looked like her. She favored their mother, but she had the same shape to her nose as their dad, as well as his height. Declan had his dad's build and some of his features, but his hair and eyes were all his mom. Truthfully, he was glad he didn't look more like the bastard.

"We'll get together soon," he promised her. "Thank you for the information. If you need anything, please call me."

"I'll keep that in mind." She hesitated. "When the girls get home, if they want to talk to you, can I call you?"

"Absolutely. You can even FaceTime me. And if you give me a heads-up, I can get Macy in on it too."

Denise beamed. "Well, I guess we'll probably talk to you later, then."

"Sounds great. Take care." He backed off the porch, waving as he turned to go back to the car. His hands felt numb as he pulled on the door handle. He sank into the seat and buckled his seatbelt, watching the house. Denise went back inside.

Seb started the engine, pulling away from the curb. "You okay?"

"Fuck if I know. He had a whole other life. We never heard from him again after he left. I can't see him being involved in Mom's death. Not now. He kept coming back to that woman, but he never had any contact with us once he left for good. Why would he suddenly kill her now?"

"I think you're probably right, but we still need to look into every angle. Maybe it's something from their past that's come back to haunt them. He could be dead too."

Declan sighed. "I know." He ran a hand down his face. "God, this is a mess."

"That seems to be the norm the last few months."

"Right? I mean, did we enter some alternate universe and not know it? It's been one weird thing after another."

"Yeah. I need a break. But first, we have a killer and an arsonist to stop. You up for hitting a few of those addresses Ms. James gave us?"

"Sure. Who knows? Maybe we'll find the asshole."

"Just don't punch him. Or at least warn me first, so I can look away. I don't want to have to arrest you again."

"I don't want that, either. Jail sucked." That was an experience he never wanted to repeat. "So, where are we going first?"

"I figure we can try a couple of the friends. Those addresses are in the neighborhood."

"Let's do it."

Seb made a series of turns and they pulled up at another house. This one looked worse than Denise's. Paint peeled off the exterior, and the porch sagged. One strong gust and it looked like it would collapse. More weeds than grass covered the yard.

"It doesn't look like anyone's home," Declan said, shutting his car door and rounding the hood.

"We're going to find out." The chain-link gate let out a squeal as Seb pushed it open. They walked up the rotted porch stairs and knocked on the door.

Declan peered through the window. Nothing moved. "I don't think they're home."

"Yeah, me either. Let's try the next one."

They headed back to the car, spending the next couple hours driving around the city. At every stop, either no one was home, or no one had seen Cole. Frustration clawed at Declan. He'd been dreading seeing his dad again, but now he just wanted to find him to ask him why he'd left and created a whole new family. Declan wasn't upset Cole abandoned him and Macy—they were better off without him—but he did want to know why Denise and her kids were different.

Seb pulled into a fast-food joint and ordered them some burgers. Declan made him drive through a Starbucks too. Part of the headache pounding behind his eyes was from a lack of caffeine. Once they'd eaten and Declan had his coffee in hand, they headed for home.

It was a long ride. Declan couldn't shut his mind off, even with his ribs aching and his head pounding. He had Seb drop him at Peppy Brewster and prepared himself to throw another bombshell at his sister for the second time in one day.

Macy's smile vanished, and her shoulders sagged. "God, what now?"

He said nothing, walking past her to push through the swinging door to the kitchen. She told the young woman working with her she would be back and followed him. He stopped at the table and leaned against it, propping his hands on the edge of the cool metal on either side of his hips.

"Dad's dead, too, isn't he?"

"Not as far as we could find out."

She frowned. "Okay. What is it, then?"

"Seb got a last known address for him from his parole officer. We went to the house. He wasn't there, but a woman answered the door.

"He has a girlfriend?"

"She's much more than that. They have three children together."

"What?" Macy's voice rose several octaves.

"A boy and two girls. Michael is nineteen. The girls, Hannah and Jessie, are twelve and seven. Their mom's name is Denise James. I gave her my card and cellphone number. I'm hoping she'll FaceTime us later so we can talk to the girls. Michael lives out of state. He's an oil field worker in North Dakota."

Macy covered her mouth with her hands. "Oh my God," she muttered from behind them before letting them fall away. "Do you think Mom knew?"

"Maybe? I'm not sure." His phone beeped, and he took it out to look at it. "Well, that's good timing. It's a text from Denise. The girls are home from school and want to talk to us."

"Call her." Macy pushed away from the table to stand next to him.

Declan touched the button to connect a FaceTime call. Denise's face filled the screen.

"Hi! I didn't expect you to get back to me so quickly."

"I was at my sister's coffee shop breaking the news about you and your children."

Macy waved. "Hello."

Denise smiled, moving through her house to the living room. "Girls. Declan called. He and Macy are on FaceTime."

They heard the murmur of young voices as she settled on

the couch. The girls' faces came into view on either side of her. They waved, and Declan's heart lurched.

"Hello! I'm Hannah," the older one said.

"I'm Jessie," the younger girl added. "You're pretty!" she said to Macy.

Declan glanced at her to see a bright smile on her face.

"Thank you. You're beautiful. You both are. It's so nice to meet you."

And they were. They both had pretty smiles and Cole's light blonde hair. Hannah had her mother's blue eyes, but Jessie's were brown like their dad's. Even seated, he could tell they both had his height too. Hannah was as tall as her mom, sitting there, and Jessie looked older than her seven years. Both girls appeared happy. Declan was glad Denise seemed like a good mother. He hoped that held true as they got to know each other.

"Your mom said you just got home from school," Macy said. "Do you like your teachers?"

The girls launched into a recap of their day, which then led to a discussion on their favorite subjects and their friends. Declan and Macy learned Hannah liked math and reading, and Jessie liked art.

Declan glanced back as the kitchen door opened. Maggie stepped through.

"Seb called and told me I should get over here. I came as soon as I could." She frowned, pausing a few feet away as she took in the FaceTime call.

He motioned her over. "Come here and meet our sisters."

Her eyes grew wide. "Your what?" Her feet carried her over to stand next to him.

"Deck found a surprise in Denver," Macy said.

Maggie looked at the phone screen, surprise on her face. "Hello."

"Hi!" Jessie chirped. "I'm Jessie. Who are you?"

"My name's Maggie."

"Maggie's a friend of ours," Declan said.

"It's nice to meet you. This is my sister, Hannah. And my mom."

"I'm Denise." The woman waved.

"It's nice to meet all of you too." Maggie looked at Declan. "That's some surprise."

"Yeah. I'll fill you in more later."

"We should probably go so you guys can get back to whatever you were doing. We'll talk again soon, though, right girls?" Denise said.

Their heads bobbed.

"That would be great," Macy said. "We'd love to have you come down for a visit. Maybe in a couple weeks? We're all in a wedding this weekend, or I'd say this Saturday would be great."

"A couple weeks would be perfect."

"Good. You girls be good for your mom."

"We're always good," Jessie quipped.

Denise laughed. "That's debatable. We'll talk to you later. Bye."

Macy, Declan, and Maggie all waved, and Declan touched the screen to end the call.

"You have other siblings?" Maggie said as soon as the screen went dark.

"Yeah. It about knocked me on my ass when Denise told me. Dad's been living a life we knew nothing about. Although, I can't call it much of a life. She said he's been in prison more than out of it." Which wasn't any different from what he and Macy experienced with him as a dad.

"But still, two kids?"

"Three. There's a nineteen-year-old boy living out of state."

Maggie blinked. "Whoa."

"Tell me about it. Are you done for the day? I need to get out of here and clear my head."

"Mostly, yes. I have a few things to finish up, but I can do them later."

"Good." He took her arm and led her toward the front of the café. "Macy, we'll see you later."

"Oh, sure. Drop bombshell number two and run away. Mmm-hmm."

He tossed her a grin as she followed behind. "At least this time it was a positive one."

"Still no less mind-blowing. I'm going to drown myself in coffee and London's macarons."

"Oooh. London made macarons for you to sell?" Maggie dug in her heels.

Declan tugged on her hand, ready to get out of town for a while. She pulled free, and he sighed, tipping his head back. "What is it with women and these cookies?"

"Oh, whatever," Macy said. "I seem to remember you hiding a container full of them from me a few months ago after you fixed London's hot water heater."

He frowned. Dammit, she would remember that. "Well, that was different. I was afraid I wouldn't get any at all if I didn't hide them."

"Okay, sure. For lying, you don't get any now." She walked over to the display case and bent over to slide open the back. She took out a macaron and handed it to Maggie. "Make sure you let him know just how delicious that is when you eat it."

Maggie giggled. "I will." She opened her purse to take out her wallet.

Declan waved her off and handed Macy his credit card. "Can I at least have some coffee?"

She took his card with a saucy smile. "Yes."

"Thank you."

It didn't take long for her to ring them up and pour him a

cup of coffee. As soon as he had the coffee in his hand, he ushered Maggie out the door. They ran through the rain to her car.

"Yuck!" She brushed raindrops off her face. "Is it ever going to stop pouring today? I thought it was supposed to change to snow."

"I don't know. And I guess it stayed too warm for a changeover." For once, Declan was glad he wasn't on duty. There were probably going to be several water rescues tonight. Slogging through floodwaters in all his gear was not his idea of fun.

"I guess I should eat this before we go anywhere." Maggie lifted the macaron to her mouth and took a bite. The crunch filled the car. Little pieces flaked off as she bit down, and she cupped her hand beneath her chin to catch them. "Mmm... yum." A smile quirked her mouth as she chewed.

He laughed. "That was pathetic. It must not be as tasty as you thought it would be."

She rolled her eyes and giggled. "I'm going to tell London you said that."

"Maybe she'll make me my own batch to prove me wrong."

"Doubtful. She'll probably ban you from her kitchen."

He shook a finger at her. "That's more likely, yes."

She stuffed the rest of the cookie in her mouth, chewing it as she buckled up and started the car. "So, where am I going? I get the feeling you don't want to go home."

"No. I need to... do something."

"What do you normally do when you're antsy?"

"Rock climbing. Skiing. Running."

"Basically, all the things you're not currently allowed to do."

"Bingo."

"Okay. So, what are we going to do? A movie?"

He shook his head. "It needs to be something physical. If I just have to sit there, my mind will wander. I need to concentrate on a task."

Maggie tapped her chin, thinking. Her face brightened after a moment. "I have an idea." She put the car in reverse and backed onto the street.

"Where are we going?"

"You'll see."

He squinted, trying to determine if he was going to like where she was taking him, but it was no use. The woman had an excellent poker face.

They traveled out of town, passing the inn and heading toward her family's ranch. She made a turn down another road before she reached the drive, though, and Declan knew where they were going.

"Duvall's? What's out there?" Knox Duvall raised some of the best horses in the country, but he couldn't imagine why Maggie would take him there. Knox didn't offer trail rides, and if that was what she was thinking, they would go to the Broken Bow. He couldn't ride, anyway, with his busted ribs.

"You'll see," she repeated.

He sighed. "Maggie. I've had enough surprises for one day."

"It's nothing bad, I promise. I find it relaxing."

"Something you do with Knox?" The first tendrils of jealousy snaked through him. Knox was a nice man, as well as unattached and good-looking.

"No. With his sister."

"Alice? I thought she lived in town." Alice Duvall was the elementary school art teacher and had her own little house just off of the downtown area.

"She does."

"I'm confused."

She giggled. "It'll all be clear soon, I promise."

"Fine." He wasn't going to quibble with her. She and Alice were good friends, having been in the same grade together. Instead, he sat back in his seat and tried to enjoy the ride. It was pretty out this way, even with the rain. The road to the Duvall ranch wound up the side of the mountain, so the overlooks were breathtaking.

A few minutes later, Maggie took the turn onto the ranch driveway. The tires made a sluicing crunch as she drove up the gravel path. At the end of the quarter-mile drive, she took the fork that led to the main house, parking near a yellow Jeep that sat beside a metal building behind the farmhouse. Lights shone in the windows, and cheery autumn decorations bracketed the door.

~

Maggie shut off the engine, unfastening her seatbelt and opening her door. "Come on." She offered him an encouraging smile. He was so afraid she was leading him to something terrible. She could only imagine what he thought it was. Probably some super girly spa treatment or something. Granted, what they were doing was a bit girly, but it wasn't that bad.

Backs hunched against the downpour, they hurried inside, stomping off the water as they entered.

"Maggie! This is a surprise. And you brought a friend." Alice smiled at them from her position at a pottery wheel. "I'd greet you two properly, but I'm a mess." She held up her clay-covered hands.

"We're making pottery?" Declan asked.

Maggie turned to him. "*Painting* pottery." She pointed to shelves full of dried clay pieces waiting to be painted. "Making pottery would require different clothes. I'm not touching that wheel in this dress and shoes."

He gave her a once over, his eyes lingering on her bare legs. She'd thought about wearing boots today, but the way Declan always looked at her in high heels made her change her mind.

Alice laughed. "That would be a sight. You trying to sling clay in that skirt. You'd either have to sit like the Queen with your legs tucked to one side or with it rucked up around your hips."

Maggie glanced at Declan at Alice's words, heat popping out on her cheeks. His blue eyes darkened, and she could tell he was imagining her like the latter. She cleared her throat and stepped toward a table, peeling off her coat.

"I hope you don't mind us showing up out of the blue like this. I know you come here after school most days, so I was hoping you'd let us paint a few pieces. We—Declan especially—need to blow off some steam."

Alice's eyes slid between them, a smile blooming on her face. She blew a tendril of her blonde hair out of her face. "There are much better ways to blow off some steam than painting pottery."

Maggie's face colored even more. Alice looked all demure and innocent with her wheat-colored hair and cornflower blue eyes, but she had a naughty streak. "Yes, well, we're not interested in those ways, so here we are."

"I call bullshit. The look on his face says that's precisely what he'd like to do. But, hey, if you want to deny it, it's none of my business." She gestured to the unfinished pottery. "Have at it. I was going to do a run through the kiln later, anyway."

Maggie refused to look at Declan. Images of him sans shirt ran through her head on a reel. He liked to walk around without one frequently. Along with shorts and lounge pants that hung low on his hips.

Was it hot in here? She fanned herself.

Doing her best to dispel those images from her mind, she walked up to the shelves and picked up a pitcher and a large square plate. They would look nice as a centerpiece on Declan's table. She set them at a workstation, then wandered over to the glazes, looking for colors she thought would complement his existing décor.

He walked up next to her. She kept her eyes on the glaze.

"Maggie."

"Hmm?" She poked through the bottles, still refusing to look at him. If she did, she wouldn't be able to keep the thoughts running through her mind off her face.

"Maggie, look at me."

She blew a breath through her nose, closing her eyes for a moment, then turned her head to meet his gaze.

Banked fire burned in his eyes. An answering heat made her cheeks burn.

"I think we need to have a serious talk about what's happening between us."

She picked up several bottles of glaze. "I agree. But not here." With one last, lingering look, she walked to her workstation. She did think they needed to talk, but boy, was she not looking forward to that. Relationships weren't her thing. And her lack of experience in the romance department was likely to come up. Confessing she'd never had sex wasn't high on the list of conversations she wanted to have with him. It was one she intended to put off as long as possible. Call her a chicken, but she didn't care. It was mortifying to confess to the man who made your body tremble with just a look that at the ripe age of twenty-eight, no one had seen her naked.

Maggie glanced at Declan through her lashes, her head bent as she worked on the plate. He'd taken up residence at the table next to her and chosen a coffee mug to paint.

He looked up and caught her watching him. A sexy smile spread over his face, and she looked away. She should have just driven him home, then holed up with her case prep.

Doing her best to keep her eyes on her project, she

decided to ombre the pitcher, using shades of blue-green. Despite what she thought, she was able to shove her feelings back in their little box and soon relaxed into her task. It helped calm her mind, not just of thoughts of Declan, but of her assault case tomorrow. She was hoping for a quick acquittal, but with the craziness of late, she was not counting on it.

"Maggie, that looks fantastic." Alice came up behind her to look at what she'd done.

"Thanks." She turned the pitcher, double-checking her transition zones. They looked pretty smooth. "I think I'm done."

"Great. You can just leave them there and I'll put them in the kiln later."

Maggie nodded, then looked at Declan, who had moved on to a full set of mugs while she worked on her stuff. "What are you going to do with all those?"

He shrugged. "Keep one and give the rest away." He smiled at her. "I'm glad you brought me here. You were right; this is relaxing."

"Good. Are you about ready to go? I'm hungry."

"You're always hungry." He chuckled.

"What can I say?" She cleaned off her brushes. "I like food." Maggie stood, picking up her glaze bottles and returning them to the shelf. Declan did the same.

"Thanks again for letting us paint," she said to Alice.

"Any time. I'll get these fired tonight and you can pick them up whenever."

"Sounds great. We'll see you later."

Alice smiled. "Bye."

It was still raining when they stepped outside. Maggie sighed. They needed the rain, but she was ready for it to end. She didn't like driving in it. Especially in the dark.

"Do you mind if we stop at the Broken Bow before going

back to town? I need to get my mail." She buckled her seatbelt and started the engine.

"No, that's fine. We can eat at Heartwood, if you want."

She wasn't sure she wanted to subject herself to the scrutiny eating there would provoke. Though Tara wasn't working because she was busy with wedding prep. And some of her sister's cedar plank salmon sounded amazing.

"That works." She pulled away from the building and headed down the drive.

The trip was quick, the two ranches only a few miles apart. Maggie turned down the lane to her family's spread, pulling over to the bank of mailboxes first. She cleaned out her box and handed it all to Declan.

"Geez, Maggie. When were you here last?"

"Um, it's been a while. A week, maybe?" She shrugged and pulled back onto the drive. "Most of my bills are on autopay, and the ones that aren't, I pay online." She pointed to the stack he rifled through. "Most of that is probably junk."

"Yeah, it looks like it." He flipped through some flyers. "Except for this." He held up a hand-addressed envelope. "It looks like a card."

She glanced over, frowning. "Why would someone send me a card? My birthday is in February. Open it."

"You sure?"

"Yes. I don't care if you see it. It's not like it's going to be some gushy letter from a lover."

He chuckled. "That would be fun."

"Just open it."

He ripped through the flap and pulled out a card. Maggie glanced over again to see his expression morph into a deep frown.

"What?"

"It's a sympathy card."

"Sympathy? No one's died. Do they have the right

Margaret Archer? Maybe they were trying to reach someone else. My name is old-fashioned."

He flipped it open, sucking in a breath as he saw what was inside. "No, they have the right woman. Jesus."

"What?" She slowed. "What is it?" His tone and the disbelief and anger on his face made her worried.

"We need to call Seb."

"Why? Declan, what's in the card?"

"Pull into the restaurant and park, then I'll show you."

She drove the remaining distance as fast as the wet gravel would allow, then pulled into the Heartwood's parking lot, angling her car into a space. She threw the gearshift into park. "Show me."

He turned the card around, passing it to her. Maggie felt all the blood drain from her face as she took in the pictures inside the card. There were four, and in all four, someone had burned out her face. Fingers numb, they fell to her lap. "Oh my God. Who would do such a thing?"

Declan's gut churned as he thought about those images. Someone wanted to do some serious harm to Maggie. "Some sick bastard, that's who. There's no return address on the envelope. Can you think of anyone who would want to hurt you?"

"I'm a criminal defense attorney. There are probably quite a few."

"Anyone in particular?"

"Not that I can think of off the top of my head." She put her fingers to her temples. "Though shock and adrenaline may have something to do with my inability to think at the moment."

He pushed his door open. "Come on. Let's go get some food and a stiff drink, and we'll call Seb."

"That sounds lovely." She got out. "The drink will have to wait, though. I have to drive us back to town."

"We could stay on the ranch. Your house is just down the lane."

She pursed her lips, considering the idea. "That has merit. But you don't have any other clothes."

Declan held the door for her and they stepped inside, shaking off the raindrops once more. "It won't be the first time I've worn the same stuff for two days in a row. I'll be fine."

The hostess smiled at them as they walked up to her. "Maggie. It's good to see you. Tara's not here, if you're looking for her."

"Hi, Kaylee. We're not. We just came to eat."

"Oh, okay. Great. Do you want a booth or a table?"

"Booth," Declan answered. "Somewhere private." He didn't want anyone overhearing the conversation they would soon have with Seb.

"Of course." She picked up two menus. "Follow me."

They crossed the dining area to a booth tucked into the corner. Declan eased into the seat while Maggie flopped down across from him.

"Can I get you two anything to drink before you order?" Kaylee handed them their menus.

"I want a strawberry margarita. A big one," Maggie said, shedding her coat.

The girl nodded, then looked at Declan.

"Jack and Coke."

"Okay. Your server will bring them out shortly." She spun on her heel, leaving them alone.

Declan took out his phone and called Seb.

"You're interrupting family game night," Seb said when he answered. "Abigail's kicking my ass, so I'm not all that upset."

Despite the situation, Declan chuckled. "Good for her. I'm going to save you a further beating. Can you come out to the Heartwood? Maggie and I stopped at the ranch to get her mail and some food. She got a threatening card you should see."

"What?"

Declan could practically see the frown on Seb's face from that one word. "Just get over here."

"Yeah." He sighed. "On my way."

"Is he coming?" Maggie asked, as Declan hung up.

"Yes." He picked up his menu, not really seeing it. His eyes strayed to the card lying atop the table. Who could it be from? She could be right that it was from some disgruntled plaintiff or client. But the burned-out face bugged him. After all the fires, it was too much of a coincidence. Why the arsonist would target Maggie, he had no clue. If the fires were about the child trafficking ring, she shouldn't be a target.

Their server showed up with their drinks, and they gave their orders. Declan asked Maggie about her day while they waited, doing his best to distract them both. He supposed he could bring up their relationship, but he wasn't sure he wanted to think about that, either. As much as he liked her and found her attractive, he was hesitant to drag her further into his family drama. Hell, the more he learned about his parents, the trashier he felt. Maggie's family was loaded. She was an attorney, for crap's sake. He was a firefighter from a hellish family. She didn't need his past clouding her life. He was better off with his solitary state. They both were. Fewer people got hurt that way.

She smiled as she talked, the beauty of it hitting him in the solar plexus, stealing his breath. He wasn't sure his reservations would make a lick of difference. She drew him in, her pretty hands holding tight to his heart.

Heavy footsteps approaching snagged his attention, and he breathed a sigh of relief. Seb stopped at their table, and Maggie slid over to make room for him. Their server followed close behind with their food. She set the plates down and smiled at Seb.

"Can I get you anything, Sheriff?"

"I'm good, thanks."

"Let me know if you change your mind."

Seb watched her go, making sure she was out of earshot before he spoke. "All right, show me this card."

Declan slid it toward him, then stuffed a bite of his steak in his mouth, chewing quickly. He wanted to eat as much as he could before his stomach soured from their conversation and food was no longer appealing.

Seb took the card out of the envelope, holding it by the edges.

"Careful, there are pictures inside," Maggie cautioned.

"Of course there are," Seb muttered. He opened the card, sucking in a breath as he got a look at them. "Goddamn. Do you know when these were taken?"

She nodded. "They were all last week. Those," she pointed to the top two, "were outside my office. The next one was at the fire station, and the fourth was at the courthouse."

Seb studied them all, then looked at the envelope. "It's postmarked in Denver, so someone didn't want to broadcast they were mailing stuff to you. We might be able to find who took them, though. The courthouse and fire station are both public places with lots of cameras. The surrounding businesses have them too. I'll have my deputies get the footage from around there and see if we can't find our shutterbug. In the meantime, you need to be careful. You're still staying with Deck, right?"

"Yes. He still can't drive."

"Good. Keep doing that." He frowned as she picked up her cocktail and took a drink. "You're not driving, though, after drinking all that, are you?"

She put the drink down and shook her head. "No. We're going to stay at my house tonight. If I'm too buzzed, I figure I can get Brady to come get us."

"I can drive that short distance," Declan said. "There's a lot less alcohol in my drink than yours, and it only kinda hurts to raise my arms now. The doctor's supposed to clear me later this week, anyway."

She frowned. "Fine. But if you hurt yourself—"

"I won't." He looked at Seb. "What are the chances this is related to our arsonist?"

Surprise crossed Seb's face. "What makes you think it is?"

"The burned-out faces. Don't most people who send this sort of thing cut the faces out or cross them out with a big X?"

He shrugged. "Usually, yes. But I've seen stalkers who burn the faces. They're most often smokers, though."

"See?" Maggie looked at Declan. "It's probably someone related to one of my cases."

"That's more likely," Seb said. "You need to go through your recent case history and make a list of anyone who might want to do you harm."

She blew out a breath. "Yeah. All right. I'll start that tomorrow after court."

"And I will get my deputies working on camera footage from the area. Maybe one of the faces will match a name you put on your list." Seb slid out of the booth, taking the card and its contents with him. "I'm going to head out. I'll drop this into evidence, then go home. Hopefully, London will have managed to win a round or two against Abigail, so she's in a good mood. That girl is ruthless."

Maggie chuckled. "What were you playing?"

"Poker."

Declan laughed. "You let Abigail play poker?"

"Who do you think taught her to play?" He grinned. "I'll see you guys later. Maggie, be careful."

"I will. Let me know what you find."

"Yep. If anything weird happens, call me."

She nodded, and he waved, leaving them alone again.

"Cards sound fun," Declan mused, turning his attention to her. "Want to play around later?"

"Maybe. I still have to finish going over my notes for tomorrow. That shouldn't take too long, though. I only have the one case. I just want to make sure I didn't miss anything. The prosecuting attorney is known for twisting words. I want to be prepared."

Declan frowned. "I thought Seb cleaned house at the prosecutor's office when he shut down that child trafficking ring." Judge Brandt hadn't been the only public official involved.

"He did, but the attorney I'm up against was clean. He's just an asshole."

"That's too bad."

"Yeah. He's one of those people who made me want to be a defense attorney. He'll stop at nothing tomorrow to put Angie in jail."

"Angie? Tulley? She's your client?"

Maggie nodded.

"I wish you hadn't taken that case."

"Why?" She frowned. "Angie acted in self-defense when her husband beat the shit out of her and one of their kids."

"Because I know Hank. He's a mean son of a bitch. With his wife in jail, his attorney could argue it was mutual, but if she walks, her testimony, and their history, could put him away for a long time."

"I know. Deck, I'm not oblivious to the risks of my job. I take precautions."

"Take more. He put a kid in the hospital when we were in high school just because the paper he made the kid write got a B instead of an A. Just—have eyes in the back of your head." He wished he could convince her to turn the case over to someone else, but he knew she never would. He would have to settle for making sure she was as prepared as possible.

"I'll keep my eyes open, I promise."

He nodded and ate another bite of steak. They finished their meals and drinks, then Declan paid the check.

"Keys," he demanded as they walked out of the restaurant.

"It's half a mile. On a private lane."

"Don't care." He held out his hand, palm up. "Keys."

She huffed and dug them out of her purse. "Fine." She slapped them into his palm.

He hit the button to unlock the doors, and they climbed inside. He backed out of the space and turned right out of the lot. At the gate separating the rest of the ranch from public access—a new feature since Tara's run-in with Jared Fetter and Tim Jacobsen—Declan punched in the code and the metal gate slid back, letting them through, closing behind them.

The drive down the lane took less than a minute. He turned into her driveway and pushed the button on the garage door opener before pulling the car into the garage.

"How'd that feel?" she asked as they got out.

"Not bad." He handed her the keys so she could unlock the interior door. "A little pain, but not much. I don't think I'll have a problem getting cleared to drive again at my appointment on Thursday."

"Good." She walked inside the house. "I know you've been eager to get your independence back." She flipped on the lights and dropped her purse on the counter.

"Yeah. Being reliant on others for a ride everywhere sucks. Not that I don't like having you around, but it's nice being able to do things for myself."

"No, I get that." She glanced around.

Declan felt some awkwardness creep in now that they were alone. The heated glances and words they shared at Alice's pottery studio filled his head. Her pupils grew large and her cheeks colored. He knew she was thinking about it, too.

Maggie cleared her throat and looked away. "Well, I'm going to go look over my notes one more time, then go to bed. There are extra blankets and pillows in the hall closet. You can either sleep in the living room on the couch, or there's a bed made up in the spare room."

"I'll take the bedroom." Two closed doors between them was better than one. "Do you have an extra toothbrush?"

She nodded. "In the bathroom cabinet."

"Okay." His gaze held hers when she didn't move. "Maggie, you need to go work." His voice was a rough whisper.

"I know," she whispered back.

He took a step toward her. It shook her from her trance, and she shifted, moving back.

"Work. I need to work," she said under her breath. "Good night, Declan."

She scampered away, and he sagged against the counter, only to straighten when she returned.

"I forgot my briefcase." She hurried past him into the garage. A car door opened, then closed, and she came back inside. She didn't stop as she darted past, only offering him a wave and a quick salutation.

Declan groaned and scrubbed his hands over his face. Part of him wanted to storm into her office and make her forget about work. But the other part of him listed all the reasons why they were a bad idea. The age gap, her job, his terrible pedigree, how she reminded him of his ex—it all combined to make his feet move toward the spare bedroom instead.

NINE

Maggie exited the courtroom, feeling victorious. The prosecutor, Kyle Bancroft, tried his best to paint her client in a poor light, but all her preparations paid off. The judge dropped all the charges against Angie.

"Maggie."

She turned at the sound of Declan's voice. "Hey. What are you doing here?"

He walked closer, looking every inch the sexy firefighter in his crisp khaki cargo pants and department polo.

"I came to see how your case went."

"It went well. Kovac dismissed the charges."

"That's great." His eyes roved the corridor, watching the people milling around them.

She crossed her arms. "You didn't really come to hear about my case, did you?"

"What? Of course I did."

She rolled her eyes and dropped her arms. "Yeah, sure." She walked toward the stairs. "That's why you're looking at every person like they're just waiting to attack me."

"Well, can you blame me?" He followed her. "Someone

sent you those pictures—pictures they took of you here—and you antagonized one of the meanest men I've ever known by defending his wife. So, yeah, I'm here to watch your back."

"And I told you I don't need you to look out for me. I do fine on my own."

"And you'll continue to do so—just with me here now, too."

"Don't you have to work?" She stepped off the last riser and trekked across the marble floor, her heels tapping a steady staccato as she walked.

"You're more important."

She stopped and turned. "No. Don't do that."

"Do what?"

"Put me ahead of your employees. I will not be the reason someone doesn't get their raise on time."

"You won't be. I still have some time. And I plan on bringing the files home to work on."

"Declan..." Maggie sighed.

He stepped closer, invading her personal space. The scent of him carried toward her on a wave of his body heat. Her eyes wanted to roll up into the back of her head in ecstasy. He smelled wonderful. She loved his woodsy aftershave.

"Humor me, Mags. Please?"

She huffed. "Fine." Whirling around, she continued her march toward the door, eager to get away from his enticing scent before she did something scandalous in the middle of a public place. "How did you get here, anyway?" she asked as they stepped outside.

"I had one of the guys drop me off. They needed to make a grocery run, so I bummed a ride."

She stopped at her car, unlocking it. "I need to go to Colorado Springs to get table decorations for Tara's wedding. Am I dropping you at the fire station, or are you coming with me?"

"I can come with you. With my injuries and the time off I already had scheduled for later this week for the wedding, the captain only wants me to finish the personnel reviews. I have until the end of the day Friday."

"All right. Hop in." She opened her door and climbed inside.

He got in, buckling up. She pulled away from the courthouse. They talked about her case and what was next for Angie Tulley and her children as she drove. Maggie hoped Angie didn't back out of testifying. She'd looked spooked today. Hank was out on bail, and Maggie had a feeling he'd threatened her somehow. Now that she was free, Maggie hoped Angie wouldn't run in the dead of night. Her husband would get a stiffer sentence, and she could put much more time and distance between them in the end if she stayed and told her side of the story.

She wove through the downtown area of Colorado Springs, eventually pulling into a parking space at a storefront.

"What are we getting here?" He looked up at the sign above the door. It read Genevieve's Antiques.

"We need vases." Tara wanted to cluster vases on each table with wildflowers and fairy lights. They found a few in Silver Gap—enough for three tables—but they needed many more.

"How many?"

"A lot." She reached for the door, opening it and stepping inside. An older woman looked up as they entered and smiled.

"Hello."

Maggie smiled back. "Hi. So, we need vases. They're for a wedding. Various sizes. Color doesn't matter too much, but we need quite a few."

The woman motioned around them. "I have them scattered all over, so you'll have to look around. I'll clear some space on the counter and you can set them all up here."

"That sounds great, thank you." Maggie looked up at Declan. "Let's start looking."

She walked over to a display near the window. Several small vases sat on a shelf. Maggie snagged them all. Declan pointed to some larger ones to their left.

"What about those?"

"They work. No bigger than that, though."

For the next twenty minutes, they combed through the store, picking dozens of vases. Maggie eyed what they had on the counter and started arranging them into clusters. The proprietor caught on to what she was doing and helped her group them until she had enough for nine tables. The woman found some boxes, and they packed them up.

Declan reached for a box, but Maggie swatted him away. "You can get the door."

"Oh, come on, Maggie. It's a box of vases."

"That weighs over twenty pounds. You can't lift that much." She squinted up at him. "And don't tell me you aren't still sore. Especially after pulling my ass out of the barn."

His mouth turned down. "Just so you know, it chafes something awful to watch you carry all these boxes while I hold the door open."

"Don't worry." She picked up the first box. "You're still macho in my eyes."

Declan chuckled and walked toward the door. "Good to know."

She breezed past him with a sunny smile.

Once they were loaded up, Maggie suggested lunch. It was after one.

"Food sounds good. Do you just want to leave the car parked here and walk? There are several good little cafes downtown."

"Sure." It was chilly, but the sun was shining, so it felt warmer than it had in several days. She locked the car, and they started down the sidewalk. Declan offered her his arm, and she took it.

"What are you in the mood for?" he asked.

"Hmm. A good soup?"

He nodded. "I know just the place." He led her to the corner, and they crossed the street. A block later, he stopped in front of a small bistro.

"How did you find out about this place?" she asked, stepping inside as he held the door for her.

"My ex, Lilah, liked to eat here."

Maggie cast a rueful smile over her shoulder at him as he walked in behind her. "Okay. I guess I can see why you might equate me with her. This looks just like my kind of place." She glanced around. "We're not going to run into her here, are we?"

"We shouldn't. Her lunch hour is over."

"What does she do, anyway?"

"She's a financial advisor for an investment firm."

"How in the world did you meet her? I'm not saying you aren't sophisticated, but firefighters and financial advisors don't usually run in the same circles."

He chuckled. "No. She was at a bachelorette party for one of her friends. They were bar hopping and came into the same bar I was in. We chatted a bit, and she gave me her number. To my surprise, she answered when I called a few days later."

"You were together a while, weren't you?" She stepped up to the counter, looking at the menu.

"About a year and a half, yeah. It was all long distance, though. We typically only saw each other on the weekends I was off."

They placed their orders and stepped off to the side to wait. Maggie leaned against the counter while Declan took up residence against a wall.

"You don't date much, do you?" she asked.

"No. I'm not that social. I like my small group of friends. The only reason I was at that bar when I met Lilah was because a Marine buddy of mine was in town. You don't really date, either, though."

"I don't. Too busy." She looked away, hoping her inexperience didn't show. Her gaze landed on a woman watching them. Maggie's eyes widened as she recognized her. "Deck." She nudged him and gestured with her head.

He turned to look and stifled a groan. "I'm sorry. I really didn't think she'd be here this late." He waved at Lilah and forced a smile.

Maggie couldn't help but stare as the other woman sauntered over. Lilah was tall and perfect. Every dark hair on her head was precisely placed. Her makeup flawless. A light gray linen dress hugged her slender frame under her black trench. Sleek black pumps and a strand of pearls finished her look.

Jealousy reared its head, but Maggie squashed it, remembering how this woman held beauty over fun, and that it was part of the reason she and Declan broke up.

"Declan. It's been a long time. How have you been?"

Geez, even her voice was perfect. Melodic, it floated through the air.

"I've been good, thank you. You look great. Things still going well for you?"

She nodded. "I made senior partner over the summer."

"Congratulations."

"Thanks. Who's your friend?"

"We've met." Maggie held out her hand. "Maggie Archer."

Lilah took her hand. "Oh, yes. I remember you now. You look a little different."

Maggie imagined she did. At the last gathering where Declan brought Lilah, Maggie had helped her dad round up some stray calves when the fence broke in a storm. She'd shown up in her ripped jeans and dirty t-shirt. "I'm not chasing cattle today, so I dressed a little nicer."

"I see that. I love your dress."

"Thanks."

"So, what brings you two to Colorado Springs?"

"We were getting vases to make table decorations."

"Oh? Is your family having another party?" Lilah looked at Maggie. "I seem to remember they were fond of their family get-togethers."

"We are, but it's more than a party. It's a wedding."

Shock crossed Lilah's face, and her eyes bounced between the two of them. Maggie thought she saw a dose of regret there too. "You two are getting married?"

"We are," Declan said, as Maggie opened her mouth to answer in the negative. She looked at him sharply.

Expression more somber now, Lilah's shoulders straightened. "Oh. Well, that's wonderful. I'm happy for you, Declan. Congratulations." She forced a smile.

"Thanks."

One of the staff members called their order number.

"That's us." Declan motioned to the counter. "It was good to see you Lilah."

"You too." He took Maggie's hand and led her around his ex.

Maggie smiled and waved.

"What the hell was that all about?" she hissed when they were out of earshot.

"Sorry. I could see on her face she was gearing up to ask me to call her. Telling her you're my fiancée is easier on both of us than me outright rejecting her. She gets to save face, and I don't have to have an uncomfortable conversation about why I don't want to date her again."

"Chicken."

"No, pragmatic. Why should I cause her embarrassment

by telling her I'm not interested? Trust me, if she was given a choice, she would prefer to think I'm engaged than that I don't want her. She's a narcissist, remember?" He reached for the tray on the counter, picking it up.

"Still, you lied. We're not even together, let alone engaged."

"Aren't we? Together, I mean?"

Heat spread throughout Maggie's body as he stared down at her, desire turning his eyes an even deeper indigo. She licked her lips. "I have no idea what we are."

His mouth flattened. "Me, either." He started toward a table by the window. "We never did have that conversation about where we stood."

She glanced around, her gaze landing briefly on Lilah, who had her back to them as she ordered. "And you think now is the right time?"

He shrugged and slid her bowl of soup and a small baguette of bread toward her. She pulled it closer and dipped her spoon into the soup.

"Do we even need to have one? I think the fire between us speaks for itself. Though I'm not sure you want to be associated with me."

Her spoon paused on its way to her mouth. "What do you mean? Why wouldn't I?"

He stirred his soup, looking down as he answered. He looked uncomfortable, but she didn't know why he would be. Declan was one of the most confident men she'd ever met.

"Well, for one, I was accused of murder. Even though I was cleared, people still look at me differently. You're a criminal attorney. And you were *my* attorney. Think how that looks to your colleagues."

She scoffed. "It's a small town, and considering who the real culprit was, *and* everything that's happened since then, I think you can rest easy about all that. Next argument."

He sighed. "Okay. What about my family? Both my parents were junkies. My mother was just murdered, my dad's in the wind after his release from prison—I don't exactly come from good stock."

She dropped her spoon in her bowl and sat back, anger churning in her gut. "So, you think I wouldn't want to be your girlfriend or whatever because your parents suck? Deck, I couldn't give a rat's ass about your family. Where you come from doesn't matter. All that does is the person you are now, and you're a good man." She picked up her spoon and took another bite. "Where is all this coming from, anyway?" she asked after she swallowed. "You've never lacked confidence before."

He took a bite of his sandwich, thinking as he chewed. "We've already established I don't date much. But when I do, it's because I really like a woman." He caught her gaze, holding it. "I've never liked a woman as much as I like you. I want to be someone you can be proud of."

Maggie's heart faltered. That was so sweet! She reached out to cover his free hand. "You already are." He stared back at her, uncertainty on his handsome face. She sighed. "This is going to take some convincing, I see."

He gave her a rueful smile. "I'm trying, Maggie. I really am, but where we come from has an impact. On others and on ourselves. I thought I was past my lousy parentage, but Mom's death and Dad's infidelity and repeated criminal offenses have brought it all back. What we have is explosive and promises to be amazing, but—" he broke off and stared into his soup again. "I don't want to drag you down."

She uttered a soft growl, sitting back. "I won't let it."

He shrugged. "It's not up to you. I know you have aspirations to run for public office someday. What would having me for a husband do to those?"

"Make people love me more. They'll see you as someone

who rose above an awful beginning to be an amazing man." She crossed her arms and glared at him. Why was he refusing to see things her way?

"Or they'll see me as someone trying to ride your coattails to a better life."

"Now you're just being ridiculous."

"No, I'm not. How many times do you see political candidates losing races because their spouses weren't up to snuff?"

She frowned. "So? Declan, holding public office is a goal, yes, but I'd rather be happy in my personal life. A job can't keep me warm at night or cheer me up when I'm sad." When he continued to sit there, stoic, she sighed. "Just promise me you'll think about it, okay?"

He made eye contact with her again. "I don't want to hurt you."

"Not giving us a chance will hurt more than losing an election." She picked up her spoon once more, knowing she'd said all she could. He would have to decide on his own if he thought they were worth pursuing.

Ten

A rms loaded, Maggie got her fingers around the knob of Peppy Brewster's back door and let herself in. It was book club night—her first—and they were making table decorations instead of discussing the book none of them read.

"Oh! Here, let me help you." London hurried forward to take a box off the stack Maggie carried.

"There are more in the car."

"We'll get them," Macy said. She motioned to Rayna, and the two of them went out to get the rest of the vases.

Tara walked over to look inside the boxes Maggie set on the table. "Oh, I like these. You guys did good."

Maggie smiled and started unpacking them. "Thanks. The shop we went to had some great stuff. Did you bring the lights and stuff?"

"Yep." Tara pointed to a box at the end of the table.

"Awesome."

The back door opened again, letting Macy and Rayna inside.

"Don't unpack all that back here. We'll have more space out front," Macy said.

"Oh. All right." Maggie put the few vases she'd pulled out back in the box and picked it up, carrying it out to the café. The others followed.

"So, what are we doing?" Rayna asked.

Tara explained what she wanted, and they spread out amongst the tables, each taking a glue gun and some vases, lights, ribbon, and flowers.

"Where did you get all these, Maggie?" Macy asked. "They're gorgeous."

"Declan and I went to Genevieve's Antiques in Colorado Springs."

"You got Declan to go shopping?"

She shrugged, bending over to plug in her glue gun. "I offered to take him to the fire station, but he said he'd rather come with me. He was worried there was going to be some backlash from the husband of a woman I represented. She was charged with aggravated assault, but argued self-defense and the judge agreed."

London wrinkled her nose. "Good. Seb told me about that case. I'm glad she's leaving the bastard."

"Me too. I hope she stays away this time."

"But Declan was worried? Was there a credible threat?" Macy asked.

"Not really, no. Hank Tulley's just mean."

"My brother's smitten."

Maggie snorted. "Maybe, but nothing's going to happen."

"Yeah, right," Tara said. "I saw the way you two looked at each other at the inn."

"Oh, I'm not denying the attraction. He's just determined he's not good enough for me." She glued a flower to the jar and picked up another one.

"What?" Macy said. Her head shot up to stare at Maggie. "Why the hell would he think that?"

"Your parents. And his arrest in June."

"That's just bullshit. Those charges were dismissed. And our parents haven't been part of our lives since we graduated."

"That's what I told him. I don't know what else to say to convince him otherwise."

"Don't say anything," Rayna said.

Maggie paused and looked up. "Huh?"

"It's not words that will convince him. It's actions. You need to show him you'll always be there."

"Okay. I wasn't planning on giving up."

"Good. Just make sure he knows you want to be more than friends, though. Or he'll construe your presence as friendship."

Macy grinned. "As much as I don't want to think about my brother's sex life, do you have any, ahem, revealing outfits?"

Maggie blushed to her roots. "No. Not like what you're thinking."

"Really?" Tara said. "Not even any holdovers from past relationships?"

She picked up another flower and kept her eyes on the jar. "I never had a reason to wear any of that stuff."

Silence greeted her admission. She chanced a glance at the others. They all stared at her, dumbfounded.

"Are you saying you've never—" Macy flipped a hand in the air, "had relations?"

Her face had to be beet red. Maggie could feel it flaming. "Yes. That's what I'm saying."

"Well, that changes things a bit." London said.

"Oh my God, I don't want to have this conversation."

"I had no idea you were still a virgin," Tara said. "How did that happen?"

Maggie shrugged, still refusing to look at them. "I never met anyone more interesting than my books."

"My brother, who would rather be alone on a mountain

or reading than go out and party, is more interesting than your books?"

Declan's easy smile and witty comebacks floated through her mind. "Well, yeah."

Macy shook her head. "Bookworms."

The others chuckled.

"I think it's great," Rayna said. "And I think you're suited for each other. You bring him out of his shell a bit, and he has that seriousness you need."

Face still flaming, she looked up. "Yeah, well, tell him that."

"Oh, I will," Macy stated.

Maggie sighed. She appreciated the support, but having Macy and the others interfere in what was between her and Declan wasn't a great idea. "Thank you, but I can handle Declan."

"Can I take you lingerie shopping?" Tara asked. A naughty smile spread over her face.

"I can buy my own lingerie."

"Oh, come on. It'll be fun. We could all go."

"And when were you proposing we do this? You're getting married in three days, then going on a honeymoon."

Tara bit her lip. "Good point." Her face brightened. "I'll just give you pointers on what to look for instead."

Maggie laughed and held up her hands. "I think I can figure out what to buy." If she even went. They weren't anywhere near that stage yet. They might never be.

The others grinned.

"Let's leave poor Maggie alone," Rayna said. "She and Declan can figure things out just fine without our interference."

"Thank you," Maggie said. She ran a line of glue around the rim of a vase, then pressed the jute into it.

"Fine," Tara sighed. She tied a bow around her vase, gluing

it in place. "So, did everyone have their final dress fitting?"

There was a chorus of yeses around the room.

"You should probably try your dress on one more time for me," Rayna told Tara. "Your belly grew."

Tara ran a hand over her extended stomach. "Tell me about it. They've been more active, too."

"Your mid-term ultrasound is tomorrow, isn't it?" London asked.

"Yes." Tara grinned. "I'm so excited."

"Are you going to find out what you're having?" Macy asked.

"If they cooperate. I want to decorate and buy clothes."

"What do you think you're having?" Maggie asked. She was so happy she got to experience Tara's pregnancy with her this time. And that it was going well. After the way her first one ended, Tara deserved to have things go smoothly.

"I honestly don't know. Because there are two, I'm carrying differently than I did with Lucy. I feel different, too. I can't tell what's because I'm having twins and what's because of their gender. It'll be a surprise to us all." She filled a vase with some stones and stuck some flowers in it as she talked.

"Do you have a preference?" London asked.

"No. I just want healthy babies." She blinked hard a few times.

Maggie's heart lurched, knowing her sister was thinking of the baby she lost. "That's what we all want. I can't wait to spoil my little nieces or nephews. Or both." She chuckled.

Tara smiled. "The rest of you need to get busy on having your own, so my kids have playmates."

Maggie glanced around, noticing the red spots on London's cheeks. She sat a little straighter. "Wait. London?"

London's head shot up. "What?" The redness bloomed brighter.

"No way!" Rayna exclaimed. A bright smile lit her face.

"Are you really?"

"I don't know what you're talking about."

"Oh, whatever," Macy said. "That right there tells us you are. And it also explains your untouched wine." She pointed at London's still full glass. "Why didn't you say something sooner?"

London's shoulders dropped, and she sat back. "We were waiting until after the wedding." She looked at Tara. "We didn't want to steal your thunder."

"I wouldn't care, you know that."

"I know, but you deserve to have your day after what you've been through."

"The sentiment is appreciated, but no secrets, remember?"

"Yeah," London sighed. "I remember." She grinned. "So, yes, I'm pregnant. The baby's due in July."

Tara squealed and clapped her hands. "Excellent. Oh, this is so exciting!"

The group fell into an animated conversation about baby names and nursery themes. Maggie's mind wandered some, imagining what it would be like to have her own child. One with Declan's deep blue eyes and easy smile. She sighed. She had to convince him they were a good idea first.

"What about you, Rayna?" Tara asked. "Have you and Thomas talked about kids?"

"We have our hands full with Emma. But we have talked about it. We want to wait until we're married. That'll give us all time to settle into a routine and find each other's quirks."

"Is she adjusting well?" Maggie asked. She could imagine it would take some time for young Emma Lund to get comfortable in her new surroundings. After years in lackluster foster homes, she was probably still expecting the other shoe to drop and take away her newfound family.

"Yeah, for the most part. We've had a couple hiccups, mostly with curfew. Her previous foster family didn't care much what she did, so long as she didn't make waves at home. We don't want her running around after dark. Having Mason close by has helped, though. She trusts him, and she's getting better about being back on time. She's a good kid."

"That's awesome," Macy said. "I love that you guys took them both in. I wish—"

A loud boom from behind the coffee shop cut her off. The building shook, and their car alarms went off.

"What the hell was that?" London asked, standing.

"It sounded like an explosion," Rayna replied.

They all hurried into the kitchen. The back door was blown in, and smoke rapidly filled the room.

Maggie covered her mouth and nose with her shirt. "Tara, London, you two stay back."

"You should too," Rayna said. "Your lungs haven't healed completely." She motioned Macy forward. "Let's check it out. Someone call 911."

London pulled her phone from her pocket. Macy and Rayna hurried toward the door, their faces covered with towels from the stack on the table. Maggie could see the glow of a fire from where she stood. Embers floated through the air and smoke rolled.

"Oh my God!" Macy looked back. "Maggie, your car blew up."

"What?" Alarmed, she hurried forward, braving the smoke. It stung her eyes and scratched the back of her throat. She held her shirt a little tighter to her face and peered past her friends to look outside. Flames shot skyward from the twisted remains of her SUV. Thick black smoke roiled around the vehicle as the engine oil burned.

The world spun, and her vision grayed as shock, and a healthy dose of fear hit her. She grabbed the doorframe for support. The sound of a firetruck pulling up out front, sirens blaring, barely registered.

"Come on, Maggie," Rayna said, turning her around. "We need to get out of here and let the firefighters do their jobs."

Her feet felt like lead, but she let Rayna usher her through the kitchen to the front of the café. Macy unlocked the front door, and they stepped outside. Firefighters hurried around, hooking up hoses. Matt Crichton walked up to them.

"What happened?"

"We were in the front, working on decorations for Tara's wedding, when we heard a boom and the building shook. We ran back to check and found Maggie's car on fire. It looks like it blew up," Macy said.

He gave a quick nod. "Okay. You guys stay out here behind the truck." He looked back and gave a sharp whistle. "Stickley, McPherson, charge the hose. We'll go through the building. The fire's out back."

Maggie hugged herself and followed the other women around the firetruck and across the street. She stared at the building, her mind elsewhere. Why would someone want to blow up her car? Was it Hank Tulley? Was he also the person who sent those photographs of her? Or did she have another unseen enemy lurking? The first shiver of fear went up her spine.

A truck screeched to a halt at the perimeter set up by the police department. It was Declan. The vehicle still rocked as he climbed out, helmet under his arm. He jogged toward her.

"Maggie!" He stopped in front of her, wrapping his hands around her arms and catching her eye. "Are you okay? What happened? I heard the address come over the scanner."

She blinked at him, then glanced at his truck. "You aren't supposed to drive."

He gave her a soft shake. "Maggie, honey, never mind that. What happened?"

She took in a breath, clearing her mind a bit. "Um, my car exploded."

"What?" Shock colored his tone and his face. His eyes roamed over the others, pausing on Macy before he turned his attention back to Maggie. "How?"

She shrugged. "I don't know. I'm going to guess it wasn't an accident, though."

He cursed and looked around. "This is Crichton's squad, right? Where is he? Never mind, I'll go find him. Stay here, okay?"

Maggie nodded. Where was she going to go? Her car was a twisted hunk of burning metal. A hysterical laugh bubbled up her throat. She swallowed hard, holding it in, knowing if she let it out, it would quickly turn into sobs she couldn't stop.

Declan weaved through the emergency vehicles on scene, looking for Crichton and finding him standing at the open door to the pumper, radio in hand.

"Crichton!"

The other man turned. He said something into the radio, then hung it up on the hook on the dash. "Hey, Briggs. Did you find your sister? She and her friends are all right."

"Yeah, I talked to them. Maggie said her car exploded."

Crichton nodded. "It did. Stickley and McPherson are putting it out now. You want to assess it once it's out?"

Declan nodded. "Any idea what happened?"

"Not yet. It definitely exploded, though. The roof and all the doors are blown off. The blast blew in the back door of the coffee shop too."

"Did it do any other damage?"

"All their cars were parked close together. The two on either side of Ms. Archer's took the brunt of the explosion and were heavily damaged. The other two cars look like they escaped the worst of it."

He ran a hand through his hair. He hoped Tara didn't drive her old Ford into town tonight. She loved that truck and had restored it herself.

The radio on the dash crackled to life. Crichton picked it up. Declan listened as Stickley gave the all-clear.

"Let's go." He didn't wait for Matt. Moving at a brisk walk, he strapped his helmet on as he made his way into the shop and through to the back door. Smoke hung heavy on the damp air as he exited and got his first glimpse of the devastation.

His heart stuttered as he took in the destruction. Maggie's car was a charred, smoking hull of what it used to be. He could see the roof panel behind the car in the small parking lot. London and Rayna's cars on either side were smashed in from the force of the doors and the pressure wave. Glass glittered in the light from the streetlamp. Smoke and steam rose in thick wisps.

"Jesus," he muttered. Declan stepped closer, doing his best to turn off his emotions and look at the scene like he would any other. He peered closer at the interior, noting the higher degree of damage near the driver's side. Dread settled deep inside him, making his heart pound.

"Stickley, look under the driver's seat and tell me what you see."

"What am I looking for, exactly?" Stickley asked as he crouched.

"Char patterns and pavement destruction."

He nodded and bent his head to peer under the car. "There's a charred area about two feet in diameter and pieces of the car embedded in the pavement." He lifted his head to look at Declan.

"Fuck." Declan wanted to punch something. "Okay. We need to call forensics. Have the police cordon off this area. Someone planted a bomb in this car."

Stickley's eyes widened. "You're sure?"

Declan nodded. "Yeah, I'm sure." He ran a hand over his jaw. Tension made the muscles in it tick. Someone just tried to kill Maggie.

The chaos around him registered, and the urge to find her again hit him hard. "I'm going to call for assistance. Don't let anyone else back here."

Stickley nodded, and Declan spun away, jogging through the coffee shop, not caring that the motion jarred his ribcage with each step. Reaching Maggie was his number one priority. Only then would he call for help. He wove through the hose lines and emergency vehicles. His shoulders dropped a fraction, and his heart slowed as he caught sight of her where he left her.

"What did you find out?" Macy asked as he reached them.

His eyes connected with Maggie's. He couldn't think of a nice way to tell her the news, so he blurted out the truth. "I think someone planted a bomb under the driver's seat."

She blanched and her knees buckled. Declan wrapped his arms around her and held her close.

"Why would someone want to hurt Maggie?" London asked. "This is insane."

"I don't know, but we'll find out." He looked down at the woman in his arms. "I need to call your brother. Are you going to be okay for a few minutes?"

Some of that famous Archer grit showed itself as she straightened. Her eyes hardened as some of the shock cleared, and she nodded. "Do what you have to and find this asshole."

He pressed a kiss to her temple, smoothing back a tendril of dark hair that fell over her face. "I will. Stay with the others. Don't wander off alone, okay?"

She nodded again.

"That goes for all of you. Stick together."

"We will," Rayna said. "None of us have a desire to be alone right now."

London and Macy murmured their agreement.

Declan let Maggie go. "Good. I'll be right back." He retraced his steps, heading for the firetruck to use its radio.

Crichton saw him coming and cursed. "I wondered if it was bad when I saw you make a beeline for the women." He held out the radio.

"Yeah, it's bad." He took the receiver. "Thanks." Pressing the mic button, he called for a forensics team. He was about to ask for a location on the sheriff when he saw the tall man walking through the crowd of emergency personnel and onlookers.

He glanced at Crichton. "There was a bomb under the driver's seat. I've got Stickley keeping people out of the area. I need to go talk to Seb."

"Man, what the hell is going on around here? First arson fires, now a bomb?" He waved a hand toward Seb. "Go talk to him. Keep me informed."

"Will do." Declan handed him the radio and hurried away, flagging Seb down.

"What happened?" Seb asked, his long legs closing the gap between them. "Where are London and the others?"

"They're safe over there." Declan pointed toward the sidewalk where the five women stood huddled together, watching the commotion.

Seb blew out a breath, relief relaxing his features. "Good. I heard you call for forensics." He motioned to the radio on his belt.

"Yeah. Someone put a bomb in Maggie's car."

Seb's eyes grew wide. "Are you serious? How bad is the damage? And why isn't she hurt? I mean, that's usually the objective of a bomb, right? To hurt or kill the target?"

Declan nodded. "I'm not sure. I think it went off prematurely, though. It was under the driver's seat."

"Shit." Seb put a hand to his forehead and spun away several paces before coming back. "Any idea who it could be? Is it our arsonist stepping up his game?"

"Not sure. It could be Hank Tulley, too."

Seb's mouth flattened, and he shook his head. "It's not. He's in my jail. Gentry brought him in just as I was leaving around six. He decided to drown his sorrows in a bottle and started a fight at a bar."

"That leaves our arsonist or some other unknown suspect."

"What's your gut say?"

Declan chewed on his bottom lip and glanced away. With Tulley out of the picture, it was too much of a coincidence for it to be a third, unknown person. "I think it's the arsonist. So far, minus my mom, everyone else is connected to your family."

"Maybe this is about her. But I don't know what connection Maggie would have to her."

"Me either. But maybe the bombing will yield some clues. It's a lot harder to set off an explosive without leaving a trail than to pour some gasoline on a building and set it on fire."

Seb sighed. "Yeah. And Katie's the best, so if there's something to be found, she'll find it." He pointed toward the coffee shop. "Show me the car."

Declan led him through the café and braced himself as he stepped out back, knowing what he would see.

Seb let out a low whistle. "Damn." He looked at Declan. "Once we're done here, we need to call a family meeting. I want you and Macy there, too. We need to make a plan to keep everyone as safe as possible."

"I agree. We'll be there." Whatever the plan entailed, Declan was going to make sure it meant Maggie stuck with him. He needed to be there to keep her safe.

Eleven

Maggie paused as she left her room and tried not to stare as Declan walked out of the bathroom, bare-chested. The bruising on his ribcage had faded, coloring the skin shades of yellow and brown now as it healed. Without the more intense discoloration, his well-defined muscles stood out. She curled her fingers and forced her hands to stay at her sides.

"Oh, sorry," he said, stepping around her to the bedroom he was using. They were at her house now. After the car bombing, they'd all decided the ranch, with its cameras and fencing, was the safest place. Declan was staying with her, and Macy moved into the main house with Maggie's parents. Thomas and Rayna were staying in his house with Mason and Emma until things settled down. Rayna even convinced her parents to take over Seb's old place, worried about them staying on the Double Moon by themselves with the threat looming over them all. Only Seb and London were living elsewhere.

She cleared her throat. "Are you about ready? We have a lot to do today." Tara had a list ten miles long of things for them to do before the rehearsal tonight. Maggie was sure they were going to be working up until it was time for that and then probably after as well.

He looked over his shoulder. "Yeah. I need to grab a shirt and eat something, then we can go."

"I'll scramble you some eggs."

"Sounds good, thanks."

She gave him a quick nod and scampered away before she walked toward him and laid her hands all over those rippling muscles. The last thirty-six hours had been torture. He refused to leave her side, but he also hadn't made any move to turn their relationship into something more. In fact, after he hugged her at Peppy Brewster, he hadn't touched her. She was rapidly coming to the conclusion Rayna was right; she needed to take the direction of their relationship into her own hands.

After Tara's wedding. She didn't have the energy to navigate both.

Maggie took four of the fresh eggs from the basket on the counter and cracked them into a bowl, adding a dash of milk and salt before whipping them with a fork. She melted some butter in a skillet, then added the eggs, stirring them as they cooked. Declan walked in while she worked. He started the coffeemaker and set the table, then poured two mugs of coffee. Once the eggs were done, she split them between the two plates he laid out, then grabbed two bananas and two yogurts, knowing they were going to need the fuel for the day ahead. Declan made himself some toast, too.

They ate fast, putting their dirty plates in the dishwasher when they finished, then hurrying out the door. Birds chirped their morning song as they walked up the lane to the barn. Maggie let it wash over her and eat away some of the stress she woke up with. Today and tomorrow would be happy times. They would celebrate love and life and family. She wouldn't let her troubles intrude on that.

As they got closer to the barn, she heard hammering and her brothers yelling directions at one another.

"What are they building?" Declan asked.

"Probably a stage. Brady was in charge of music, and knowing him, I'm betting there will be live entertainment." Her brother loved music and was even in a band in his teens until the demands of college and running a ranch took away most of his free time. Now, he just played for himself, singing and playing guitar in the evenings and at casual family gatherings.

"You don't know who he hired?"

She shook her head. They entered the barn to see a platform going up at the far end. Brady carried a two-by-four toward a frame on the ground. Thomas and Seb stood at the far corner, Seb holding two boards while Thomas screwed them together. A saw started up off to the right where Jace cut more boards to use as crossbeams for support.

"Wow. They've been busy," Declan said.

Maggie smiled. "Brady probably started on his own at sunup. It looks like he put some support columns together to string lights on." She motioned to the four-by-four posts leaning against the barn wall, strung together in twos by a length of two-by-four. She imagined he was going to attach them to the stage base on three sides, then add some lighting and other decorations.

"About time you two showed up."

Maggie turned to see Macy standing behind them, carrying several folding chairs.

"Decide to sleep in?" She grinned. "Or do other things?"

Maggie's face flamed, even though she had no reason to be embarrassed. "Tara said eight. It's seven fifty-three. We're not late."

"You are when Brady's in charge. He woke me up at five-thirty."

"Wait," Declan said. "I thought you were staying with Lee and Jenny?"

Macy set the chairs down and waved a hand. "Oh, that. I was, but I was sleeping on the couch. The kids take up all their extra bedrooms now. Brady has a spare room and offered it to me when he found out."

Maggie couldn't help the grin that spread over her face. "Yeah? How's that working out?" She knew Macy had a crush on her brother. Everyone did. Except Brady.

"Fine, except he's an early riser. Like ungodly early. I hear his shower come on at four every morning." A flush crept up her neck, and Maggie knew she was thinking about Brady in the shower. Macy cleared her throat. "We're setting up tables now. Why don't you grab some chairs? You can carry those, can't you, Deck?"

He nodded. "Most likely. I got cleared for light lifting and driving at my appointment yesterday."

"Sweet. Everything's in Lee's truck outside." She pointed back the way they came. London and Rayna entered the barn with their own stacks of chairs. The foster kids living with the Archers followed them, carrying tables.

They followed her out of the barn to get to work. For the next few hours, they set up tables, chairs, and decorations. With all of them working, they accomplished much more than Maggie thought they would. It helped that Tara put Brady in charge of setup. The man could organize anything to within an inch of its life. She had the final say on everything, but Brady knew her well enough to know what she wanted, and she made few changes to his plans.

When they broke for lunch, all they had left to decorate were the rafters. Tara wanted lights strung through them. She also had some large floral arrangements to put on the support beams. But for the moment, it was break time.

Maggie piled a plate high with a ham sandwich, chips, and

a pickle before sinking into a chair at a table with a groan. It felt nice to sit. She picked up her sandwich and took a bite, glancing up as Declan came up beside her. He put a bottle of water down in front of her, then sat down.

She swallowed. "Thanks."

He nodded and picked up his own sandwich. Maggie crunched a chip and looked around at all their handiwork. The space looked great. She could imagine how it would look once they finished. It would be amazing and definitely reflect her sister and Jace.

"How are your ribs?" she asked Declan, looking at him.

"Sore, but not too bad. I'm good."

"Did the doctor say when you could return to full duty?" She didn't ask that question yesterday when she took him to see his surgeon. He walked out of the clinic with a big smile and demanded to drive.

"At least two more weeks. I am allowed to do some light exercise now, though. He gave me some strengthening exercises to do."

Maggie was about to ask if he tried them yet, when Seb's phone rang. It was likely nothing, but she got nervous now any time his phone chirped.

Everyone else must have felt the same way, because all conversation stopped as he answered.

"Yeah, Katie?"

Maggie held her breath. She hoped Katie found something to point them toward whoever blew up her car.

"Okay, thanks."

He hung up and looked around at everyone before zeroing in on her. "No usable fingerprints or DNA, but she was able to piece together a detonator. It was a cellphone. And she found an intact SIM card. I need to go put together a warrant to give to the phone service providers in the area for phone call data from the time of the explosion." He stood, bending over London to give her a quick kiss.

"Do you need me to come?" Jace asked.

"No, I should be fine. I'll pull in Wilder and Gentry if I need help. Unless the world crashes down around us, you are off until you get back from your honeymoon."

London smacked his leg. "Hush. Don't jinx us!"

He grimaced. "Sorry. I'll see you guys later."

They waved and murmured goodbyes as he dashed out of the barn. Maggie pushed her plate away, her appetite gone now with the mention of her car. She knew her mood should be buoyed that he had a lead, but it just brought back the fear. That someone could get to her so easily was unsettling. She still didn't know why she wasn't dead.

Needing to do something, she got up.

"You didn't finish your lunch," Declan said.

"I wasn't as hungry as I thought I was. I'm going to get back to work."

"That's bullshit. You eat more than some men I know." He stood next to her and took hold of her elbow, ushering her away from the others.

"Deck, what are you doing?" she hissed.

"You're going to tell me what's bothering you." He dumped both their plates in the trash on the way out of the barn and led her around the side, where it was quiet. "Talk. What's wrong?"

She huffed and stared past his shoulder at the pasture beyond. "Nothing. We had a big breakfast, so I didn't want as much lunch."

"Try again, Mags."

She crossed her arms and cocked a hip, glaring up at him. "I'm fine."

"No, you're not. I can read you like a book, remember?"

Dammit. He was right. It was annoying. She dropped her

arms and looked at the sky for a moment. "Fine. Talk of the bomb brought back all the fear, okay? I thought I was past it, but it's all come flooding back. It's scary how close someone came. How close *I* came to—" She broke off, unable to voice the thought aloud.

"Damn, Maggie." Declan's voice was soft. He gathered her to his chest.

She wrapped her arms around his waist, sniffing.

"I'm sorry, honey. I know Seb's doing everything he can to find this guy. And no one's going to get to you so long as I'm around."

She hugged him tighter. "I know." She lifted her head. "I appreciate that. You make me feel safe. It's why I haven't balked at you staying with me, even though you don't need me anymore."

He lifted a hand and buried it in her hair. "I'm not so sure about that." His eyes flicked to her mouth, heat flaring in their blue depths.

Maggie felt an answering heat build low in her belly. She wanted him to kiss her.

Take charge.

Rayna's words floated through her mind.

All right, fine. She tipped her face up, stood on her toes, and sealed her mouth to his.

He made a soft grunt of surprise at the contact, but relaxed into the embrace. In a blink, he took control. His hands cradled her head as he plundered her mouth. She went from zero to sixty in an instant. Her fingers toyed with the hem of his shirt, sliding beneath to touch the skin at his waist. She'd been dreaming about the golden skin of his torso for weeks now. She was going to touch it while she had the chance.

Careful of his tender ribs, she slid her hands up his back, loving the feel of silken skin over hard muscle. His hands traveled south to hold her hips. He pulled her into him, and Maggie felt the evidence of his desire against her abdomen. A thrill went through her, sending shivers down her spine. She wished they were back at her house.

Laughter from in the barn intruded on their moment, breaking them apart. Declan stared down at her, his eyes hooded.

"That wasn't supposed to happen."

"Why not?"

"I'm no good for you, Maggie. You don't want my history clouding your life. We're better as friends."

"The fuck we are. How about you let me decide that?"

Surprise at her outburst widened his eyes, but she was tired of him making excuses for why they shouldn't be together. "I don't care who your parents are. And anyone who knows you, knows you would never hurt someone deliberately."

"Maggie—"

She held up a hand. "I don't want to argue, Declan. Let's just go back inside." He still held her, so she stared up at him, waiting for him to release her.

"Dammit." He let her go and stepped back.

She walked around him and headed for the door.

"You're not going to quit, are you?"

"Nope." She spun around. "I like you. Enough to set all my insecurities about men aside and take a chance. I don't want to be friends. I want more. I just need you to realize you're more than your family." Turning around, she marched back to the barn. Her hands shook as the realization she told him how she really felt hit her. Boldness in a relationship was not something she was accustomed to. But no one had ever mattered the way Declan did. She wasn't going to give up.

TWELVE

Declan stood between Thomas and Alex as they rehearsed Tara and Jace's wedding ceremony with the minister. He couldn't keep his eyes off Maggie, who stood next to her sister as the maid-of-honor. She'd changed from her shorts and t-shirt to a soft pink, knee-length sundress for the rehearsal. Strappy heeled sandals adorned her feet, adding to her long legs and driving him crazy.

He couldn't stop thinking about what she said earlier. Declan wanted to believe his past didn't matter, but he feared what would happen a few years from now when she decided to enter the political ring. Her opponent would undoubtedly use it against her. He didn't want to be the reason she lost.

But he'd be damned if he could stay away.

Declan forced his attention off her and onto the altar. The minister explained the ceremony, then had them walk down the aisle in reverse order. Deck stepped into the aisle and held out an arm to London.

She smiled up at him and took it. "Don't look so grim. People will think you don't approve of this marriage."

"What? Oh, sorry. My mind is elsewhere."

She giggled. "I can tell. She looks very pretty this evening."

"Yeah, Tara looks great. Pregnancy looks good on her."

"It does, but she isn't who I was talking about, and you know it." She cast a sideways glance at him as they walked.

A corner of his mouth lifted. "I do."

"When are you going to do something about it?"

He sighed. "Not you too."

"I just want you both to be happy. I think you make a good couple."

"But will that be the case when Maggie's in the public eye?"

"Maggie will be happy so long as she's with you. Her career doesn't define her, you should know that."

Maybe not, but Maggie deserved to be and do whatever she wanted. He didn't want to hold her back.

They reached the end of the aisle, and London let go of his arm. "Just think about what I said, okay?"

He nodded. "I will."

"Good." She smiled and turned away to find her husband.

Declan sighed, his thoughts jumbled. He wished he had a magic ball that would let him see the future.

He stepped toward the others, intending to mingle, when darkness descended over the barn as all the lights went out. The younger children screamed, and unease skittered up Declan's spine.

"Everyone stay calm and don't move," Lee said. "Brady, let's check the electrical box. Maybe all these extra lights tripped a breaker."

Brady's phone lit up as he turned on his flashlight app. Glass broke and the whoosh of fire blooming to life followed close behind. Flames raced along the ground at the opening to the barn doors. The tink of more glass breaking sounded on the other side of the barn, and smoke began to filter in.

"We're trapped!" One of the kids shouted.

"No, we're not," Declan said. "We're in a barn." He turned on his phone flashlight and aimed it at Brady. "There any tools still in here?"

Realization of what he was getting at crossed Brady's face. "Yes." He darted away, Declan hot on his heels. They stopped at a supply room, which they soon discovered was locked.

Brady growled in frustration, but it didn't slow him down. He used his size to their advantage and shouldered it open.

"Axes, hammers, anything that can break through the walls," Declan said, stepping forward to grab an axe off the wall.

"Yep."

The two of them gathered a variety of tools and ran back to the others. Thick smoke filled the room, reducing visibility. They passed out what they gathered.

"Come on." Brady motioned them toward one of the side walls.

"Two teams," Declan said. "We attack two points and take turns, so no one tires out."

"Why can't we go out a window?" Mason asked.

"Because there's fire under every one." The arsonist would make sure they had no easy way out. Busting through a wall was their best chance. Declan was thankful Tara wanted to hold her wedding in one of the older barns. If they were in one of the new barns, which were made of steel beams and sheet metal, they'd have a lot harder time breaking out.

They lined up about fifteen feet apart and attacked the wall. Declan hung back, holding the light on the wall and assessing their progress. Fire licked up the front and back walls, and smaller blazes were taking hold beneath the windows. He could see the flicker of flames through the glass.

Jace and Brady both broke through the wall with their axes. After making several splits in the wood, they stepped aside and let Thomas and Seb bust the wall open wider with sledgehammers. In minutes, they had two holes big enough to climb through.

It was none too soon, either. They were all coughing from the smoke now. Declan tried to suppress his coughs, but pain still lanced through his chest. He looked at Maggie, worried about how she was handling the smoke after her recent encounter. She coughed, but no harder than anyone else.

Brady and Seb pushed their way through the holes, then leaned back in.

"Give us the kids," Seb said.

They passed the children through, including Emma and Abigail. London and Tara went next, then the rest of the group followed.

As soon as Declan cleared the barn, he called dispatch to report the fire and request medical assistance.

"Is everyone okay?" Seb yelled.

Through their coughs, everyone nodded.

"Are you calling in the fire?" he asked Declan.

"Yeah."

"Ask for a police response, too." He looked over the group. "Jace, Brady, Thomas, Mason, come with me. Dad, you and Deck stay with the others. We're going to check the other buildings."

A thought occurred to Declan. "I'll request the bomb squad from the state police. Just to be safe."

"Sounds good. For now, everyone stay outside. Let's go, guys." He jogged off, giving orders to the others as they went.

Declan put in the request for help, then hung up and went to check on the others, starting with the children. They were shaken, but their respiratory issues were minor.

He stopped in front of Tara, who sat in the grass, and crouched to her level. "You okay?"

She nodded, coughing lightly. "Yeah. Just shook up." Tears formed in her eyes. "Why does this keep happening? Why is it every time something good happens, some asshole comes along and ruins it?"

"It's not ruined." He put a hand on her knee. "You still have Jace. The minister survived."

She laughed.

"You can get married anywhere, so long as you have those two things. The rest is just trappings."

"Thank you." She patted his hand. "I needed to hear that."

He smiled. "Good. Now, are you sure you're okay? No issues breathing?"

"No. Just coughing."

"Babies moving?"

She laid a hand over her belly. "Yep. They're agitated, just like their momma."

"Okay. If something changes, let me know. You should probably go to the hospital anyway and let them check you and the twins out."

"How about I sit in an ambulance and let them monitor me for a bit?"

"And go if they think you should based on what they see."

"Deal. Now, go check on my sister. She's coughing harder than anyone."

He glanced up, finding Maggie in the crowd. Tara was right. She was trying hard to control it, but it looked like she was fighting a losing battle.

Declan pushed to his feet and walked her way. "Maggie, you should sit." He helped her down into the grass. She continued to cough. "Where's your inhaler?"

"At home."

"Where?"

"In my purse." She coughed hard. "On the counter."

"She okay?" Macy walked up, concern on her face.

"She needs her inhaler. Can you sit with her while I go get it?"

"Of course." Macy dropped to the ground.

"I'll be right back." He took off at a run, ignoring the twinges in his chest as he hurried down the lane to the houses. Ribs on fire from breathing hard and coughing, he entered the code to get in the garage and let himself inside. He dumped the contents of her purse on the counter, plucking the inhaler from the mess, then dashed back out, closing the garage door.

As he cleared the house, movement to his left caught his attention. He paused and stared into the growing darkness. The silhouette of a man moved behind Thomas's house further down the lane.

"Hey!"

The figure paused, then broke into a run, going deeper onto Broken Bow land. Declan started after him, but realized he couldn't chase the man and get Maggie her inhaler.

"Dammit!" Concern for Maggie won, and he turned around, heading back to the burning barn. He took out his phone as he ran, calling Seb.

"There's someone headed into the hills from the houses," he said, not bothering with a greeting when Seb answered. "I saw him behind Thomas's house when I went to get Maggie's inhaler."

"Copy. We'll head that way. Thanks." He hung up.

Declan heard the first sirens as he reached the others. He said a prayer of thanks, glad for the backup. Maybe they could find the person he saw.

He came to a halt in front of Maggie and handed her the inhaler. She took two puffs, and her breathing calmed.

"Feeling better?"

She nodded, taking several slow, deep breaths. "Yes. Thank you."

"I need to go help coordinate the fire response. Stay here?"

Again, she nodded.

He squeezed her hand and hurried off toward the fire engines.

"We have to stop meeting like this," Crichton said as Declan ran up.

"No shit. Ignition points are front and back doors and under every window. Sonofabitch tried to trap us."

Crichton barked orders at his men on where to attack the flames, then turned to Declan. "How did you get out?"

"Hacked our way through the wall."

"Damn. Good thing you were in the barn. If it had been one of the houses, you might not have made it out."

"That's no lie. We're going to have to rig up some alarms. This was too close." He didn't know how they would accomplish that on a ranch the size of the Broken Bow, but they had to do something.

"Anyone hurt?"

"No. Just some minor smoke inhalation. Tara should be looked at since she's pregnant. And Maggie, since she had a recent exposure. Oh, and London too. Maggie told me yesterday she's expecting as well."

"I'll get the medics on it. The kids all okay?"

"Yeah. We kept them low and evacuated them first, so they escaped the worst of it."

"Good. Go sit with your woman. I've got this."

Declan glanced between the burning barn and the Archer clan grouped in the field, torn. He wanted to work the fire, but he wanted to be with Maggie, too.

His desire to be with her won out. "Come get me when you're ready to do the survey. I doubt we'll find anything I'm not already expecting, but I still want to look."

"You got it. Go."

Declan jogged back to his friends, one eye on the fire. Anger made his spine rigid. He was going to bring this bastard down.

Sweat trickled between Maggie's breasts as she leaned against the wall in Brady's office in the main barn. Soot lent a fine grit to her skin. She couldn't wait to get into the shower and wash off the grime. But she wanted to see the ranch security footage first. Seb and his deputies had little luck finding the perpetrator. The K-9 traced a scent away from the houses about half a mile, then lost it. Seb thought they had a vehicle waiting. The good news, though, was that the bomb squad didn't find any hidden devices elsewhere on the ranch. Maggie had a feeling Declan chased the man away before he could plant any.

"Can we make this quick?" Macy asked. "We're crammed in here like sardines, and it's hot."

"Typing as fast as I can, babe," Brady muttered. His fingers flew over the keyboard as he pulled up the footage.

She flicked him in the ear. "Not your babe."

"Ow!" He ducked away from her hand. "Knock it off, Mace."

"Don't call me babe." A naughty grin spread over her pretty face. "Unless you mean it."

His face flushed. Maggie smothered a smile. It was so funny to watch her big, burly brother blush.

He kept his mouth shut and his eyes on the computer screen.

"Queue it up to just before the fire erupted," Seb said.

Brady moved the cursor on the video, queueing all the feeds up to a few minutes before flames were visible, then split the feeds between three monitors so they were easier to assess. They all leaned in as he hit play.

On the center display, a figure ran into view. A man walked the perimeter of the barn with a gas can, pouring the fuel beneath the windows. He disappeared from view for a minute, then showed up again at the corner of the barn, where he lit two Molotov cocktails. He ran forward and threw them into the open doorway of the barn, then dashed around back to throw a third at the closed doors.

"Damn. There's no good shot of his face," Jace said.

"Not at the barn." Brady isolated the barn feeds and put them on a side screen. "But there's better lighting near the houses." He put the feeds from the housing area on the center screen and hit play. They watched for several minutes before the man showed up. He checked each house, attempting to go inside, but because of all the trouble lately, everyone had locked their doors before leaving.

The cameras caught Declan arriving. Brady moved to the camera nearest Thomas's house. The man checked the windows, then froze when he saw Declan, only taking off when Declan spotted him.

"Can you zoom in on his face?" Seb asked.

"Yep." Brady scrolled the wheel on the mouse, zeroing in on the man's face.

Declan gasped. "What the fuck?" he growled.

"What?" Seb asked.

"How did I not see it?" Declan pointed at the screen. "That's one of my rookies, Jameson Gehring."

"Seriously?" Seb leaned closer to the screen. "How did he get hired? Don't you guys screen for firebugs?"

"Yes. I don't know how he passed the psych test."

"If he's a sociopath and highly intelligent, it wouldn't be difficult for him to fake it well," Maggie said. "I read several case studies in law school on arsonists and serial killers. Those who were sociopaths fooled even those closest to them for years."

"This means you have his home address, right?" Seb said.

Declan nodded. "It's in my office at the fire station."

"Good. Let's go." He looked around at the others, his eyes stopping on Tara. "I need to borrow Jace."

She sighed. "I figured." She turned around to look up at her fiancé. "Be careful, please? I really would like to get married tomorrow."

"Babe, the only way that won't happen is if I'm dead. And I don't plan on dying." He pressed a kiss to her lips. "I love you. I'll be back as soon as I can."

Maggie felt tears swim in her eyes as she took in the look of love on her sister's face. Not only was it a beautiful sight, but one she never thought she'd see on Tara again. Jace had really opened her up and helped her heal.

"Bring him back in one piece, Sebastian," Tara said.

"I will."

Declan touched Maggie's shoulder, gaining her attention. She nodded as he silently said goodbye. The three of them left, taking some of the energy in the room with them. They were in waiting mode now.

Jenny clapped her hands, getting their attention. "All right. Now that we have that handled, it's time to move on to how we're going to salvage this wedding. Obviously, we can't have it in the barn now. The weather's going to be nice, if a bit chilly, so how about we set up out back of the main house? We have all those canopies we take camping. We can set them up and put the space heaters we use in the barns under them."

"What about tables and chairs?" Lee asked. "They were all in the barn."

"We can use our dining sets, and I'm sure our friends and neighbors won't mind bringing their own." She looked at Tara. "What do you say, honey? I know it's not the wedding you dreamed of, but we can still make it beautiful."

"I say we go for it. It'll be memorable, that's for sure."

Jenny beamed. "Let's get busy." She ushered them all out of the room and took control, issuing orders better than any drill sergeant ever could.

In moments, Maggie held everyone's house keys. She and

Macy climbed into Declan's truck to retrieve chairs from their homes. Thomas and Brady would go back for the tables later. There wouldn't be a dining chair left in any of them once they were done.

Despite the late hour, a renewed vigor filled her. They would do what they could to make Tara's wedding the best it could be under the circumstances.

After visiting all the homes, they drove back to the main house and offloaded their loot. Thomas and Brady had several canopies set up, and Jenny was on a ladder, stringing her Christmas lights around the first one.

"You have the house keys?" Thomas asked, coming up to her. "Brady and I are going to go get all the kitchen tables now."

"They're in the center console." She picked up two more chairs and walked toward the canopies.

Tara sat on a chair, untangling more lights.

"This is going to look great," Maggie said, depositing the chairs. "Maybe not what you dreamed of, but still amazing."

"I know." Tara looked up with a smile. "I have Jace and my family. That's all that's important."

Maggie stepped over and wrapped her in a hug. "I love you, T. You're going to have the best wedding ever."

Tara snorted. "I love you too, but no, I won't. It's going to look like a redneck shotgun wedding." She pulled back to look up at her. "But it's going to be a blast."

Maggie laughed. "That it will."

Thirteen

Declan marched into his office at the fire station, Seb and Jace on his heels. They turned heads as they filed past, but he didn't care. The staff would all find out what was happening soon enough. He unlocked his door, flipping on the lights as he entered, and made a beeline for the filing cabinet. He opened the drawer with the personnel files and found Gehring's.

"Here you go." He held the folder out to Seb.

Seb opened it, scanning it for Gehring's address. "It's an apartment at that new complex by the highway." He glanced up at Jace. "Should make it easy. One entry point."

"And lots of people in the way," Jace added. "What are the chances he's there?"

"Slim to none. Not after being spotted."

"You should have the bomb squad sweep the place before you go in," Declan said. "He might have run back there long enough to grab some stuff and rig the place. You don't want to set something off inadvertently."

"That's a good point," Jace said. "They haven't left yet, have they?"

Seb shook his head. "No. They were checking the last couple barns when we left the ranch."

"Detour them to that apartment complex," Declan said. "The barns can wait. There could be a bomb just waiting to go off where there are dozens of people."

Seb was already dialing. His conversation was brief.

"They're going to meet us there."

"Good." Declan moved toward the door.

"Where are you going?" Seb asked. "I still need to coordinate my team."

Declan glanced over his shoulder. "To talk to my staff. Someone has to know something."

Seb looked at Jace. "Go with him."

Not waiting for Jace to follow, Declan walked out. He entered the common room and let out a sharp whistle. Crichton's entire squad turned.

"Tell me what you know about Jameson Gehring."

They looked at him, confused.

"Gehring's part of your squad, sir," Stickley said.

"I'm aware, but some of you have to know him."

"We went to a bar together once," McPherson said.

"Where did you go?" Jace asked, taking out his phone to take notes.

McPherson named the bar. "I only went with him once. To be honest, he's a little strange."

"How so?"

"I don't know. It was just the way he interacted with people. Like they were there to amuse him. We had a couple drinks, then I called a cab and left."

"He say anything personal while you were with him? Tell you about some place he liked to go?"

"He mentioned camping with his dad."

"Did he say where?"

"Just the mountains."

"What about friends or girlfriends? Did he mention either of those?"

"No. Wait. While we were at the bar, I asked him if he saw anyone he liked. He shrugged and said one or two. But he was dismissive almost. He just shrugged it off like he didn't care. I asked him if he had a girl waiting. He said there was someone once, but it didn't work out, and he wasn't ready for another relationship."

"His file says he's from Cheyenne," Declan said. "Is that what he told you?"

McPherson nodded.

"I'll check it out," Jace said. "Maybe I can find someone there who knows him. Find the girlfriend, too."

"You mean maybe Seb can. You're leaving for two weeks tomorrow, remember?"

Jace cursed. "Yeah." He ran a hand through his hair. "I'm tired, sorry. I'll pass along all the info." He sighed. "Can you think of anything else?" he asked McPherson.

"No, but if I do, I'll call the sheriff."

Declan scanned the room. "Anyone else know anything that can help us?"

There was a chorus of no's.

"Why are you looking for him?" Stickley asked.

"He's the one who tried to barbecue us tonight," Jace replied. "Come on, Deck. Let's go check out his apartment and hand this off. I don't know about you, but I'm ready to go to bed."

He definitely was. This day felt like it would never end.

"You know, I've been thinking," Declan said as they walked back to his office to find Seb. "I'm not sure Gehring acted alone."

Jace frowned. "What makes you say that?"

"Because he was with me at the first fire. And he was at the station all day before that. Our shift started at seven that morning. None of us left the station unless we were on a run."

"You're sure about that? He couldn't have run out for a bit and no one noticed?"

"Theoretically, he could have, but I don't think he would have chanced it. If he left, and we got a call while he was gone, it would have led to questions about where he'd been. He would have wanted to avoid suspicion."

"Dammit."

Seb stepped out of Declan's office. "Why are you cursing? What happened?"

"Declan made a good point. Gehring has a partner."

"What?"

Declan explained his theory.

Seb groaned. "Yeah, that makes sense. Okay. Jace, text me what you got from the firefighters. I'll give it to Gentry and Wilder in the morning. Let's get over to Gehring's apartment. I have patrol units en route to set up a safety perimeter and the bomb squad's on its way."

The three of them filed out of the building, climbing into Seb's truck. They crossed town in just a few minutes, pulling into the complex as the first cruisers arrived on scene. Declan ran to Gehring's door while Seb and Jace started evacuating the building.

Crouching, Declan shone his penlight at the doorknob, looking for wires. It looked clean. He rose and perused the doorframe, but nothing looked amiss. That didn't mean there wasn't something inside. He wasn't going to open it. He'd let the bomb squad use their scope to look behind the door first.

The noise around him grew as families streamed out of their apartments. Declan stepped away from the door to look at Gehring's front window, checking for more signs it was booby-trapped. Again, it all seemed fine, but the blinds were drawn, so he was limited to what was visible from the outside.

A loud engine broke through the voices. Declan turned to see the bomb squad tactical vehicle roll into the parking lot. He jogged away from the building to meet them.

"What have we got?" their commander asked when Declan reached them.

"Possible explosive device. Single entry point. No visible tripwires." He turned and led the man toward the apartment building. The rest of the team followed with their gear.

"This is the apartment." Declan pointed to Gehring's door. "We know he's capable of building a bomb, but it's unknown if he left one here."

"We'll use our scope camera and check out the door for wires and motion detectors." The man glanced around. "Are all the residents out of the building?"

"Seb and Jace went door-to-door, so they should be." People mulled in the parking lot. Declan didn't see his friends, though. "I think they might be clearing the adjacent buildings now."

The commander nodded. "We'll camera the apartment. Once we get the all-clear from Sheriff Archer, we'll breach."

"Sounds good. I'll find Sebastian." Declan hurried away and let the bomb squad get to work. He found Seb two buildings over.

"Can you evacuate the residents in the building behind this one?"

Declan nodded. "Yes. Once the buildings are clear, let the bomb squad know. Their commander said he's waiting on your word before they enter Gehring's apartment."

"This building and the one behind it are all we have left."

"Got it." Declan turned and headed for the next building. He ran from apartment to apartment, knocking on doors and evacuating residents. In less than ten minutes, all the tenants were behind a police line in the parking lot.

He made his way back to Seb's truck, which had become a makeshift command post. Seb raised an eyebrow in question, silently asking if the building was clear. Declan nodded. "They're all out."

Seb picked up his radio and sent the all-clear to the bomb squad.

"I take it they didn't find any tripwires?"

"No. Maybe we'll get lucky and there won't be anything here."

"I think it depends on how fast he fled." Declan leaned against the truck's front bumper and crossed his arms, settling in to wait. Fifteen tense minutes passed before the radio crackled to life.

"Apartment's clear. We're going to sweep the public spaces, but you can send your men in here."

"Copy." Seb clipped the radio to his belt. "Let's go see what your rookie left behind." He pushed away from the truck and led the way up the sidewalk to the apartment. Jace and Declan followed him inside.

"There's not much here," Jace remarked as they got their first look inside.

He was right, Declan noted. The place had a worn sofa with a tray table in front of it. Both sat across from a large TV mounted on the wall.

"Fan out. See if there's a clue where he went or what he's planning."

Declan wandered into the kitchen while Jace and Seb went down the hall. He opened cupboards and the fridge. He peeked inside some open cereal and cracker boxes and the can of coffee, but didn't find anything he shouldn't. Disappointed, he walked back into the living room, giving it a quick once over and peering inside the wall vents. Nothing.

Seb and Jace came back after searching the bedroom and bathroom.

"Anything?" Seb asked.

Declan and Jace shook their heads.

"Well, Damn. Okay. Let's head home. We'll regroup tomorrow."

Declan wasn't going to argue. He was beat.

FOURTEEN

The soft whir of the garage door opening and closing reached Maggie's ears as she lay in bed. It was after three a.m., and she should be sound asleep after the day she had. But even after a hot shower and a shot of whiskey, she was wide awake. She was antsy. And she missed Declan's presence. It didn't matter that they hadn't shared a bed since the night Thomas's clinic burned. Knowing he was in the same house gave her a measure of peace. Without him there, her anxiety ran rampant and kept her awake.

But he's home now.

His footsteps echoed on the hardwood floors as he walked across the living room and down the hall to the spare bedroom.

She squeezed her eyes shut, trying to tap into that peace he brought.

The bathroom door shut and the shower started.

Images of his body, naked and wet, flooded her mind. She stifled a groan. Now she was awake for another reason. Her body burned as it remembered his touch. She wanted so much more from him. If she were more confident, she would march into the bathroom and join him. But her virgin sensibilities overruled her libido. She had no idea how to seduce a man. Especially one who was exhausted and thought he wasn't good enough for her.

She rolled onto her side and covered her head with a pillow, trying to drown out the sound of the water. Maybe if she couldn't hear it, she wouldn't think about him in the shower.

Water glistening on ripped muscles. Getting caught in the springy hair on his chest. And lower.

"Fuck." She held the pillow tighter to her ear and tried to think about case law. Nothing was more dull than legal jargon.

The water cut off, and she breathed a sigh of relief. He would get dressed and go to bed, and she would be able to *finally* fall asleep.

A soft knock sounded on her door.

No!

Eyes wide, she peaked out from under the pillow. Maybe if she was silent, he would go away. Did she want him to, though? How big of a fool would she make of herself as she stammered through a conversation with him?

The door creaked open.

"Maggie? Are you awake?" he whispered.

For half a second, she debated feigning sleep. But she wasn't a chicken. She pulled the pillow away and sat up. "Yeah."

He pushed the door open and stepped inside. "Can't sleep?"

"No. My mind won't shut off."

In the light coming from the pole lights on the lane outside, she saw him drum his fingers against his leg. He glanced out the window, then looked at her. She could just see the lights glittering in his eyes in the darkness.

"You want some company?"

Every hormone she'd managed to put back in its box surged free again. She fought to corral them. "Um. I'm not sure that's a great idea."

"You didn't have any problem climbing into my bed."

"Yeah, well, we were both injured."

"So, it was safe, is what you're saying?" He walked closer, standing over her. "Maybe I don't want safe, Mags."

She swallowed hard. "You don't?"

He kneeled on the bed and leaned over her. "No. I don't." His mouth crashed onto hers and all those hormones flew out of their box again.

Feelings she never felt before washed over her. But one thought still managed to make its way through her muddled brain. She pushed him back.

He frowned down at her. "What's wrong?"

"Why did you change your mind?"

His expression cleared. "A conversation with Tara. Through everything that happened, and even though she was disappointed she wouldn't get the wedding she dreamed of, she was okay with that because she had Jace. Everything important to her was safe. And it made me realize just how important you are to me. I'm still not sure I'm the best man for you, but I'm willing to give this a try."

A try? "I don't want a try, Declan. I didn't wait my entire adult life to give myself to a man for a try. It's all or nothing."

He blinked. "Wait. You've never had sex?"

"Oh my God, that's what you got from that speech?" She let her hands drop from his shoulders and sank into the mattress.

"Well, it's important."

"So is the other thing!"

He sighed and rolled to lie down beside her. "Maggie—"

"Don't Maggie me." Fired up now, she sat up and looked at him. "I don't know any other way to get it through your thick skull that I don't care about who your family is or where you come from. It's you I care about. If, in the future, your background becomes an issue in my career, then I'll know that particular path wasn't meant for me. I don't want a life without you in it. It's not—"

She didn't get to finish her sentence, and honestly, she was just ranting, anyway. He swept over her, fusing his mouth to hers once more.

"I don't want a life without you, either," he said, breaking away. "Can we agree to just figure things out as we go?"

She smiled up at him. "So long as we go together, yes."

"How about we start now?" His hands ghosted down her sides.

Maggie shivered. "Okay." Her voice came out on a sigh.

He kissed her again. His hands dove beneath her shirt to sear her bare flesh. She clawed at his t-shirt, eager to feel his firm, sleek muscles. He sat up and whipped it over his head. Her hands went to his chest to toy with his nipples through his dark chest hair.

"Like what you see?"

"God, yes."

"Good. Your turn." He tugged at the hem of her night-shirt with one finger.

Maggie sat up, bringing her face close to his once more. She leaned forward and nipped at his bottom lip. He growled and tried to kiss her again, but she broke away to take off her shirt. The sight of her bare breasts stopped him in his tracks.

"You're so damn beautiful. I don't deserve you, but I'm going to cherish every moment."

He cupped her breasts, sending shivers of desire through Maggie's body. She speared her fingers into his hair and held on as he leaned in to taste them. His hot breath fanned over her sensitive skin, making goosebumps erupt. She bit her lip to hold back a moan.

Declan noticed. "Don't hold back, baby. I want to know what feels good."

She nodded.

His bright smile quickly turned naughty. "Should we see if I can make you scream?"

Maggie blushed from the roots of her hair to her toes. What was she doing? She had next to no experience, and Declan was sex on a stick. He dated women who looked like supermodels. She was no slouch, but Lilah was on another level. Maggie was just a bookworm.

"Earth to Maggie."

"What?" She looked at him.

"I lost you. Where did you go?"

"Sorry. I'm just a little nervous. I don't have much experience with men."

He brushed her hair away and wrapped a hand around the back of her neck. "We don't have to do this if you aren't ready."

Oh, she was ready. So ready she felt like a champagne cork about to pop. "I don't want to stop. Can we just go slow?"

"Absolutely." He tugged her close. "The last thing I want to do is hurt or scare you."

She raised her hands to feather her fingers over his biceps as he leaned in. "I trust you."

The words were barely out of her mouth when he kissed her, this time with purpose.

Maggie framed his face, pulling him down with her to the bed. His weight settled against her, cocooning her in his heat. He trailed kisses along her jaw and down her neck to lave her breasts. She let out the moan she held back earlier and threaded her fingers into his thick hair. He smiled against her breast.

"That's more like it."

It would be the first of many, she was sure.

He trailed hot kisses down the valley between her breasts and over her abdomen, ratcheting up the fire burning in Maggie's core to new heights. When he kept going, she stiffened. "Declan?"

"This is new too?" He glanced up at her, eyes glittering.

She gave a quick nod.

His teeth flashed in the low light. "Excellent. Call me a caveman, but I like knowing no other man has had the privilege."

Before she could respond, he lowered his head and kissed and nipped his way past her hips, taking her panties with him. Every inch closer to her center sent the tension spiraling higher. His nose teased that little bundle of nerves, sending a wave of pleasure soaring through her veins, lifting her hips from the bed.

A low hum of satisfaction escaped his chest. He parted her folds with his hand and pressed his tongue to her heated flesh.

Maggie thought she would explode. Colors danced in front of her eyes, blinding her to everything but the feel of his mouth doing naughty things to her body. He toyed with her, then added two fingers to her channel, stretching her as he found that hidden spot deep inside. In just a few strokes, the colors exploded into a blinding light as her first orgasm ripped through her. She shouted his name as she soared over the edge.

While she came down from her high, he climbed off the bed to shuck his shorts and boxers. Her eyes widened as she got her first look at him. He was already erect, his shaft long and thick. More moisture flooded her core. She didn't want to beg, but if he didn't rejoin her in the next few seconds, she would.

He put a knee on the bed, then stopped. A soft whine escaped her.

"I need to go get my wallet."

Confused, she frowned, then realized why. "Oh, right.

Actually, I have some." She pointed to the nightstand. "Wishful thinking last week."

He yanked open the drawer and fished out the box. "I like that you're a planner," he said with a crooked smile. He tore open the box and ripped a packet free of the strip before tearing open the foil and sheathing himself.

"Are you ready for this? For me?"

"If you had clothes on, I'd yank you on top of me."

His smile flashed again. "Well, let's not keep you waiting." He crawled back over her, settling between her legs.

Her eyes rolled back when he nudged her entrance. But it was his fingers that slid inside. Her head snapped down to look at him. "I know we agreed to slow, but this is just torture now."

"Not torture." He nuzzled her ear, nibbling on the lobe as his fingers slid through her slick heat. "I just want to make sure I don't hurt you."

A sliver of apprehension tensed her muscles. Once he started his assault on her senses, though, the pain of losing her virginity became the furthest thing from her mind.

"I'll be careful, I swear." He pulled his fingers free, smearing her wetness around her entrance. Grasping himself, he positioned the tip and edged inside.

A delicious burn started as she stretched to accommodate him. She moaned. Her heartbeat sped up in response to the building pleasure. He eased in a little further, and Maggie felt the resistance. He pulled back, then stroked forward several times, stretching her walls. She felt a pop and a sharp jolt of pain as he slid deeper.

"You all right?" he asked, voice strained as he held himself still within her.

She nodded. "Keep going. It doesn't hurt." The opposite was true. Except for the quick burst of pain, it felt better than anything ever had.

Taking her at her word, he slid out, then pushed back in with one stroke. Her hips rose to meet his, and he took it as a sign she was a hundred percent on board. His thrusts sped up, sending her higher up the mountain. Maggie wrapped her legs around his waist, and he hit that spot that sent her to the moon in a split second. She let out a little shout, which spurred him on. In another handful of strokes, she flew over the edge. As she rode the waves of white-hot pleasure, he grasped her hips and continued to pump into her. Veins bulged in his neck, and he shouted her name as his climax hit.

As the intensity faded, Maggie's bones liquified. "That was intense."

Declan barked a laugh and rolled to her side. "Understatement." He turned his head to look at her. "You okay?"

She offered him a soft smile. "Never better. How about you? Those ribs got a workout."

"They're burning, but nothing too terrible. I'll live." He sat up. "I'll be right back." He went into the bathroom to dispose of the condom, then rejoined her.

Maggie draped an arm over his stomach and propped her head on his shoulder. A yawn cracked her jaw. He followed with a bigger one.

"We should probably sleep."

His low voice rumbled over her nerve endings, sending a thrill through her. Would she ever get enough of this man? He just set her on fire and left her in a pile of sated goo, and she already wanted him again.

Another yawn overtook her. Some of the desire faded as fatigue finally settled in. "Yeah. We have a lot to do tomorrow."

He pressed a kiss to the top of her head. "Sweet dreams, Mags."

She smiled against his shoulder, closing her eyes. "Mmm. G'night."

FIFTEEN

With a groan, Declan dropped into a chair on the edge of the dance floor. Maggie ran off with her sister to help Tara use the restroom in her cumbersome wedding dress. He was taking full advantage of her absence to sit for a few minutes. All the activity made his ribs ache. Plus, he was dog-tired. He and Maggie didn't drop off to sleep until nearly four. They were up at six to finish prepping.

A soft smile spread over his face as he thought about the night before. He would have gladly gone with no sleep for sex with Maggie. What they shared was intense. Mind-blowingly wonderful. And scary. He wanted it all with her, but he still felt inadequate. She was amazing. Smart, funny, sexy, kind—she ticked all the boxes for everything he wanted in a woman. But digging into his family's past made him feel like trash next to her. He prayed she meant what she said about it not mattering. He was past the point of being able to walk away.

A beer appeared in front of his face, startling him from his musings. He looked up to see Jenny.

She smiled. "You looked thirsty."

"Thanks." He took the bottle and put it to his mouth,

gulping down some of the cool liquid. Despite the cool temps, he was a little warm from dancing in a suit.

"This shindig turned out pretty well," she said, sitting down next to him and taking a drink of her own beer. "It helps we have great music." She nodded toward the stage. "I still can't believe Brady got Knox to talk Asa Mitchell into performing."

Declan was surprised, too, when he saw the country superstar getting out of an SUV with Knox earlier. He knew the man was friends with both Knox and Brady because of ranch business, but he didn't know they were that close. "Me too, but I'm glad, though. Tara was really surprised and pleased he was willing to sing at her wedding. I also think Brady might regret the decision to ask him." He motioned to where Asa now stood with Macy, deep in conversation. He'd stepped off the stage and let Abigail's boyfriend Trent and his band take over for a few minutes. Brady stood ten feet away, glaring at Macy as she laughed at something Asa said.

A broad smile split Jenny's face. "Well, well, well. The plot thickens. He does look rather perturbed that she's talking to him, doesn't he?"

"The funny thing is, he has nothing to worry about."

"Really?"

"Yes. If he'd get his head out of his ass, he'd realize she only has eyes for him. I'm waiting for her to tire of him ignoring her and confront him." He was surprised she hadn't already. Especially since shy Maggie had done that exact thing with him.

"What's wrong?"

He frowned and looked at her. "What do you mean?"

"You have something on your mind. I can see it. Your face clouded over all of a sudden. What's wrong?"

Declan opened his mouth, then shut it, unsure how to phrase the thoughts running through his head. "I'm sure you've noticed Maggie and I have... something going on."

She nodded, smiling. "I have. I think it's wonderful."

"You do?"

"Of course. Why wouldn't I?"

"Maggie said the same thing."

"I'm not following."

He sighed. "We've been circling each other since June. When she moved in to help me, it brought it all to a head. I didn't want to get involved because my past could hurt her future."

"That's a load of horseshit."

Declan barked a laugh, then held up a hand. "Sorry. I see Tara and Maggie come by their attitudes honestly."

A sardonic tilt lifted a corner of Jenny's mouth. "That's quite likely, yes. But don't try to change the subject. Maggie doesn't care about your past. And if she does, she and I need to have a chat."

"She says she doesn't, but I'm not worried what she thinks so much as how it will harm her reputation. I know she wants to run for office. Having me around could hinder her chances of getting elected. She said if that's the case, it won't bother her, but I'm not so sure. I guess what's really bothering me is how to get past it. I want to be part of her life, but I don't want to get in the way of her dreams."

"Declan," she covered his hand with hers, "does she make you happy?"

"Yes." That was a no-brainer. His entire life was brighter with her in it.

"Do you make her happy?"

"I think so."

"Then anything else is just icing on the cake. You're worried she'll come to resent you, right?"

He nodded.

"She won't. Maggie was raised to value God and people over everything else. If loving you keeps her from becoming an elected official, she'll take it as a sign that wasn't her path after all."

"That's pretty much what she said."

Jenny tapped his arm. "There you go. You have nothing to be worried about. Enjoy having my daughter's love."

He didn't want to tell her how much he already had.

She giggled as she took in his expression. "I'm not even going to ask."

"Thank you."

"So what exactly about your past has you so worried? The bogus murder charge?"

Thankful for the reprieve—he did *not* want to discuss his sex life with his girlfriend's mother—he pounced on the change in topic. "That and my parents. My mom, who spent her life as a junkie and an alcoholic, turns up murdered in an arson fire. And my dad has been in and out of prison my entire life and has a secret family."

"Maggie mentioned that. It sounds like you've embraced the role of big brother, though. Well, I guess you already were with Macy, but you know what I mean."

"Yeah. Hannah and Jessie seem great. I can't wait to spend some more time with them. I'm sure I'll like Michael, too, once I meet him."

Jenny shook her head. "For all your father's faults, he produced some great kids."

Her praise made him smile. He valued her opinion of him more than just about anyone. "How well did you know my dad? He wasn't around much."

"Well enough, I suppose. Lee hired him one summer. He would have kept him on—he was a good worker when he was sober—but we had some cattle go missing. Lee and a couple hands staked out the pastures and caught Cole rustling."

Declan's eyes widened. "I didn't know that."

"I'm not surprised. You were pretty young still. That was

the first time your dad went to prison. Cole pleaded with Lee to let him go, but he'd stolen nearly ten thousand dollars' worth of cattle.

"God. I'm so sorry."

"It's not your fault."

"No, but I still feel like I should apologize. He's my family."

"Cole Briggs barely qualifies as your parent, Declan. He wasn't around enough to truly be your family. Haven't you learned family is what you make it?"

He frowned. She had a point. He felt more at home with Lee and Jenny than he ever had with his parents. A sudden thought hit him, and he laughed. "So, does that mean I'm dating my sister?"

She laughed. "Thank goodness there's no blood relation."

"For sure."

The swish of chiffon drew his attention, and he turned his head to see Maggie and Tara walking through the grass. They both looked stunning, but he couldn't take his eyes off Maggie. He'd stared at her throughout the ceremony too. She was beautiful in her cranberry bridesmaid's dress. It sat just off her shoulders, dipping low in front, and hugged her body all the way past her knees. She had her hair pulled back in a sleek ponytail, with strands of wildflowers running through it. Silver three-inch heels finished her outfit, making sure his eyes kept straying to her long legs. He kept envisioning her in those heels and nothing else.

She looked his way and caught him watching her. A pretty smile lit her face, and she excused herself from Tara to walk toward him.

"Excuse me," he said, rising.

"Declan."

Jenny's hand on his made him pause. He looked down.

"You are a good man. Maggie knows that, and you need to remember it."

He bent down and placed a kiss on her cheek. "Thank you, Jenny. For everything."

"You're welcome, dear."

With a smile, he turned away.

"What were you two talking about?" Maggie asked as he met her in front of the cake table.

He touched the edge of the silver board the red velvet cake sat on with one finger and shrugged. "This and that."

She hummed. "Secretive. Okay."

"No secret. Just stuff. She's a wise woman."

"She is." She gave him a curious look, then grinned. Leaning in, she twisted his tie between her fingers. "So, do you think it would be poor form for the maid-of-honor to leave before the happy couple?"

Declan chuckled, locking his hands behind her waist. "It would, but I think they're leaving soon." He nodded toward Tara, who rubbed at her back while Jace looked on, concerned.

"Perfect." She turned back to him to twine her arms around his neck. She pressed a quick kiss to his mouth.

"Don't start that. Not yet," he muttered, pulling back with a smile.

She gave him a naughty grin.

Jace let out a sharp whistle, drawing everyone's attention.

"I want to thank you all for coming despite the last-minute change of plans. We feel very blessed to have you be part of our day."

"That being said," Tara continued, "we're going to leave you all to party on without us. After such a late night, we're both ready to crash. Thank you again for coming."

To applause and cheers, they walked out of the yard into the main house.

"So, does this mean we can leave now?" Maggie whispered in his ear.

Prickles of heat raced along the back of his neck and down his spine. "Hell, yes." He looked down at her. "Don't we need to stay to clean up, though?"

"Mom said we're just going to put the food away and take out the trash to keep the animals out, then do the rest of the take down tomorrow."

He growled. "It could be a couple hours yet before that happens. Even without the bride and groom, people don't want to leave. Asa's getting ready to play another set." He pointed at the stage, where Asa had his guitar in hand, standing off to the side while Trent's band finished their song.

She took his hand and walked backward. A wicked smile spread over her face. "Well, I guess we have a couple hours to kill."

Declan fought to keep his body under control at what she proposed. They were in public, and he didn't want to make it blatantly obvious why they were walking away from the party. Expression neutral, he kept their pace slow as they walked away from the crowd. Once they disappeared into the growing twilight, he picked up the pace and tugged her toward the nearby outbuildings.

"In here?" He pointed to a shed near the grain storage bins.

"That works."

He twisted the knob, thanking his lucky stars it wasn't locked, and let them in. Declan yanked her inside, shut the door, and pushed her up against it, fusing his mouth to hers.

She moaned as his hands roamed her body, sending his arousal to another level.

"Is there a light in here?" he asked, moving his mouth down her neck and nuzzling her cleavage.

She let out a strangled groan as he dipped his tongue

beneath the neckline of her dress. Her hand slapped at the wall moments before the lights flickered on.

"Excellent. Now I can see you in nothing but those heels." He stepped back, eyeing her up and down. "Take off your dress."

Maggie reached an arm up behind herself for the zipper, thrusting her breasts forward.

"God, Maggie. You're killing me."

Her smile was naughty as she drew the zipper down. The neckline sagged, and Declan didn't wait. He slid his hands inside and pushed the dress down her arms, exposing her chest to his hungry view. Reaching around her, he unsnapped her strapless bra and tossed it to the ground, then palmed her breasts in his hands. She wove her hands in his hair and kissed him.

Declan tucked his hands in her dress and tugged it down past her hips, taking her panties with it. It hit the floor with a soft swish. He stepped back to look at her, taking in her long, supple body clad only in her silver heels.

"Damn, I love your legs."

She crooked a finger. "Come here so I can wrap them around you."

In one step, he was in front of her, laving her nipple with his tongue. "Who taught you to talk dirty like that?"

She gave a throaty laugh. "Have you met my sister?"

He smiled against her breast.

"And you have on too many clothes." She tugged his shirt from his waistband.

"Agreed." He shucked his coat and unbuckled his pants while she worked the buttons on his shirt. Taking the condom from his wallet, he tossed the billfold onto the pile of fabric at their feet.

Maggie snatched the foil packet from his hands. "Let me."

The first touch of her fingers on his shaft almost sent him

over the edge. "Don't linger, or this is going to end before it starts."

Another wicked smile cut across her face. She gave him a hard squeeze, sending dots of light dancing through his vision, then rolled the condom down his length. As soon as he was sheathed, he grasped her by the backs of her thighs and lifted her against the door, ignoring the sharp twinge in his ribs. She wrapped those long, heel-clad legs around him.

"Please, Deck. I can't wait."

He couldn't either. In one long stroke, he seated himself inside her. Her breathy moan kicked him into motion. Their coupling was fast and electric as he drove them both higher. He shifted to get a better angle and put a hand on the door. The roughness of the wood registered, and he slowed.

She growled. "Why did you stop?"

"The door's rough. I don't want to hurt you."

"I don't care."

"I do." He looked around desperately, hoping for some other surface. A small table sat nestled against the far wall. "There." He locked his hands around her hips and stumbled over to it.

"It's not high enough. You're too tall."

She squirmed again, and Declan's eyes fluttered. He needed to think of something. Fast. Unwrapping her legs, he set her feet on the floor, then spun her around and bent her over the table. The added height from her heels put her at the perfect angle.

"You okay like this?" He ran a finger over her womanhood, keeping her aroused.

Maggie moaned, leaning on her forearms as she glanced back at him. "Hell, yes."

"Good." He stepped up behind her and slid inside her tight channel once more. It was a quick trip to the top at this angle and position. Within moments, they were both flying over the edge. He held her hips pressed to his as he pumped into her, letting the waves of his climax crash over him.

"Ugh. I think I died," she moaned.

Declan's legs sagged, and he leaned over her back, resting next to her on the table, trying to catch his breath. "Same, honey. Wow."

She giggled. "I really hope no one walks in right now. They're going to get an eyeful of our asses if they do."

He laughed. "Among other things." Some of the starch came back to his legs, and he straightened, putting a hand to his ribs as they protested. That interlude was worth the pain, though. "Should we head back?"

She stood and wrapped her arms around his shoulders, pressing against him. The flames of arousal licked back to life, sending his blood pulsing through his veins.

"Not yet. They won't miss us for a while. Maybe we can try that door thing again. I'll wear your jacket."

He spun them around and backed her toward the door. "Heels and a suit coat? You're like my fantasy come to life."

She laughed. "But I'm very, very real."

He cupped her jaw, running a thumb over her full lower lip, and held her gaze. She felt like a dream, but she wasn't. "I know." He leaned down to give her a tender kiss. The arousal turned to a slow burn. He smiled against her mouth. Whiling away another hour or so was going to be easy. And fun.

Sixteen

Feet aching, Maggie stepped out the back door of her law office, taking in her surroundings. The lot was empty except for her borrowed car. Her phone trilled from her purse as she pulled the door closed. She fished it out as she walked to the car, frowning when she saw Angie Tulley's number on the screen.

Opening her car door, she peered beneath the seat, looking for anything out of place before climbing in. Once locked inside, she answered.

"Hello?"

"Oh, Maggie, thank God. I didn't know who else to call." Angie's voice carried over the line, breathless and panicked.

"What's wrong?"

"I think Hank found us."

"What? Did you call the sheriff's department and report it?"

"I did, but they can't do anything. I don't have anything concrete, really. It's just a feeling. Every time I've gone outside the last couple days, I feel someone watching me. And I swear I saw someone in the trees this morning. That's when I called the police. They sent a deputy out, but he didn't find anything. I don't know what to do. I mean, is this all in my head?"

"It could be, but it could also be your instincts telling you something's wrong. Maybe we should move you guys. You were cleared of your charges, so there's no reason you can't leave the area. You can come back when it's time to testify against Hank."

"But where would we go? I don't know how to go about any of this. If it weren't for the women's shelter and their help in getting us this house, we'd be on the street." Her voice wobbled.

"You're doing fine, Angie. Take a breath. We'll get this figured out. I'm going to drive up there right now, and we'll hash out a plan, okay?"

"Really? Oh, that would be wonderful. I really appreciate it."

"Of course. I'll be there in about an hour."

"Okay, great. Thank you!"

"Yep, see you soon." Maggie hung up and immediately dialed Declan.

"Hey. You on your way home?" he asked when he picked up.

"Not yet. I need to go visit Angie Tulley. She's getting twitchy up in the mountains by herself. I'm going to help her come up with a plan to get out of the area. She needs to start over and she's just overwhelmed."

He sighed. "Yeah. I get that. You really shouldn't go up there by yourself, though, and I'm stuck at the station until morning. Can one of your brothers go?"

"Probably not." She glanced at her watch. "But Macy might be free. It's past closing time for the coffee shop."

He hummed. "I'd rather one of your brothers went."

She started her car. "Declan, I just need someone to be an extra set of eyes. I can take care of myself."

"Famous last words, Mags. I know you can fend off an attacker. I've seen you practice your katas. But you're still more vulnerable than one of your gigantic brothers."

"I will call them and see if they're free, but I'm going no matter what. I can't ask her to come into town and risk Hank seeing her. He made bail finally."

"Great." He sighed again. "Okay. Just... be careful. And send me a text or two while you're gone, so I know you're safe? It's been quiet the last week since we identified Gehring in the surveillance footage, but I'm still nervous. He wasn't acting alone."

"I know and I will. I'll be back before you know it."

"Yeah, yeah. Call your brothers."

She couldn't help but smile at the droll note in his voice. "Doing it now. I'll see you in the morning."

They bid each other goodbye, and she hung up, then dialed Thomas. Seb was in Colorado Springs for another meeting today, and Brady was likely still out on the range.

He picked up on the fourth ring. "Hey, Mags. What's up?"

"Are you free to come with me on a little trip up the mountain?"

"Not really, no. I finally got some replacement equipment and am working on my client backlog. I have several more appointments this evening. Did you try Brady?"

"Not yet. I'll call him next."

"Okay. What about Declan?"

"He's working. He's back on full shifts and won't be home until morning."

"Well, don't go up there alone. Seb still hasn't found Gehring."

"I know. I'll find someone. Go back to work. I'll talk to you later."

"Be careful."

"I will. Bye." She hung up with a sigh and called Brady. His phone rang, but rolled to voicemail. Well, Macy it was. Maggie scrolled through her contacts to find Macy's number and touched the phone icon.

Macy picked up on the second ring. "Hey! What's up?"

"Are you free for the evening?"

"Yeah." Macy drew out the word. "Why?"

"I need to go help Angie Tulley form a plan to move away. I don't want to go alone because of everything happening."

"That's a good idea. Yeah, I can go with you. Did you want to leave now?"

"As soon as I grab a burger from Boone's, yes."

"Sounds good. I'll be ready when you get here."

"Thanks, Macy."

"No problem. See you in a few."

Maggie bade her goodbye, then texted Declan. She put her SUV in gear and headed for the diner. After picking up a burger and a milkshake, she drove to Macy's house. True to her word, Macy stepped out the front door as Maggie pulled in, ready to go.

"Do you want me to drive so you can eat?" Macy asked.

"That would be great." Maggie got out and rounded the hood, settling into the passenger seat.

Macy buckled herself in and backed out of her driveway. Maggie told her to head out of town toward the ranch, then peeled back the wrapper on her burger and took a bite.

"So, why the spur-of-the-moment thing? I'm assuming it is, anyway. I imagine if it wasn't, Declan would go with you."

"Yeah, it is. Angie called and said she felt like she was being watched. I figured getting her out of town sooner rather than later was a good idea, in case she wasn't imagining things. She's never had to do anything like this before, though, and is a little lost."

"I bet. She married Hank right out of high school. You're a good person, Maggie."

"Thanks. I just want her to feel safe. She's been through enough."

"We'll get her straightened out and set up right."

That was the plan. Maggie hoped it was that simple.

"So." There was a load of curiosity in that one word.

Maggie gave Macy a side look, knowing where she was going with the conversation.

"I couldn't help but notice you and my brother sneaking away at the wedding last week. I've been so busy I haven't had a chance to talk to either of you for very long. Spill it, sister."

"Uh-uh." She shifted in her seat, heat pooling in her core as she thought about their time in the shed.

Macy laughed. "I'm both delighted and disgusted. Declan deserves to be happy, and you make him that way. But I don't want to think about his sex life. Forgive me if I don't ask for details."

It was Maggie's turn to laugh. "No problem. I'm not keen on sharing."

"Do you love him?"

That word—love—bounced around Maggie's brain. She knew she felt as giddy as a teenager with her first crush every time he was near. And he was all she could think about. At work for the last several days, she had to force herself to concentrate. Even then, she caught herself staring off into space, thinking about him more than she cared to admit.

But Maggie had never been in love. She didn't have anything to compare it to.

"I'm not sure." She shrugged. "I know I can't imagine life without him now. I don't want to, either. These past few weeks have been amazing, even though we spent the first few just taking care of each other's broken bodies."

"That's how you know it's real. When it's the companionship you crave. Don't get me wrong, the sex should be fantastic, but it's not what matters most."

"No. I want to be with him, even if we're doing nothing."

Macy grinned. "Welcome to the family, dear girl."

Maggie's eyes widened. "Whoa, now. Marriage is a ways off."

"Hmm, maybe not as far as you think. Declan's thirty-six. And he's always wanted kids."

The reality of the seriousness of her relationship crashed into Maggie in that moment. So did the desire to be the woman who gave him those children.

"All I ask is that I get to babysit often. At the rate I'm going, my friend's kids are the only ones I'll ever get to love on and cuddle."

"Nah. One of these days, you'll get tired of waiting on Brady to make a move and you'll do it for him. I'm surprised you haven't already."

"What? That's not—I'm not—"

"Oh, don't even try to deny it. I know you told Rayna, Tara, and London how you feel about him. And it's obvious to anyone with eyes."

Macy huffed. "Except him."

"For a smart man, he's oblivious. I think that has more to do with the blinders he put on after his divorce, though. He doesn't want to get hurt again. It doesn't help that he's shy. I don't know how that happened in our family, but it did. If you're serious about him, you might have to make the first move."

"I know." Macy sighed and let her head fall back against the headrest. "It's just weird. Not only because I'm not used to being the one doing the pursuing, but because we're friends."

Maggie laughed. "That should not be weird."

"No?"

"No. All our other friends and siblings are hooking up. Why not you and Brady?"

Macy giggled. "That's true. I didn't think about it like that." She shrugged. "I guess that gives me something to think about."

She wasn't the only one with something to think about now. That "L" word wouldn't stop bouncing around Maggie's head.

Rain pelted the windshield as Maggie pulled into Macy's drive. The wipers made a steady swish-thump, and the car dinged as Macy opened her door.

"Thanks again for going with me," Maggie said.

"Anytime. I think we got her moving in the right direction. Filling out all those online applications in different cities was a great start." She swung her legs out of the car, clutching her purse. "I'll see you later." She waggled her fingers. "Bye." Slamming the door, she took off through the rain.

Maggie waited until Macy was inside before backing out onto the road and pointing the car toward the ranch. The rain increased as she got out of town. She turned her wipers up and slowed down. Driving in the rain sucked, but at least it wasn't snow. That would come all too soon.

Headlights appeared in her rearview mirror, coming up on her fast. "Geez." She kept one eye on the mirror as she navigated the winding road. "Don't they realize how treacherous it is in this weather? Probably some tourist." She shook her head. Accommodations in the area needed to come with a course on driving on mountain roads in bad weather.

The lights loomed larger as the vehicle caught up to her.

She hit her flashers to signal the car to go around her, but it just rode her bumper. Maggie moved her hands to a more defensive position on the wheel and sat straighter. What the hell was this guy up to? She wished she could speed up—she was only about three miles from the ranch—but there was a sharp curve coming up. In this weather, taking that curve too fast would spell disaster.

She slowed as she got closer to the curve. To her relief, the car pulled into the other lane. It wasn't a good place to pass, but she just wanted them to go around her. She relaxed a fraction until she realized the car wasn't passing, but driving beside her. Maggie hit her brakes, and the other car shot forward. Its brake lights flared, and it swung back into her lane ahead of her, still slowing. She slowed to a crawl. The other car's backup lights lit up. Her heart rate kicked up and her breathing quickened as horror washed over her. They were going to hit her!

Adrenaline flooded her veins, and she threw her car into reverse, praying no one came up behind her. She flung an arm over the passenger seat and steered the SUV backward down the road, weaving all over her lane. Her car lurched as the other vehicle struck the front bumper. She let out a scream as she fought for control. Once she stopped weaving, she pressed harder on the accelerator.

Oh my God! What was going on?

She tamped down the panic clawing its way up her throat and concentrated on driving. A side road appeared, and she whipped her car into it, still driving in reverse. The other car zoomed past on the highway, brakes screeching as it slowed. She shoved the gearshift into drive and rocketed back out onto the main road, flooring the accelerator. It didn't give her much of a lead on the car behind her, but she hoped it was enough to get her safely through the curves coming up. Once past those, she could fly the rest of the way to the ranch.

A glance in her rearview mirror revealed the other car catching up once again. Even though she was entering the curves, she sped up. Her tires squealed, and the vehicle threatened to tip as she dove around the bends, the dark SUV right on her tail. She flew around a curve just as the other car tapped her back bumper. The trees whizzed by in a blur as her car spun wildly over the wet pavement. She skittered off the road into the ditch, coming to a jarring stop.

Dazed and dizzy, she fumbled with her seatbelt. She had to get out of the car before the person in the other vehicle came back for her. The belt released with a click, and she pushed at her door to get out. The car was at an angle in the deep ditch, so gravity wasn't on her side. She shifted to get her legs under her and used her height to try to open the door. She only got it open a crack before it flew out of her hand.

Maggie let out a shout of surprise. Rain dripped in on her as she looked up. The face that filled the doorway made her do a double-take. *No. It couldn't be...*

"Hello, Maggie. Remember me?" The man reached in to grab her collar.

Maggie screamed and squirmed, grabbing onto the car's frame as he attempted to haul her out. "Let go!"

He braced his feet and pulled harder, tangling a hand in her hair.

She grabbed his wrist as fire raced along her scalp. "Please, stop! What do you want?"

He got her out of the car and pushed her against it, leaning into her, breathing hard from the struggle. "You're quite feisty. I can understand what my son sees in you." He backed up, taking hold of her arm in a bruising grip. "His mother was feisty too. It got her killed. Don't be like Sherri."

Horror flooded her veins, turning her legs to noodles, as she realized Cole killed Sherri. Probably Jed too. He would kill her as well if she didn't cooperate. She fought the panic that wanted to take over and forced some starch back into her spine. "What do you want, Cole?"

He smiled an evil smile. "Smart too. Whoo-ee, you're the total package, aren't ya?" He shook his head. "Where he got his taste in women, I'll never know. That Lilah was an even prissier version of you."

Maggie's eyes widened. "How do you know about her?"

"I keep tabs on all my kids. Make sure they're not going down the wrong path. Declan—that boy has definitely strayed down the wrong path."

"Wh-what do you mean?"

He leaned in, his expression dark and menacing. "He's involved with you."

She reared back like he slapped her. "What's wrong with me?"

"You're an Archer." He tugged on her arm. "Come on. We need to get out of here before someone comes along."

Maggie planted her feet.

Cole spun around and punched her without warning. She let out a shout and dropped to her knees in the mud. *Dammit.* Maggie covered her jaw with a hand. She should have seen that coming. He had her flustered, though. It wasn't every day her boyfriend's dad admitted to murder and tried to kidnap her.

"Remember what I said about feisty? Word to the wise, pretty lady. Fight it."

Anger made her blood boil. She would do what he said. For now. But the minute she saw an opening, she would take it.

"Get up." He pulled at her arm.

Maggie pretended to be off balance, falling down again. She knew she was pushing it, but every second counted.

"Those heels are ridiculous. Kick them off."

"But they're Manolos." She didn't care if she ruined her shoes. She just wanted to stall.

He shook her, and she knew her time was up.

"Okay, okay." She rose and stepped out of her shoes.

As soon as her feet cleared the leather, he pulled her toward his SUV, an older model beast that had seen better days even before he rammed her. He took a pair of handcuffs from the front seat and clamped them over her wrists, then opened the back door and put her inside. He pulled a roll of duct tape off the floorboard and bound her ankles, dashing her hopes of diving out of the car. He tore off another piece and went for her face. Maggie moved away.

"Is that really necessary?"

He paused, then shrugged and rolled the tape up, tossing it onto the ground. "I guess not. Where we're going, no one will hear you." His eyes narrowed. "But if you annoy me on the ride there, you'll get more than duct tape when we stop. Understand?"

She nodded. "Quiet as a mouse, I swear."

He stepped back and slammed the door shut, then ran around to the driver's side and hopped in. The car lurched forward as he took off. She realized he was still heading toward the Broken Bow and scooted as close to the window as she could. Seb put a camera on the driveway entrance. If Cole stayed on this road, he would drive right through the camera's field of vision.

Her heart thudded in her chest as she stared out the window, praying he didn't turn off before they went past. When the pole light at the end of the drive came into view, elation made her adrenaline spike. She pressed herself to the window, turning her face to look at the property as they drove by the gate.

Cole laughed. "Say goodbye to home. You'll probably never see it again."

Tears welled in her eyes, but that burn of anger glowed

brighter. "Why didn't you just kill me? And why send me threatening messages or blow up my car? What do you want?"

She saw his face pull in the rearview mirror. "That was a misguided attempt to take you out of the picture. The plan now, though, is a simple one. I need my son to come to me. Alone. Taking you is the best way to accomplish that."

She swallowed hard. "What are you going to do to Declan?"

"Set him straight."

"What does that mean?"

"It means, he'll either see things my way or not at all. He has to pick a side."

"Side? What side? I don't understand what's going on."

"Enough questions. It'll all be explained once Declan arrives."

"Can I ask one more?"

He sighed. "Sure."

"What part does Jameson Gehring play in all this?"

Cole laughed. It started low and slow in his chest and built until he was hunched forward and wiping a tear from his face. Maggie was still confused. More so now than ever.

He glanced back and shook a finger. "You'll have to wait for that one, too."

Frustration cut into the anger she felt. She slumped in the seat, watching their route, her mind spinning. Nothing made sense. How did Cole know Jameson? And what did her family have to do with any of it?

SEVENTEEN

Fire tones drew Declan's attention away from his computer screen. Dispatch came over the loudspeaker, calling for an engine and ambulance response to a crash on the highway near the Broken Bow. He pushed away from his desk and ran out to the truck bay, donning his turnout gear. He was so glad to be back on limited duties. He still couldn't run into a fire carrying a hose, but he could go on calls. He'd been going a little cross-eyed, staring at computers and twiddling his thumbs while the rest of his crew saw all the action.

Gear on, he climbed into the front passenger seat of the firetruck and radioed their status as Reeves pulled out of the garage, siren blaring. The ambulance pulled out behind them.

"How much you want to bet someone took the curves too fast?"

Declan let out a snort. "I'm not taking that bet. On a night like tonight and the location of the wreck—that's pretty much on top of that area." Those curves were notorious for crashes in bad weather. Even with the signs in place, tourists still took them much too fast, not realizing how sharp the switchbacks were. He just hoped the people in the car walked away from the crash. Many had not.

Reeves blazed out of town and down the wet road, getting them to the crash site in under ten minutes. A pickup sat on the highway, its flashers on, and a man exited the vehicle as they drove up. Declan could just make out a silver car in the ditch from their position.

Once Reeves pulled to a stop, Declan hopped out and walked over to greet the man.

"You find the wreck?"

The man nodded. "I was just passing through and saw the car."

"Any injuries?"

"That's the thing. It's empty."

Declan frowned, a hint of unease filling him. "What?"

"Yeah. The door was open, and there's a purse inside. I didn't touch it, though. Just called for help."

"Okay. We'll check it out, thanks. You can wait in your car if you want to stay out of the rain."

The man nodded, and Declan jogged around him to check out the other vehicle. His steps slowed as he took in the make and model. It looked like Maggie's borrowed SUV. Adrenaline dumped, and he ran forward.

Please, God, no!

"Lou?" Reeves stepped back as Declan pushed past him to look inside. Dread filled him as he saw Maggie's purse resting against the passenger door.

"It's Maggie's car." He backed away and glanced around, looking for any sign of her. A pair of brown leather pumps laid just past the front bumper. His eyes traveled down the road. Maybe she started walking. He looked back at the car. But why would she leave her purse behind?

"Are you sure?" Sam asked.

Declan nodded. "Yeah. That's her bag inside, and those are

the shoes she put on this morning." He pointed to the heels lying in the mud.

"Where did she go?" He looked up and down the road. "Maybe she decided to walk home? The ranch is only a couple miles past here."

Declan shook his head. "I could see her kicking off the shoes, but not leaving her bag. I'm going to call Seb. Don't touch the car. He's probably going to want to have forensics process it." He backed away and headed for the truck. Pulling himself into his seat, he grabbed the radio and asked them to connect him to the sheriff. Seb came on the line a minute later.

"Engine 2, this is Sheriff Archer."

"Seb, it's Deck. You need to get on the highway and head toward the ranch. Maggie's missing."

A long pause greeted his words. "Say again."

"Maggie's car is in a ditch, and she's not with it."

"And she didn't walk away."

"I don't think so. She left her purse."

"Copy. I'll have someone from the ranch drive that way to look for her on that end. I'm on my way."

"Copy. Engine 2 out." He hung the mic up, then pressed the heels of his hands to his eyes, stemming the tears welling there. He had an awful feeling. The urge to punch something had him balling his fists. He took a deep breath, welcoming the ache in his chest as a distraction from the pain invading his heart. Dammit, where could she be? Who had her? And why?

His cell rang from the cargo pocket on his Dickies. He fished it out and frowned at the unfamiliar number, then slid his thumb over the screen.

"Hello?"

"Son, I'm glad you took my call."

Shock rendered Declan speechless.

"I have something of yours." Declan heard rustling, then his dad's muffled voice.

"Say hello."

"Declan?"

"Maggie?" Declan's heart stuttered, then kicked into over-drive. "Oh, thank God you're safe. Why did you leave your purse and your shoes? I thought—"

Cole's laugh stopped him. "Oh, she's not safe, my boy. The opposite, in fact."

"What? What do you mean? Dad, what's going on? Is Maggie okay?"

"She's fine. For now. Whether she stays that way depends on you."

"Huh? What the hell are you talking about?"

"Really, Declan? I thought you were smarter than this. You're sitting at an accident scene right now, aren't you? And it's Maggie's car?"

"Yes. How did you know that?"

"I'm the one who ran her off the road."

"Wait. Why would you do that?" Understanding dawned, even as he asked. Horror and dread were quick on its heels. "Dad. No. Why?"

"I'll explain when I see you. I need you to meet me at the following coordinates." He rattled them off. Declan repeated them in his head so he wouldn't forget. "Don't take too long to get here. I might think you're not coming and decide to cut my losses."

"I'll be there. Just don't hurt her. Please."

"I'll be waiting. And I don't think I need to tell you not to share those coordinates, do I?"

The line went dead, and Declan stared at the phone for a moment before exploding into action. He opened the notepad app on his phone and wrote down the coordinates, then scrambled out of the truck.

How the hell was he going to get away from here? He couldn't exactly take the firetruck. Not only would everyone notice, but it was equipped with GPS. As much as he wanted Seb to track Cole down, he feared it would happen before Declan could get Maggie to safety.

A quick glance around showed the only possibility was the man who found her car. Deck wasn't about to leave, though, without leaving behind some breadcrumbs for Seb to follow.

"Sam!" Declan jogged over to Reeves, who stood guard near the car, waiting for the police to arrive. "I just got off the horn with Seb. He wants the witness to come to the station to give a statement. I'm useless to you here, so I'm going to ride back with him. I need to *do* something."

"I get that. I hope you find her soon. We'll be good here."

"Thanks, man." He started to walk away, then paused. "One more thing. I forgot to tell Seb earlier that I ran into Cole. He said to tell everyone hi. Can you relay that to the sheriff? I'm afraid I'll forget again with everything going on."

"Uh, sure." Sam frowned, looking confused, but didn't question him.

"Thanks. We all go back a long time." He waved and jogged away, heading for the man in the truck. Declan motioned for him to roll the window down.

"What's up?"

"The sheriff wants you to go into town and give your statement at the station."

"Oh. Um, I guess I can do that. I'm not from around here, though. Can you tell me where it is?"

Perfect. "Actually, I can do one better. Another emergency came up I need to be at, but I need a ride back to town. The fire station is near the sheriff's department. Can you give me a ride and I'll give you directions?"

"That works. Hop in."

"Great, thanks." Declan ran around the hood and got in. "I appreciate this. I'm the only supervisor on duty tonight, so I'm spread thin."

"Not a problem." He started the truck and held a hand out to Declan. "Name's Robby."

Declan shook his hand. "Declan. Nice to meet you."

They made small talk for the rest of the drive into town. At one point, Declan ducked down, pretending to check his boot when he saw headlights coming at them. The last thing he needed was for Seb to see him and turn around.

Robby pulled up to the fire station and Declan got out. "Thanks for the ride. The sheriff's department is just up the street. Just tell the desk sergeant who you are and why you're there. She'll do the rest."

"Sounds good. Thanks."

With a nod, Declan shut the door and hurried inside. He shucked his gear and snagged his truck keys from his office, avoiding anyone still left in the station. Once in his truck, he plugged the coordinates into the GPS app on his phone and peeled out of the parking lot. He had to take a couple detours to get around the accident scene and avoid unwanted attention.

Driving as fast as he dared, he drove deeper into the mountains, soon turning off onto a dirt road. His tires slid in the mud, and he fought to keep the vehicle out of the ditch. Crashing wouldn't help Maggie. He slogged through.

The coordinates led him down a two-track that cut up the side of the mountain. Thankful for his four-wheel drive, he bounced over the uneven terrain through the trees until an old, but well-maintained cabin came into view. He parked near the porch and got out, scanning his surroundings as he knocked on the door. The man who answered—though not who he expected to see—wasn't a surprise.

"Hey, brother. Good to see you. Come on in." Jameson Gehring held the door wide so Declan could pass through.

He eyed the younger man as he entered. "We're not brothers. That title's reserved for firefighters who put *out* fires, not set them."

Jameson chuckled, but didn't reply.

Declan looked around the room and frowned. "Where's Maggie? And my dad?"

"Maggie's tied up in the bathroom. He went to get her." No sooner were the words out of his mouth than the bathroom door opened. Cole pushed Maggie out ahead of him, a pistol pointed at her side.

"Are you all right?" he asked, his eyes roving over her face, pausing on the bruise forming on her jaw.

She nodded, her expression carefully schooled. He could tell she was scared, but she was doing her best to keep it off her face. He admired her grit.

"I'm fine."

"See? Unharmed as I promised," Cole said. "Have a seat, boy."

Declan crossed his arms and planted his feet. Cole rolled his eyes. "Have it your way. It doesn't matter."

"Just explain what the fuck you're doing. And why."

"Why? I'll tell you why." He shook Maggie's arm like a rag doll. "Her family ruined my life."

Maggie scoffed. "I find that hard to believe."

So did Declan. "I agree. What makes you say that?"

"Did you know her daddy's the reason I went to prison the first time? He set me down a path I can't shake."

"No, you're the reason you went to prison. Jenny told me you rustled a bunch of cattle from them. And you have no one to blame but yourself for continuing your life of crime. Plus, you've roped this poor sap into things now." He hooked a thumb toward Gehring. "What I don't get is how your grudge against Lee translates into the need to take your anger out on the entire Archer family and their friends."

Twin pops of red bloomed on Cole's cheeks. His light gray eyes turned to hardened steel. He shoved Maggie toward Jameson and advanced on Declan until they were nose to nose. "I'll tell you why. Because their family needs to suffer like mine suffered. Like you suffered." He jabbed a finger into Declan's chest. "None of my children got a fair shake at life because of them. I had plans for all the money from those cattle. It's not like they would have missed a few head. They're worth millions! I was going to take you all away from this hellhole. Buy a boat and start a fishing charter service. But Lee ruined all that. And once I got out, no one would hire me. I wronged an Archer, and it made me unemployable around here. It's why I eventually left."

Declan held his ground as his father spewed hatred toward Maggie's family in his face. He felt sorry for him. To hold so much bitterness for so long had twisted him up inside. He wished someone had helped his dad see the truth years ago— that there was no one to blame for the way his life turned out except himself.

"I tried to start over," Cole continued. "But I couldn't escape the stigma of being an ex-con. And even in Denver, the Archer name carries weight. Once potential employers caught wind of *who* I wronged, they kicked me to the curb."

"I met your mistress and your daughters," Declan said, trying to turn the conversation. He doubted he could convince him to turn himself in, but maybe he could get Cole to let them go.

"I know." He smiled. "They're good girls. Denise did a wonderful job with them. I wish I could have been there more."

"You talked to her?" He didn't think they had any regular contact.

"No. Michael told me after she told him you came calling."

"Oh. I'd like to meet him, too. She said he was an oil field worker up north."

Jameson laughed. "That's what I wanted her to think."

Declan paused, frowning. He ran the kid's words back. *What?*

Jameson laughed harder. "All these months and you never suspected. I guess I can understand. We don't look much alike. You look more like your mom. I'm a good mix of my parents, though, don't you think?" He turned his head and ran a finger along his jaw, arching a brow, then turned back to grin at Declan.

"You're Michael?"

The kid nodded.

"How did you pass the background check to get your job?"

He shrugged. "Dad knew the right people to get the right papers. With those in hand, it was easy."

Declan stumbled over to the chair and sat. He propped his elbows on his knees and ran his hands through his hair as utter disbelief stole his voice.

"Why are you part of his vendetta?" Maggie asked. "You've never met any of us."

"Because I heard all my life how the Archers ruined our lives. I just wanted what was rightfully ours. This whole thing was my idea."

Declan's head shot up to glare at Cole. "You're so concerned about your kids' lives, but you used me to get to the Archers?" He snorted. "I feel really loved, Dad."

"I used you because you turned traitor. You and Macy both did. It was just easier to find an in with you than her."

"Well, what the fuck did you expect? You abandoned us. First by committing crimes and going to prison, then later when you just up and fucking left. Mom was high or wasted all the damn time. The Archers practically raised us. Maybe if you'd owned up to your mistakes and tried to be a better man, we wouldn't have looked to them for guidance. I would have loved to have a dad who was there."

Michael walked forward and before Declan could react, slugged him in the jaw, knocking him from the chair.

"Show our dad some respect. You have no idea what his life was like. What my life was like. You had your precious Archers to fall back on. We had no safety net."

Declan rubbed his jaw and glared up at his younger half-brother. He rose to his feet, looming over the kid. Michael didn't quite have his height, and Declan had about thirty pounds of muscle on him. "You touch me again, and we're going to have a problem."

Michael grinned and backed up, taking hold of Maggie's arm again. "Not so long as I have her."

"He's not the one you should be worried about," Maggie said. "Uncuff me. Let's see what happens."

"There's that feistiness again," Cole said. "So spunky." He looked at Declan. "I bet she's spicy in bed. Trust me when I tell you, you want a more timid woman." He shook his head. "It'll come back to bite you later if you don't."

"He killed your mother, Deck," Maggie said. "I'm guessing Jed Stafford, too."

"What? Is that true?" He turned away from Michael to face his father. "Why?"

"She learned of my plans for the Archers and was going to warn them. Seems she had a soft spot for them as well. Jed stumbled over Michael and me together, and he recognized me. Michael followed him and killed him. When I realized who he was, well, it seemed like the perfect start to toying with the Archers."

"You bastard," Declan bit out through his teeth.

"Why do you care? It's not like you cared about her."

"At least she stuck around."

Cole laughed. "But how often was she sober? A couple days a year, maybe?" He shook his head. "I should have done it long ago and saved you some teenage angst."

Declan felt like he was getting nowhere. They were just talking in circles now, and it wasn't what was important. "Enough about all that. What do you want? Why are we here?"

"Wondering why I kept your lady alive?"

He nodded.

"It's simple. If you want to live—and keep your girl alive—you need to help us."

"Yeah, no. You're just going to let us go once everything's all said and done? I don't think so."

Cole shrugged. "I can just kill her now." He pulled back the hammer on his gun and pointed it at Maggie.

"No, wait!" Declan held his hands out. "Tell me what you want me to do."

"That's better." Cole grinned. "You interrupted Michael before he could finish his job last week. I need you to get him on the ranch so he can finish it. I also need you to bring me Lee."

Declan looked at Maggie. She stood in Michael's grip, her expression hard, but her eyes pleaded with him as tears rolled down her face. Whether she wanted him to cooperate or not, he didn't know. But if he had to hazard a guess, he doubted she wanted him to do what Cole wanted. He didn't want to put her family in danger any more than she did, but he couldn't stand here and watch her die.

"What's it going to be, son? Are you going to help, or do you watch the love of your life die right now?"

"What is he going to do once I get him on the ranch? Torch more buildings?"

"Something like that," Cole hedged.

Declan had a feeling his sadistic half-brother had much

more in mind for the Archers than just some fires. But he couldn't sign Maggie's death warrant.

"Fine. I'll do it."

"Declan." Maggie's voice came out a strangled whisper.

"I'm sorry, honey. I can't—" Emotion choked off his words. "I'm sorry."

Michael let Maggie go and moved toward Declan, shoving him toward the door. "Let's go."

He cast one last look over his shoulder at Maggie as Michael pushed him outside, praying she would still be alive when he returned. *If* he returned.

"We'll take your truck, so they aren't suspicious." He opened the back of the ancient SUV parked next to the building and took out a blanket, tarp, and a radio, tossing them into the back of Declan's pickup. "Back up to the shed."

Declan did as he asked, watching as Michael threw two duffels into the back, then hopped into the bed. He rapped on the rear window with his knuckles, and Declan slid it open.

"I'm going to ride under the tarp. We end up anywhere but on the Broken Bow, or I see any of your buddies behind us, I'll radio dad and tell him to shoot Maggie. And, just in case you're thinking about pulling over and trying to over-power me, if Dad doesn't hear from me within a preset time-frame, Maggie dies." He gave Declan a hard look. "Give me your phone."

God, he didn't want to, but he fished it from his pocket, anyway, and handed it over. Michael took it, then hunkered down under the blanket and tarp.

Muttering curses under his breath, Declan shut the window, gritting his teeth, and shifted the truck into drive, pulling away from the cabin. On the way down the mountain, he hit every rock and dip he could see in the rain. It would not bother him at all if the kid bounced right out of the truck bed.

How the dirtbag hiding back there could be related to their sweet sisters, Declan didn't know.

He made the turn onto the dirt road and did his best not to slide off as he steered them down to the highway. Once his tires hit the pavement, he punched the accelerator. His fire radio caught his eye. He thought about using it, but didn't know if Cole was monitoring the traffic. Declan remembered seeing a police scanner on the table.

He banged a hand on the steering wheel. "Fuck!" He needed a plan. And fast. The pole light at the end of the ranch drive came into view, and he slowed. Turning onto the drive, he rocketed down the lane, past the restaurant, only stopping to get through the new gate to the family compound. He entered his code into the box. The heavy iron gates swung open, and he drove in, pulling off once they were on the other side, out of the cameras' view.

Declan knocked on the window and slid it open. "We're here. Where am I going?"

Michael's head popped out of the tarp. "The houses. Pull into Maggie's garage." He ducked back under the tarp.

He heard the squawk of the radio as Michael called Cole. He put the truck in gear and drove down the lane. In less than a minute, he pulled into the garage. He cut the engine and closed the overhead door. When he climbed out, Michael was already out from under the tarp. The younger man hopped over the side and lifted the two duffels out.

"You going to tell me your plan, or am I just supposed to follow you around like some whipped puppy?"

Michael crouched over a bag and unzipped it. He glanced up and grinned. "We're going to set some bombs."

"You're a sick, sadistic bastard."

"Yeah?" Michael rose with two of the pipe bombs in his hands. He shoved one into Declan's chest. "Well, you're my brother, so what's that say about you?"

"That I'm unfortunate. But I'm nothing like you."

"You think Maggie's going to think that? Especially after she learns you helped blow up her family's ranch?"

Those same doubts he'd been fighting reared their heads. He shoved them back into their box. There was no way he was going to set bombs on the Broken Bow. Michael had checked in with Dad. He took a menacing step toward his brother.

Michael jumped back, waving the radio. "Nuh-uh-uh. He wants regular updates."

Declan bared his teeth as he growled.

Michael laughed. "Let's go."

Biting his tongue, he followed. Michael turned on the bomb he held and set it near the interior door. Declan glanced at it and noted the remote detonator as well as the timer that still flashed zero.

"When you arm that, how much time do we have to get clear?"

"Five minutes." He scooped up the duffels and walked out the back door of the garage.

They crept along the house, going down the line, setting bombs at the front and back doors of each house. With each successive one they set, Declan's jaw clenched tighter. If Michael armed all these, he was going to have a hell of a time defusing them all before they blew.

"You realize all this is being caught on camera, right?" Declan pointed at the pole mounted outside Jace and Tara's. A camera sat attached to it about halfway up.

Michael nodded. "I do now. I wasn't aware there was so much security the first time I was here. But it doesn't matter now. From what I can tell, it's a passive system, so unless they're staring at the monitors right this second, they don't know we're here. By the time they figure it out, Dad and I will be long gone." He pushed Declan forward. "Keep moving."

Seb's house was last. Michael set bombs at the front and

back doors, then ushered Declan toward the main house. They ran through the rain and darkness to reach the porch. Michael clomped up the steps and knocked.

"What the hell are you doing?"

"We need Lee. No better way to get him than through the front door."

Declan groaned and scrubbed a hand over his face. He needed to get Lee alone—to explain—but that was looking less and less likely. Michael had a plan, and Declan was just along for the ride.

The door swung open. Declan said a prayer of thanks that it was Lee and not Jenny who answered. He couldn't fathom what Michael would do to her.

Lee stared at the young man with a frown, which turned curious when he saw Declan. "Declan. Did you find Maggie? And who's this? He looks familiar."

"Oh, he found her all right. Mr. Archer, I'd like to introduce myself. I'm Michael James, Declan's brother."

Lee smiled and held out a hand. "It's nice to meet you. Were you with Declan when he heard Maggie was missing?"

"Not exactly." Michael took Lee's hand and yanked him outside.

"What the hell?" Lee exclaimed.

"I should mention I go by another name. You might be more familiar with it. Jameson Gehring."

Lee's eyes widened. He looked at Declan. "What's going on?"

"No time for that. We have a schedule to keep. He'll explain on the way." Michael grabbed a handful of Lee's shirt and dragged him off the porch.

"Let go of me! What the hell is going on? Declan?"

Despite his squirming, Michael kept a solid grip on Lee. With his other hand, he brought his radio up to tell Cole he had the eldest Archer, and they were on their way back.

Declan had a plan, too. And it was time to implement it. He stepped behind his brother, waiting as he fumbled with the truck's door handle. Distracted, he didn't see Declan rush him. Anger fueling him, Declan grabbed Michael by the collar and yanked him back, spinning him around. He leveled a punch on the kid's jaw that sent him to the ground. Michael jumped up, staying just out of Declan's reach.

"Big mistake, brother." He took a cell phone from his pocket and turned it on. "We were going to wait to blow the place until we were clear of the area, but I guess now's as good a time as any." His thumb hovered over the keypad.

"The hell it is," Lee said, running up and tackling Michael.

The phone went flying as the older man wrestled with him. Declan scooped it up, powering it down, then jumped into the fray. He pulled Michael off the ground, away from Lee, and twisted his arm up behind his back.

"You know, your plan was actually pretty good," Declan said. "But you had one fatal flaw."

"Oh, yeah?" Pain laced Michael's voice as Declan leaned on his arm. "What's that?"

"You were too arrogant."

"Whatever, man." He glared at Declan over his shoulder. "You're as bad as them. Dad was never going to let you go, you know. Maggie's probably already dead."

Declan knew that was a distinct possibility. He'd been trying not to think about it. "For your sake, you better hope she's not. I'm not normally a violent man, but I'll have no problem snuffing out your and Dad's miserable lives if he laid a finger on her."

"Man, she must be a helluva good fuck for you to commit murder over."

Declan saw red. He shoved Michael's arm higher and heard a pop as his forearm broke. Michael screamed. His legs sagged, but that only increased his pain, so he stood on his toes.

"Say another word about her, and I'll do more than break your arm. Get in the truck." He shoved him forward. Michael let out a shout of pain and lurched forward.

Lee ran around them to open the door. "You want to tell me what's going on now?"

"In a second. There's a rope in the toolbox. Get it."

Lee jumped into the bed and opened the bed box, pulling out a length of rope. He hopped down and helped Declan tie up Michael. They put him in the backseat on the floor, then got in the front.

"Explain, Declan. Now."

"Where's Jenny?" he countered.

"At the inn. Please tell me what's going on."

"My dad's the one behind the fires." Declan put the car in gear and shot down the drive. "He's pissed at you for sending him to prison all those years ago. His vendetta carried over to dipshit back there who planned all of this. Maggie's at a hunting cabin up the mountain with Dad, and he's threatening to kill her if I don't help Michael. Which reminds me, we need to evacuate the ranch. We put a bunch of bombs on all the houses before coming here. They're active, but I don't think they're armed. I think I got the phone away from him before he could send the signal."

Lee sat next to him, wide-eyed, and stared for a moment. "Is that all?" He swallowed hard. "We need to call Seb." He patted his pocket. "I don't have my phone. It's in the house."

"He took mine. I think it's in the truck bed." He braked.

"I'll just use the radio." Lee reached for the mic on the dash.

"No!" He put the truck in park. "Dad had a police scanner at the cabin. I think he's monitoring the traffic. We need to use other means. I'll get my phone." He climbed out and vaulted into his truck bed, scrabbling through the tarp and blanket for the device. It clattered on the metal as he lifted the blanket and shook it. He scooped it up and jumped down, climbing inside the cab.

"Call him. Put it on speaker." He tossed the phone at Lee and put the car in drive, only slowing for the gates to open.

"Where the fuck are you?" Seb's angry greeting echoed through the truck. "Reeves said you left the scene with the witness. That I wanted him to give his statement at the station. Oh, and that Cole said hello. The only Cole I know is your dad. What does he have to do with any of this shit?"

"Dad took Maggie. My brother is Jameson Gehring, whose real name is Michael James. I'm in my truck headed up the mountain, with him trussed up like a turkey in the backseat. Your dad is with me. Oh, and there's about a dozen bombs on the ranch, so you might want to call the bomb squad."

Silence met his speech. "Sweet Jesus. Okay. I'll radio dispatch—"

"You can't use police radios. Dad's got a scanner. Until I get Maggie away from him, it's not safe."

"Phones it is, got it. I'll get the bomb techs there. Where do I need to send backup for you?"

"Lee, open the notepad app and read him those coordinates."

The other man did as asked.

"Send them in quiet, Sebastian, unless you hear from me."

"I will. I'd tell you to wait for backup, but having been in your shoes, I know that won't happen. Just be careful."

"Yep." He nodded at Lee, who said goodbye and hung up.

"I'm sorry, Declan."

"For what?"

"This is my fault. If I hadn't pressed charges on your father—"

"No. This is on him. I'm sure he had opportunities to go straight after he got out of prison for stealing your cattle. He chose to continue down the wrong path and to be bitter about it."

"Still. I could have offered him help after he got out. Tried to do—something."

"I doubt he would have accepted help. He had years in jail to stew over his perceived slight. Who knows? He might have used that to get back at you sooner."

"Then maybe my daughter wouldn't be in danger."

"We're going to get her back." They had to. Declan couldn't live without her. He loved that woman more than anything. He would spend the rest of his life proving to her he was nothing like his father and brother if she'd let him.

EIGHTEEN

Rain pelted the windows. Maggie sat tied up in the wooden rocker and watched Cole string det cord from a bomb made of gasoline cans in the center of the room to the doors and windows. Once Declan returned with her dad, her chances of escape would dwindle drastically. She had to do something. Now.

"I'm sorry."

He paused and looked at her. "Huh? Why?"

"For my dad. I'm sorry. I've been thinking about what you said. You're right. He should have let you go. He's always been a bit of a stickler for what's proper. I'm kind of amazed he never disowned Tara and Thomas. They were hellions growing up."

A corner of his mouth ticked up. "I remember."

"They got in lots of trouble with him, though. They even spent some time in jail. They stole one of the ranch vehicles. Dad made sure they sat in the county jail." For only a few hours until he could get there, but he didn't need to know that.

"Seriously?" He shook his head. "What kind of man calls the cops on his own kids?"

"Oh, I agree. I might live on the ranch, but he and I don't see eye-to-eye. I've been saving up to move away."

"Really?" Skepticism dripped off the word. "Didn't you just open your law practice? With daddy's help?"

Damn. He was more informed than she thought. She did some fast thinking.

"I needed some experience before I tried to set up in a larger city, and I didn't want to work for anyone else. He offered the capital, so I took him up on it. But trust me, I'm going to hightail it out of here one day soon and never look back."

"Good for you. This place is a hole. Sucks the life right out of you."

She nodded. "Absolutely." She shifted in her seat. "Um, I don't suppose I could use the bathroom, could I? I drank about a gallon of coffee earlier."

He studied her for a moment. Maggie did her best to keep any emotion off her face except for the desire to pee. Finally, he nodded and untied her, but left the handcuffs on. She raised her hands. He shook his head.

"Those stay on. I'm not dumb."

She let them fall into her lap. "I'm not trying to fool you. I feel for you. I'd happily drive away from here and never tell a soul anything. Dad can face the consequences of his actions on his own," she said, perpetuating the injured princess thing she was going for. He needed to think she was on his side if she was going to get the jump on him. She stood up and crossed to the bathroom, shutting herself inside.

Maggie's eyes roved the small space, looking for anything to aid her in escape. The window was much too small for her to fit through, so that was out. The room was rather sparse. There wasn't even a toothbrush on the sink.

Her gaze stopped on the toilet. As quietly as she could with her bound hands, she lifted the lid off the tank and peered inside. "Yes!" she hissed. She set the lid down, then reached in and pulled out the pin holding the chain on the plunger. She worked it into the keyhole on her cuffs, trying to pop the lock. The cuff gave a soft click and loosened. She quickly pulled it off and doubled it up on her other wrist to keep it out of the way. She'd worry about getting them completely off later.

Standing, she shoved the pin in her dress pocket, then flushed the toilet by pulling up on the arm. She flipped on the faucet, to keep up the appearance that all was well, and counted to twenty. After she shut it off, she counted to ten, then took a deep breath. Things were about to get real.

She opened the door, covering her free hand with the cuffed one as she walked out. Instead of going back to her chair, though, she wandered to the window.

"Hey. Where are you going? Sit back in the chair."

Maggie stayed where she was. She needed him to come to her.

His boots clomped over the wooden floor. "Are you deaf? I said sit down." He touched her shoulder.

Maggie whirled, knocking his arm away. She brought her other hand up to slam the heel into his nose. Blood spurted, immediate and bright. He staggered back, covering his face. She didn't wait for him to recover, advancing instead. She grabbed his head, pulling it down as she brought her knee up, smashing his nose again. She kicked him in the balls, then delivered a roundhouse kick to the side of his head. He dropped like a sack of potatoes.

Breathing hard, more from the adrenaline than the exertion, she nudged him to make sure he was out, then retrieved the handcuff key from his pocket and unlocked her cuffs. They fell to the floor with a thunk.

Headlights flashed through the window. She ran forward and peeked outside to see Declan's pickup pull in. Dammit, she wasn't ready yet!

She grabbed Cole by the ankles and pulled him across the floor toward the bathroom. *Jesus, he's heavy.* Maggie prayed she could get him out of sight before Michael walked in.

Car doors slammed, spurring her to move faster. She got him in the miniscule room, but realized he was too tall to lie prone and still close the door.

"Fucking men and their fucking height," she muttered as she scrambled over him. "Why do they have to be so damn tall?" She grabbed his shirt at the shoulders and lifted his upper body, leaning him against the sink cabinet just as boots sounded on the porch. She shut the door and flew to the rocker, sitting down as the door creaked open.

Maggie tried to slow her breathing, expecting Michael to walk through. But the doorway stayed empty. She frowned, staring outside.

"Hello?"

Silence met her query, so she tried again. "Is anyone there?"

Declan's voice followed after a beat. "Maggie?" He peered around the doorframe, his eyes surveying the room. He stepped into the cabin, her dad behind him. "Where's Dad?"

She stood up. "Unconscious in the bathroom. Where's Michael?"

"Tied up in my truck."

She ran forward and launched herself at him. He caught her, burying his nose in her hair.

"Are you okay? Did he hurt you?"

"I'm fine." She pulled away to hug her dad. He squeezed her tight.

"I'm so glad you're all right, girl. We were so worried when they found your car."

"I'm okay, though. And it's over."

"It is." He released her. "I'm going to let Seb know. Then I want a word with Cole." He walked just outside the door to make the call.

Declan pulled her to him and kissed her. Maggie savored the feel of his mouth on hers. She wanted to feel it every day for the rest of her life.

"Are you sure you're okay?" he asked, pulling back.

She ran her hands through his hair. "Completely. How about you? How are those ribs?"

"They ache, but I'm okay."

"Good. I couldn't handle it if something happened to you. I love you, Declan Briggs. So much."

He smoothed her hair away from her face. "I love you too," he whispered. "I don't deserve you, but I promise I will spend my days making you happy."

She kissed him. "Just you being near makes me happy, so that won't be hard."

The bathroom door banged open. They jerked apart and turned to see Cole stumble out into the main room, blood covering the lower half of his face and staining his shirt. He had a detonator in his hand.

"Dad. Dad, don't." Declan shoved Maggie behind him and took several steps toward Cole.

She made a mad grab for Declan's clothes to hold him back, but he moved out of her reach.

"Please. It doesn't have to end this way," Declan pleaded as he moved toward his dad.

"Why shouldn't it? I'll take out an Archer—the baby of the family—and I won't go back to prison. And as a bonus, Lee's still alive and will have to live with knowing he couldn't save his daughter. You should leave, though, son. Despite your terrible judgement, you don't need to die. Losing her will be enough of a punishment."

"No. If you blow yourself up, you're going to have to take me with you."

A strangled sound escaped Maggie. She kept her feet planted, though, and let Declan talk. She knew if she moved forward, Cole might just push that button.

"I already killed your mother. Don't think I won't kill you too."

"You've made it perfectly clear you think I'm a traitor." He edged closer. "But that doesn't mean I want you to die."

"Cole. Put down the detonator," Lee said from the doorway. "Let's talk this out."

"There's nothing to talk about. I'm not going back to prison." His thumb edged closer to the button.

Maggie's heart stopped only to restart at three times the speed.

"Dad! Please. Think about the girls. Do you really want to leave Hannah and Jessie without their dad?"

Cole scoffed. "Denise keeps them away from me most of the time. Sends them to some friend of hers when I'm around. I don't think they'll care whether I live or die."

"They'll care. Trust me." He took a few more steps closer.

"What are you doing?"

"What do you mean?" Declan froze.

Maggie held her breath.

"Boy, you never could lie worth a shit. Stop moving. Enough of this."

The next few seconds happened in slow motion. Declan shouted for Lee to get her out of the cabin as he ran forward. Her dad grabbed her by the waist and dove out of the house. They hit the ground hard. She didn't have time to recover before he took a fistful of her dress and pulled her backward toward the truck.

Halfway across the yard, the cabin exploded. Flames shot

out the windows and open door, and part of the roof blew off and flames leaped into the night sky through the rain.

"Declan!" Tears blurred her vision as she stared at the flames.

Pieces of the building rained down, and Lee pushed her to the ground, folding himself over her like a shield. She pushed against him. "Dad, please! Let me go! I have to get to him. Please!"

"No, baby. You have to stay here. You'll never make it past the door." He held her close as she sobbed into his chest.

Sirens sounded over the roar of the fire, heralding Sebastian's arrival with his deputies. Lee helped her stand as Seb pulled into the clearing. He shot out of his SUV as it rocked to a stop.

"What happened?"

"Cole blew up the cabin," Lee said, holding Maggie upright. "He and Declan were inside."

"What? No." Seb started forward, but Lee laid a hand on his arm.

"Son, no. It's too hot."

Seb glanced back, then looked at the fire. Through her haze, she saw the pain cross his face as he realized he had to leave his friend in that inferno.

"God, no." He ran a hand through his hair and paced in front of them.

Maggie sagged against her dad, staring at the fire. The pain of losing the man she loved overwhelmed her nerves like a third-degree burn. It left the wound raw but numb. Empty inside, she watched the flames flicker and snap in the doorway. As she stared, a shadow appeared.

She poked Lee. "Hey. Hey, what's that?" She pointed at the cabin.

Lee turned, and Seb stopped pacing to look where she gestured. Maggie's heart faltered, and she scarcely breathed.

The shadow grew, and she watched a man emerge from the flames carrying someone.

"Oh my God," Lee breathed.

The three of them ran forward. Maggie couldn't tell if it was Declan or Cole who walked out. They were built similarly, and towels draped both of them. When she got closer, she recognized Declan's clothes.

Seb and Lee helped him away from the burning building, taking Cole off his shoulders. Maggie ripped the wet towel off Declan's head and framed his soot-streaked face in her hands. She ran her fingers over his cheeks and brows and down his nose, reassuring herself he was real. "How?"

"I dove at him, and it knocked us into the bathroom." He coughed hard, wincing. "Somehow, I kicked the door shut while I had a hold of his hand, but he punched my ribs. I looked up in time to see him grin wildly as he pushed the button. I had just enough time to jump into the shower stall. It put an extra buffer between me and the blast." He coughed again. "Is he alive? I just wet some towels, draped them over us, and walked out."

"He's breathing," Seb said. "Barely." He pressed the mic button on his radio and asked for an ETA on the medics.

Declan coughed, but kneeled next to his father, checking his pulse and assessing his injuries. Commotion from his truck drew their attention. Maggie looked over to see Michael pressed against the window, yelling.

"Let him out," Declan said. He took his keys from his pocket and passed them to Seb.

Seb unlocked the vehicle and walked over, removing the young man from the backseat. Michael hurried forward as fast as Seb allowed and dropped next to an unconscious Cole.

"Dad?" Tears welled in the young man's eyes. He looked up at Declan, all traces of the angry kid gone. "Is he going to be okay?"

"I don't know. He wanted to die, Michael. I'm not sure he has a will to live."

"This wasn't the plan," Michael whispered, staring down at their dad. "It was the Archers who were supposed to die. We were going to start over somewhere else. Where no one knew who we were."

"You could have done that without murdering anyone," Declan said.

Michael curled in on himself, cradling his broken arm as he quietly cried. Declan stood and tucked Maggie beneath his arm while they waited on the ambulance. He could hear it on the highway. His gaze took in the surrounding destruction, and some of the tension left him. It was finally over.

Epilogue

Nerves assailed Declan as he stared outside. Flurries floated through the air under a steel gray sky. A bigger storm was coming, but it was half a day away, thankfully.

"Hey, you ready?"

He turned to see Macy in the doorway. She looked beautiful in her deep blue chiffon dress. It fit snug to her waist, then flared away to float around her legs like a cloud. Their younger sisters flanked her, wearing identical dresses and gigantic smiles.

"Yeah, are you ready? We're ready!" Jessie bounced. The wreath of flowers on her head tilted and Macy set it back in place.

He smiled at her. "You are? You don't look ready. Where are your flowers?"

Jessie scrunched her nose. "Mommy has them. The petals kept falling off while I held them."

Hannah giggled. "That's because you couldn't stop bouncing."

Jessie threw up her hands. "I'm excited!"

They all laughed. Declan scooped her up. "Well, let's go find them and get this show on the road, huh?"

The little girl pumped her fist. "Yes!"

He led them through the church hallway to the sanctuary and found Denise. Her previously dull blonde hair was now a more natural light brown, and she wore a mint green sweater dress and tall brown boots. Over the last couple months, he and Macy had helped get her and the girls out of the hellhole they lived in. Seb offered them his house on the ranch, and Macy hired her at the coffee shop. The girls loved living amongst the Archers and having access to the farm animals.

Denise proved to be a good woman who fell prey to a charismatic man's silver tongue. Out from under his influence and in a better place than that dilapidated house and crime-riddled neighborhood, she flourished. Macy raved about her work ethic and her ability to learn new things quickly. And she was a wonderful mother. The girls adored her, and Declan and Macy now viewed her as a sister. She was a bit young for them to see her as a stepmother figure.

"I need my flowers, Mommy." Declan set Jessie on her feet, and she ran to her mother.

Denise looked up and smiled. She handed Jessie her flowers. "Be careful with them this time."

"I will." The girl whirled around. Another petal fell off. She took Macy's hand. "Let's go line up!"

"I guess we're going," Macy said, looking back over her shoulder, laughing, as Jessie hauled her to the vestibule.

Declan grinned as he watched them go.

"They all look beautiful."

He turned to look at Denise.

"You don't look so bad, either." A sad smile crossed her face. "A lot like your father, actually."

He didn't want the reminder of his dad on a day like today, but he couldn't help but feel for the woman who, at one time, loved him. He laid a hand on her shoulder. "I'm sorry."

She waved a hand. "Don't be. He's a handsome man. It's what drew me to him in the first place. I just wish he was as *good* of a man as you are. Thank you for all you've done for me and the girls. I can't say that enough. And thank you for including them in your wedding. They were so excited to be asked to be junior bridesmaids."

"It wouldn't feel right without them." And that was the truth. The girls had become a huge part of his life in the last few months. He was glad Maggie recognized that and asked them to be part of their day.

She sniffed and wiped away a tear. "You have been so good to us. Especially me, which still boggles my mind. I raised that monster. After all he did—"

"Hush," Declan interjected softly. "Michael's deeds were his own. He and Dad can't ever hurt us again. Dad will never see the light of day, and Michael will be an old man. It's over." Once Cole recovered from his injuries, he pled guilty to arson and murder. The judge sentenced him to life without parole. Michael fought the charges, but lost. He awaited sentencing, and Declan expected him to serve at least thirty years for his role. It was time to move on.

She reached up and squeezed his hand on her shoulder. "I will be forever grateful." She sniffed again and gestured toward the altar where his groomsmen and the minister stood. "Go take your place and marry that girl."

He grinned. "I can do that." He gave her shoulder a gentle squeeze and walked up front.

"Nervous?" Brady asked.

Declan looked at his best man. "Actually, no. Not anymore." The nerves he felt a few minutes ago were gone. He knew they were doing the right thing, even if it was fast. When he proposed a week after the cabin explosion, the close call was still fresh for them both. He didn't want to waste time dating when he knew she was it for him. He would take every day together she gave him. That niggling thought she would eventually come to her senses and realize he wasn't good enough sat in the back of his mind until his sisters showed up in the ready room. Seeing the girls dressed as bridesmaids—at Maggie's request—finally helped him see she accepted him and all his faults. Family included.

Music swelled, and he turned his attention to the back of the church. Hannah and Jessie walked forward, arm-in-arm, enormous smiles on their faces. Macy, Rayna, and London followed. Tara, as matron-of-honor, brought up the rear. Behind her, he caught a glimpse of white. Lee stepped through the doors, facing away. He held up an arm, and Maggie stepped forward.

Declan's breath left him on a whoosh. She looked breathtaking in her simple white satin mermaid-style gown. A single strand of pearls adorned her neck, and she had her dark hair swept into a loose chignon, leaving her shoulders bare.

"Damn," Brady said. "My little sister really is all grown up."

She walked toward them, a broad smile on her face, and her eyes locked on Declan's. It felt like an eternity before she reached him. Lee passed her hand to him, and he helped her take the steps to the altar.

"You look beautiful."

She beamed. "So do you."

They faced the minister. He smiled at them as he began his speech about ever-lasting love and companionship. Declan barely heard him. Maggie captivated him wholly and completely. He recited his vows in a clear voice and listened to her profess hers for all to hear. The wedding ring felt cool against his skin, but like it belonged there. When the minister proclaimed them husband and wife, he stepped forward and took his new wife into his arms. She smiled up at him, lifting her face for his kiss. Declan felt the brand all the way to his toes.

"I love you, Mrs. Briggs," he murmured as he pulled back.

She rested her forehead against his. "I love you too, Mr. Briggs."

He gave her another quick peck as raucous cheers and whistles broke out around them. They pulled apart, and he laughed in utter delight and happiness. For years, he knew something was missing. He enjoyed life, but there was always a piece unsettled. It took him a long time to figure out what, but with Maggie, he finally knew. He'd found his family. He was home.

~

Keep reading for a sneak peek of *Light of Dawn*, book 6 in the *Broken Bow* series.

Thank you for reading Scorched! I hope you enjoyed it.

Want to read an EXCLUSIVE and FREE book? Sign up for my mailing list. You can find the sign-up form on my website, <u>ashleyaquinn.com</u>. My list also receives sneak peeks of my latest work and access to exclusive giveaways. Also, please consider leaving a rating or review on Amazon and or Goodreads. It would be greatly appreciated!

Thanks again for reading!
    - Ashley

~

Keep reading for a sneak peek at Book 6, Light of Dawn in the Broken Bow Series.

LIGHT OF DAWN

BROKEN BOW
BOOK 6

ONE

"Stupid son-of-a..." Macy Brigg's voice trailed off as she tried to pop off the bottom plate on her espresso machine. She worked her flathead screwdriver between it and the machine's side, but it refused to budge. "Why won't you move?" She tipped her head to peer underneath. It had to be hung up on something.

"What are you doing?" Brady Archer's low voice cut through the sound of her tinkering.

Macy shrieked and straightened, turning to glare at him. "Jesus, Brady. Did you ghost through the door or something? I didn't hear you come in."

"It jingled." He hooked a thumb over his shoulder to point at the door with its bell.

She was sure it did. But she'd been absorbed in trying to fix her damn espresso machine. She set down her tools. "You want a coffee?"

He nodded. "What's wrong with it?" He pointed to the machine she was trying to fix.

"It sprung a leak. I'm trying to change out a fitting, but I can't get the bottom plate off to do it. I swear, I'm going to buy a new one. This one gives me nothing but problems." She poured him a large cup of black coffee as she spoke.

He frowned. "You want me to look at it?"

She waved a hand as she passed him the cup. "No, I'll figure it out. Just like every other time I've had to fix it."

His mouth turned down as he took the coffee. "You shouldn't have to keep fixing it. What's breaking?" He put the cup down on the counter and walked around to her side.

Macy stepped back as he invaded her space, her body going on red alert at his proximity. The man sent her hormones into overdrive with his gigantic frame, thick arms, and even thicker thighs. Then there was his face. With his square jaw, defined cheekbones, and dark beard, he could have just walked off the set of some biker drama. Brady Archer was sex personified.

He brushed past her, and Macy sighed. He didn't even know it. It was *maddening*.

"This the piece you're trying to take off?" He touched the chrome plate hanging crookedly from the bottom of the machine.

She nodded.

He bent nearly in half to peer at the underside. "You got a flashlight?"

"Yeah." She fished one from her toolbox and handed it to him.

He took off his hat and tossed it onto the display case, then clicked on the light, shining it up at the bottom. He picked up the screwdriver and dropped to his knees. Putting the small light between his teeth, he pushed up on the metal, looking for where it was hung up.

"Does this side panel come off?" he asked, taking the light out of his mouth.

"Only that bigger piece. You'd have to take apart a lot more of the frame to get that other piece off."

He grunted and fiddled with the plate, working the screwdriver between it and the frame. "It's caught on something."

"Duh."

He threw an annoyed glance at her, then went back to work. After a few more seconds of wiggling the screwdriver while supporting the plate, it popped free.

"Ha! Take that, you stupid machine!" Macy said.

Brady pulled the plate down and over the steam nozzles to look at it. "It's bent back here." He looked up at her. "What did you do to it?"

"I didn't do anything."

"It didn't bend itself, Mace."

"Maybe it bent the last time I had to take it off and put it back on. I don't know." She held out her hands, palms up. "I probably wasn't as gentle as I could have been. It was the third time I replaced the same part." She sighed. "This makes number four."

"That's not right. It shouldn't break that often." He looked at the machine, then back at her. "Show me where it's breaking. Maybe there's a different problem."

"If there is, I haven't been able to find it, even with help from the manufacturer's customer service and YouTube."

"Don't you have a warranty?"

"I do. But it doesn't cover replacement unless there's a catastrophic failure. The parts are covered, but I have to fix it, or find someone who can."

He frowned. "And after the fourth time you called for the same issue, they don't consider that catastrophic?"

"No. It still functions once the part is replaced. Trust me, it's cheaper for them to send me the new valves than to replace the entire machine."

"I bet. Okay. Show me where the problem is."

She leaned in to point at the valve he exposed, trying not to let the smell of him unnerve her. It was an intoxicating scent of leather, hay, and man. "That valve. Under that brass box is the fitting for the water pipe. The steamer nozzle comes off the front. It's leaking from the back. I replace the valve and it's fine for a couple months, then all of a sudden it's dripping a steady stream again."

Brady stared at the machine and scratched his head before picking up the wrench she'd laid out. He twisted off the fitting and removed the valve, shining the light in it. "I don't see any issue with the valve. It and the washer look fine." He turned his attention to the machine. "You said it's the rear of the valve that leaks?"

"Yep."

He leaned in closer, shining the light on the pipe he took the valve off of. "Have you replaced this pipe?"

"No." She leaned in. "Should I have?"

"I think so. Look at the threading on it." He pointed to the side. "See how it looks funny?"

"Yeah."

"It's rolled."

He turned to look at her at the same time she looked at him. Her eyes darted to his lips, which were inches away. She straightened, her face flaming, and cleared her throat. "How did that happen?"

"My guess is they over-tightened the valve when they put the machine together. You need a new water pipe if you ever want it to stop leaking."

Macy groaned. "I'll have to take the entire machine apart for that. That pipe winds through its innards."

"It won't be hard. Order the part, and I'll do it."

She wasn't sure she wanted to be indebted to him, but it would be nice not to have to take the machine apart and put it back together herself. She could do it, but it would take a million pictures, copious notes, and several hours. She could ask her brother, Declan, but he and Maggie just got married, and she hated to intrude on their evenings.

"You're sure? It'll take a couple hours, so it'll need to be in the evening."

He shrugged. "I'm sure. Feed me dinner and we'll call it square."

"Deal."

"Okay. Now, where's the new valve? Let's see if we can get this thing to work for now."

She handed him the part. "I need to take some pictures of the pipe threads to send to customer service before you put that on." She took out her phone and snapped a few pictures, then stepped back. "So, if it's the pipe, how come replacing the valve helps?"

"It's not so much the valve as it's the rubber washer in it. It gets compressed and loses some of its give the longer it's in there and the more you use the machine. Once that happens, because of the rolled threads, the valve gets loose and it leaks." He screwed on the new valve, then the steamer nozzle.

"Well, whatever the reason, I'm glad it won't leak for the foreseeable future. I'll call customer service and get the water pipe ordered today."

"Just let me know when it comes in, and I'll make time to come fix it." He reassembled the rest of the machine. Macy was a little perturbed that he did it in half the time it normally took her.

"Okay." She stepped back as he stood, looming tall over her. She spotted his coffee on the counter and picked it up to hand to him. "Thanks for fixing my machine. I appreciate it. Coffee's on me today."

He took the cup. "Thanks." He took a sip, watching her.

She tried not to squirm. Why did he always have to do that silent, brooding thing? It drove her nuts. He was a hard man to read, so she couldn't tell what he was thinking.

"I should get going." He picked up his hat and set it on his head, then turned and walked around the counter. "I need to get back to the ranch. Call me when that part comes in." He glanced back. "Or if it breaks again. I'll do what I can to keep it running."

Macy nodded. "Thanks, Brady."

He touched two fingers to his hat brim and pushed through the door. The bell jingled as he exited at the same time the kitchen door opened behind her. She glanced back and smiled as she saw Denise James come through.

"Was that Brady?"

"Yeah. He stopped in for coffee and fixed the espresso machine. For now, anyway. He found a bigger problem with it."

She frowned. "Is it okay to use?"

"It's fine. The threading on the pipe going into the valve is rolled, so it doesn't line up right. The new valve will hold it at bay for a bit until the washer ages some."

"Oh. All right." She walked closer, tying her apron on.

"Kids get off to school okay?"

"Yes. They were quite eager to start their day. You and Declan telling them you're taking them camping in a couple weeks lit a fire under them. They don't dilly dally anymore. They want the days to pass quickly, so it's time for that trip."

Macy smiled. "I want that too. Declan and I are looking forward to it." They'd been planning this trip for a couple months. Ever since Denise and the girls moved to Silver Gap. The first thing Jessie asked—after whether she could ride a horse—was when they could go camping. Hannah echoed it, and the next thing Macy knew, she and Declan were planning a camping trip.

But she didn't mind. She was eager to spend time with them. Getting to know her younger sisters was amazing. After everything that happened in November, she was grateful for the opportunity. And her blossoming friendship with the girls' mother was a wonderful bonus. Denise was proving to be a hard worker and a good friend. It was great to see her thriving in her new surroundings.

The bell over the door dinged, admitting several people, and shaking Macy from her thoughts.

"Looks like the rush is on its way."

"Yep. I'm going to go email the pictures I took of the pipe to customer service before we get slammed. I'll be right back."

Denise nodded, stepping toward the register to greet their customers. "I got this. Go."

Macy smiled and scampered through the kitchen door to where it was quiet. She jotted a quick email to her customer service rep and uploaded the pictures, then hit send. Noise from the café increased, and she frowned. What was going on?

She stepped through the door to see the district attorney, Daniel Kerr, frowning at Denise, coffee soaking his front.

"Oh my goodness. What happened?" Macy rushed forward, grabbing a towel and handing it to him.

He dabbed at the liquid staining his clothes. "My coffee spilled."

Denise looked at Macy with watery eyes. "I'm so sorry. I went to hand him back his card and my hand hit the cup."

She touched the other woman on the shoulder. "It was an accident. I'm sure Mr. Kerr understands." Macy glanced at the D.A., daring him to contradict her.

He returned her stare as he swiped at his clothes. "Yes. An accident."

"See?" Macy said. "No harm done except to his clothes. But he lives close, so I'm sure he'll be able to run home and change." She spun around and grabbed a large empty cup, filling it full of the house brew coffee Kerr liked. She snapped a lid on it and held it out to him. "I know you already paid, so next one is on the house."

He traded her the towel for the coffee. "Thank you." With a nod, he turned and left.

Denise's shoulders dropped, and she looked up at Macy. "I can't believe I did that. I feel terrible. I hope it didn't hurt too much. He kept frowning so hard."

Macy rolled her eyes. "He wasn't in pain. He's just a grumpy bastard."

That surprised a laugh from Denise.

Macy smiled. "It's true. I don't think he's a very happy man."

"Well, regardless, I still feel terrible." She bit her lip. "Do you think he'd appreciate it if I made him a pie?"

Macy's eyebrows shot up. "You want to bake Daniel Kerr a pie?"

Denise frowned. "Is that bad?"

"No. I just can't see him eating pie. Not because I don't think yours would be good," she rushed to assure Denise, "but because he's got a stick up his ass that's lodged tight." Macy didn't have a high opinion of the man. He struck her as a jerk even before he tried to railroad her brother for murder and kidnapping. He was lucky she let him walk through the door.

"Really?" Denise glanced at the door. "He doesn't seem that way to me. He's always been polite. A little reserved maybe, but not rude."

"Why, Denise, do you have a crush on the D.A.?" Macy grinned.

Denise blushed. "I'll admit, he's not bad to look at, but he'd never be interested in a woman like me."

"Don't sell yourself short. You've really turned your life around. And you're a good person. So you made a bad decision years and years ago to get involved with my dad. He's out of your life now. And you have the benefit of never having been arrested, despite your involvement with him. Any man would be proud to be with a strong woman like you. Kerr's just a stuffed suit who wouldn't know a good thing if it bit him on the ass. Someone better will come along. You'll see."

Denise laughed. "I love your optimism, Macy."

"Choosing to be happy is all we have."

"Hmm." Denise arched a brow at her. "Are you doing that? Because I think if you wanted to be truly happy, Brady wouldn't have walked out that door without a kiss."

Macy's face turned red.

"I don't know what you're waiting for," Denise continued. "You two are obviously attracted to each other." She shook her head. "I'm not taking any relationship advice from you until you follow your own."

"Then you're doomed to wait. Brady Archer isn't interested in me. And I have no desire to embarrass myself in front of him."

Denise patted her shoulder. "You keep telling yourself that. I've seen the way he looks at you. You're as blind as he is." She turned away to help the next customer, leaving Macy to contemplate her words.

Did Brady have feelings for her? She'd certainly never seen any indication of that. The man needed to go to Vegas and enter a poker tournament. His face gave away nothing.

The bell over the door tinkled again, admitting several more people. Macy shrugged off her thoughts. They would have to wait. Right now, the morning rush was upon them and required her full attention.

With Denise by her side as well as two other young women she employed, Macy slogged through the rush. Tara waddled through the door near the end of it.

"What are you doing here? You're supposed to be taking it easy." Tara's due date was only two weeks away, and her doctor told her to rest as much as possible in an attempt to control some of the swelling she experienced now that the end of her pregnancy was near.

"I have been. But I can only stare at the walls of my living room so much before I go a little stir crazy. A trip to town to talk to you and get a decaf latte won't hurt anything. I'll go right back to the couch when I get home."

Macy grinned and punched the button on her coffee grinder to grind up some decaf espresso beans. "Sure you will. On your way past London's, no doubt."

Tara lifted a shoulder, a smile tugging at one corner of her mouth. "She might have mentioned the other day that she was making cinnamon rolls for breakfast today."

Macy's mouth watered. "Lucky. I'm stuck here and can't go get one."

"She might bring some over after her guests eat if you ask nicely." Tara started to smile, then put a hand on her back and grimaced.

"You okay?" Macy paused in pouring the milk into the latte as she took in her friend's expression.

Tara rubbed the small of her back. "Yeah. I've just had a backache the last day or so. It's getting worse. My body is done carrying Jace's giant spawn."

Macy giggled. "Have you seen your brothers? Not all of their size comes from your husband."

Tara grimaced again before she could reply. She held her back with one hand and handed Denise her credit card with the other.

"This back pain—is it coming in waves?" Denise asked. "Or does it just get worse with movement?"

"Waves."

Denise grinned. "Well, I don't think you'll have to carry his spawn much longer. I think you're in labor."

Tara's eyes grew large. "What? No. I can't be. This doesn't feel anything like labor pains. The ones I had with Lucy were excruciating."

"Every pregnancy is different. And you're carrying twins.

To term."

"Are you sure?" Macy asked.

Denise nodded. "I had back pain with Hannah before the contractions started. I thought it was just from carrying the extra weight, too, until I went in for my doctor's appointment and the doctor told me I was in labor."

Macy popped a lid on the latte and hurried around the counter. She took Tara by the elbow and led her to a table. "You should sit. And we need to call Jace."

"No!" Tara sank into a chair and took the latte from Macy's hand. "He will freak if you call him and tell him I'm in labor without a plan of action. Let me call my doctor first and see what she says. *Then*, I'll call Jace." She set the coffee down and opened her purse to take out her phone. "Oh!" At her surprised cry, she hunched forward.

"What?" Macy crouched in front of her. "What's wrong?"

Tara looked up, shock etched on her face. "My water broke."

Macy glanced down to see a small puddle forming on the floor and more fluid dripping off the chair. "Crap!" She rose. "Okay. We need to get you to the hospital."

"Go," Denise said. "The girls and I will hold down the fort."

"Okay, good. Thank you." Macy inhaled a deep breath through her nose, trying to steady her rioting emotions. "Can you get me a few bar towels to protect the car seat?"

Denise nodded and hurried away. Macy took Tara by the forearms and helped her stand. "Can you walk?"

Hunched, Tara nodded. "So long as we go slow. Damn. It feels like there's a boulder between my hips now."

"Well, they're not floating anymore, so I'm not surprised. Just hold on to me and we'll get you to the car." She wrapped an arm around Tara's waist and clutched her hand. Denise followed them to the door with the towels, holding it open.

Just over the threshold, Tara stopped, groaning. Her grip on Macy's hand tightened, her knuckles turning white. "Oh, God!"

Macy glanced at Denise. "Find her keys."

Denise slid Tara's purse off her arm and opened it, rooting through the contents to find the key ring.

Tara blew out a breath and straightened as much as she was able. "Okay. It passed. Let's go before another one hits."

As fast as they were able, they moved down the sidewalk to Tara's SUV. Denise unlocked it and opened the passenger door, spreading the towels over the seat. Macy helped her friend inside, then took Tara's purse and keys from Denise, running around the hood to jump in the driver's seat. "I'll call you later," she told the other woman.

"You better. We'll all want an update."

Macy nodded and shut the door. She started the engine and put the car in reverse, backing onto the street. "You doing okay?" She glanced over at her friend.

Tara nodded, rubbing her hands over her distended abdomen. "Yeah. A little in shock, but I'm okay. I guess I should call Jace now."

Macy chuckled and made the turn onto the road that ran in front of the hospital. "Probably wouldn't be a bad idea. I could just swing into the police station and pick him up."

Tara giggled. "That would be a sight." She took her phone from her purse. "Seeing as I'm leaking all over the front seat, I'll just call him before I do irreparable damage to the upholstery." She touched a couple icons on her phone, then put it to her ear.

"Hey, babe. So, I went to town to get a coffee and went into labor in Peppy Brewster."

Macy could hear his shout of surprise come through loud and clear.

"I'm fine. Macy's driving me to the hospital now. In fact, we just pulled in." She paused to listen.

Macy pulled up to the portico at the emergency department.

"Okay. See you in a minute." She hung up and looked at Macy. "He's on his way."

"Good." She put the car in park. "I'm going to get you a wheelchair."

Tara groaned. "I'm not an invalid."

"No, but Jace will kill me if I make you walk."

Tara tried to smile, but her face soured and she sucked in a breath as another contraction took hold. Macy jumped out of the car. Time to move. She dashed through the ER doors. The girl at the desk looked up.

"I've got Tara Travers outside. She's in labor." Macy headed for a cluster of wheelchairs, grabbing one.

"I'll page obstetrics," the woman said.

Macy wheeled the chair outside and helped Tara out of the car. She fell into the chair with a groan. "Ugh. I'm already ready for this to be over."

"It will be soon." Macy patted her on the shoulder. "Then you'll have two beautiful babies to love on."

Tara was silent. Macy glanced down to see a tear roll down her friend's cheek. She stopped the chair. "Hey. What's wrong?"

"Nothing." Tara waved a hand. "It just hit me. In a few hours, I'll be a mom. There will be two babies in my house. I can hardly believe it. The last time I was in this position, I knew things wouldn't turn out that way."

Macy bent down and wrapped her arms around Tara's shoulders to give her a hug. "I'm so happy for you, T. You deserve this. You're going to be the best mom."

Tara patted her arm and sniffed. "Thank you. Now, wheel me inside so I can get them out of me."

Macy laughed and straightened. She pushed the chair toward the doors, which swished open to admit them. As they crossed the threshold, she heard boots pounding on the pavement and turned to see Jace running toward them at full speed. He flew through the door and skidded to a stop.

"Are you okay?" He dropped to his knees next to his wife.

"I'm fine. According to Denise, though, my backache was early labor. My water broke at the coffee shop and now I'm having contractions."

"Well, shit."

She reached out to touch his cheek. "Are you ready for this? We're going to be parents again."

He laid his hand over hers. "I'm so ready. I can't wait to meet our babies."

Macy fanned her face as tears threatened. "You two are going to make me cry."

Jace smiled and stood up. "God forbid." He glanced around. "Let's get this show on the road." He took over the handlebars on the wheelchair and steered Tara toward the registration desk.

The woman smiled. "I already called obstetrics. Someone should be down shortly to get you."

"Thank you," Tara said. Jace turned her around and pushed her over to a bank of chairs to wait.

"I'm going to run to your house and get your hospital bag," Macy said.

"It's in the master bedroom closet," Tara said.

"Is there anything else you want me to grab?"

"No. Everything is in that bag."

"Okay. I'll be back soon."

"Thanks, Macy," Jace said.

"Any time." She gave Tara's hand a squeeze, then retreated outside. Excitement strummed through her, quickening her pace. It was baby time.

ABOUT THE AUTHOR

Ashley started writing in her teens and never stopped. Her first novel, Smoky Mountain Murder, came out in 2016, and she has since published two more series and has plans for more. When not writing, you can find her with her nose stuck in a book or watching some terrible disaster movie on SyFy. An avid baseball fan, she also enjoys crafting and cooking. She lives in Ohio with her husband, two kids, three cats, and one very wild shepherd mix.

Website: https://ashleyaquinn.com

goodreads.com/ashleyaquinn
amazon.com/Ashley-A-Quinn/e/B07HCT4QST

Also by Ashley A Quinn

Foggy Mountain Intrigue

Smoky Mountain Murder

Smoky Mountain Baby

Smoky Mountain Stalker

Smoky Mountain Doctor

Smoky Mountain K-9

Smoky Mountain Judge

The Broken Bow

A Beautiful End

Wildfire

In Plain Sight

Close Quarters

Scorched

Light of Dawn

Pine Ridge

Sweetness

Loner

Shark

Katydid

Homespun